RITTENHOUSE WRITERS

Rittenhouse Writers

Reflections on a Fiction Workshop

JAMES RAHN

With Ten Stories
from the Rittenhouse Writers' Group

PAUL DRY BOOKS
Philadelphia 2016

First Paul Dry Books Edition, 2016

Paul Dry Books, Inc.
Philadelphia, Pennsylvania
www.pauldrybooks.com

*Author's note: The names of certain individuals have been changed
to protect their privacy.*

Printed in the United States of America

Library of Congress Cataloging-in-Publication Data

Names: Rahn, James, author. | Rittenhouse Writers' Group (Philadelphia, Pa.)
Title: Rittenhouse writers : reflections on a fiction workshop, with ten stories from
    the Rittenhouse Writers' Group / James Rahn.
Description: Philadelphia : Paul Dry Books, 2016.
Identifiers: LCCN 2016001899 | ISBN 9781589881129 (paperback)
Subjects: LCSH: Rahn, James. | Authors, American—21st century—Biography. |
    English teachers—Pennsylvania—Philadelphia—Biography. | Short stories,
    American—Pennsylvania—Philadelphia. | American fiction—Pennsylvania—
    Philadelphia. | American fiction—20th century. | American fiction—21st
    century. | BISAC: BIOGRAPHY & AUTOBIOGRAPHY / Literary. |
    BIOGRAPHY & AUTOBIOGRAPHY / Personal Memoirs. | BIOGRAPHY
    & AUTOBIOGRAPHY / Educators. | FICTION / Anthologies (multiple
    authors).
Classification: LCC PS3618.A384 Z46 2016 | DDC 808.3071/074811—dc23
LC record available at http://lccn.loc.gov/2016001899

To the Rittenhouse Writers' Group
and
to Marlyn, McCall, and Adrienne

Contents

PART ONE

⌒

1

I ARRIVED AT the Ethical Society building on a cool, blustery Monday night in October. It was 6:30; my class was due to start at 7:00. Through the glass doors I saw a dark foyer. I tried the doors and they were locked. I rang the buzzer and nothing happened. I rang it again. Nothing.

I noticed an intercom jutting from the wall and I pressed the call button. Nothing happened. I started to sweat. My heart began to pound. I pressed it again. Finally a man's staticky voice came through. "Yeahhh?"

"I'm teaching a class tonight and can't get in the building."

"A class? No one told me about a class."

"It's a writers' group. Students are going to be here in half an hour."

"What?"

"A writers' group."

Then . . . silence. I buzzed again.

The man's voice crackled through the speaker, "What do you want?"

"I'M TEACHING A CLASS. SOMEBODY'S GOTTA OPEN THE DOOR FOR ME."

He sighed loudly and said he'd be down.

Ten minutes later he stepped out of the shadows, a thick-chested, white-haired Quasimodo-looking man. He was unsmiling, clearly irritated. He pushed open the door, repeating that he didn't know any group was supposed to be meeting that night. I knew I should

try to calm him down, but I wasn't calm myself. I was twitching like
a Chihuahua in a cold rain, without the little poncho. He flicked
on a light, walked me upstairs to the classroom, tottering and muttering, "They don't tell me shit." He opened the classroom door and
switched on more lights. One of the overhead fluorescents began
fluttering. I looked up. His eyes followed. "Not tonight. Can't do
it tonight."

"Got an extra bulb? I'll do it," I said.

"Not allowed. You might get hurt. Then we get sued. But I'm not
doing nothing tonight."

There was a large wooden table in the middle of the room, shy
several chairs.

"Any more chairs?" I asked.

He pointed to another room. "In there. I can't help you. Got a bad
back. They already make me do more than I'm supposed to."

"A shame," I said. Was there anything more this guy *couldn't* do?

I wanted to tell him to fuck off, but held back. My first night, the
first class of my new workshop that I'd managed to get a few people
to attend. I could've used a little help, even if it was only janitorial,
even if it came from Quasimodo.

I got the chairs. The man disappeared, and the room came into
sharper focus: candy wrappers on the floor, an overflowing trashcan,
what looked like watercolor stains on the table; on the wall a portrait
of a man, lean-faced, grim, staring down at me with unforgiving eyes.

I had to make the room a little tidier. I picked up the wrappers and
squashed them into the trashcan. I dragged it into the hallway to hide
it, then discovered the ladies' room right next door. I grabbed some
toilet paper, wet it, and was swabbing the table when a woman, fifty-
ish, arrived. She was dark-haired, smiling. I smiled back.

"Is this the writers' group?" she asked. She smelled of smoke.

"In fact it is." I shook her hand. "Welcome," I said. "Sit down, relax." I gestured toward a chair. "Excuse me for a minute. I'll be right
back." I ran downstairs to the men's room to wash up, take a moment to steady myself, and study one last time the introduction I'd
typed up.

⌐⌐

THIS WAS 1988. I'd just finished grad school at Columbia and didn't know what to do next. I had an MFA in writing fiction, but what was I going to turn that into? A novel? Freelancing? Teaching? Maybe. I didn't have a place to live, didn't have much money. What I did have was fifty thousand dollars in student loans that I owed the university.

My girlfriend, Adrienne, lived in Philadelphia. She said I could stay with her. She had a job and loved me and would tolerate me . . . for a while. So I moved to Philly. I applied for a bunch of jobs: copyediting, resume writing, teaching English Comp. Nobody wanted me.

Some guys I knew from grad school had started a fiction workshop in New York. They'd actually managed to attract some students. Like me, they had minimal teaching chops, and hadn't published much. I called and asked how they'd done it. Since I'd already moved out of town and wouldn't be competing with them, they told me.

I thought maybe I should try it. I'd taken numerous workshops so I knew the format. I also had some ideas about what worked and what I would change. The workshops had been a little too free-wheeling— meaning the instructors let students say almost anything to each other. Having witnessed too many tears and near fist-fights after particularly harsh critiques, I decided I wanted better control of the class. My instructors had put too much emphasis on craft. It was certainly essential but not the most important thing, in my opinion. I'd focus on the emotional heart of a story, where the writer appeared most engaged with his material, where I felt the story's energy was the strongest. I'd speak about *intent*, both the writer's intent and the story's intent, which are often different. I knew I could critique the hell out of stories, but with my students I'd do it gently, gently—the iron fist in the velvet glove.

Like my New York pals, my credentials were slim. I had my MFA, had tutored some undergrads and edited their work—that was about it. My publishing history wasn't much more impressive: a few magazine articles and some genre stories. I hadn't published any literary fiction, something most of us in grad school saw as our eventual goal.

Also, I'd never really taught before. I'd led a couple of individual classes, but never a semester-long course. The bigger problem was that I'd always gotten nervous—visibly nervous—in front of a group. I thought, People will see my ineptitude, my ignorance, and know I'm an impostor. I'll be rejected. Leading a senior seminar in college I'd sweated through two headbands and a beret. My head shook like it'd come unhinged from my neck. Reciting Torah during my Bar Mitzvah I'd suddenly forgotten everything and stopped abruptly. My mother stared heavenward, right hand clutching her throat . . . a minute later the words emerged from my larynx.

Teaching wouldn't be easy, but I thought I'd probably be able to do it. At least I could put together a plan to do it. If nobody signed up then I wouldn't have to worry.

I decided to focus the workshop on fiction writing, particularly literary fiction. Where, generally speaking, the characters drive the story; the plot emerges from conflict, from the strengths and foibles of the characters; and usually something changes by the end: characters gain insight or the reader understands something new and crucial about them.

I decided on Rittenhouse Writers' Group as a name. I chose it because Rittenhouse Square, a small, beautiful, upscale tree-filled park, was near where I was living with Adrienne. The name had nothing to do with a play on the word "written" (though the connection may have been inspired subliminally).

Then I had to find a place for the group to meet. Our apartment was small, and Adrienne didn't like the idea of inviting a bunch of strangers in. I checked out the nearby library, some high-rises and their common rooms, some church basements. Finally I found the Ethical Society which was right on Rittenhouse Square—that made the name even more apt. It was an old four-story former Quaker meeting hall. Elegant white stucco exterior. Gray flagstone steps leading up to a high archway. Leaded glass doors that gave onto a grand auditorium. The upstairs classroom was a bit tatty, with chipped white windowsills and stained red carpets, but I liked the high ceiling, the feeling of expansiveness. The room felt right for a group of striving writers. The Ethical folks I met I liked. They were a humanist organization, accepting all kinds of people. I imagined Rittenhouse Writers' Group that way too.

Next I needed to write a description to mail out to anyone who was interested. It took me a few days to capture my vision for the group and how I felt about writing. I needed the right words, the right tone; something honest, not too salesy. I used lines like: "Find out what works and what doesn't in your fiction. We emphasize support rather than criticism."

I supplied my credentials which, as I said, were slim.

I included my publishing history. Also slim.

I added a page of particulars about the workshop: dates, time, location, price.

I designed a registration form.

The package was complete. Now I had to spread the word.

I printed up some very spare flyers: "Fiction Workshop, led by James Rahn, MFA, Columbia." Under that I added *"Limited Enrollment,"* which I hoped would entice people. Along the bottom I printed my phone number on tear-offs. Adrienne drove me around in her little red Civic and I posted the flyers all over the city, in diners, coffee houses, libraries, bookstores. Periodically I checked to see how many chads had been torn off or whether someone had covered up my ad with their own. Sometimes I'd show up just a day or so later and my flyer would already have been ripped down, a tiny fragment like "Fic" all that remained. I also placed box ads in the local free presses, but to pay for them I had to borrow money.

I hooked up an answering machine to Adrienne's phone. The recording intoned, "You have reached the Rittenhouse Writers' Group. At the sound of the beep, please leave your message." When Adrienne's friends and co-workers heard it, they wondered what was going on.

The first person to respond spoke with a soft British accent. He said he worked as an investment banker and had graduated with an MBA from the Wharton School at Penn. He'd won the university's first-place prize for fiction in a competition that included submissions from all the graduate and undergraduate departments. Impressive . . . maybe. But who knew what the Penn prize really meant? Maybe he was the only one who'd submitted. I sent him a brochure and he signed up. That was exciting—my first student. Eventually six others signed up, a housewife, three recent college graduates, a photographer, and an ad saleswoman for the *Philadelphia Inquirer*.

Now that I had students, I'd have to teach. I could feel the bees begin to buzz in my gut.

I wrote a bang-up introduction to read at the start of the first meeting, using materials from grad school as well as my own ideas. I emphasized things like: Fiction is an *intensification of reality*. It heats up a situation and makes it burn so hot you feel what the characters feel. Fiction isn't reality; it's verisimilitude. It requires a greater order than in real life or nonfiction. In fiction you have to convince us of an inner truth. In nonfiction the truth is assumed.

I wrote about *intent*—the author's conception of the story, where ideally he makes choices that he understands, full of implications and revelations that he also understands.

I wrote about *point of view*, and some of the advantages and disadvantages of the various perspectives.

I stated that *plot equals conflict*. Characters should collide with each other, and with previously hidden aspects of themselves. These collisions expose the depths of the characters and often lead them to change.

I asserted the need for enhanced *sensory description*. In beginners' writing, sight is often overused. Including all the senses vivifies the scene.

Then I drew up a page about some of the formal elements: voice, theme, symbol, structure, setting, character. Identifying the most compelling formal element is a way to begin to talk about a piece.

Everything I'd written I figured would take about half an hour to present.

Last, I selected two stories I loved, by well-known authors. I planned to have students read them so that I could illustrate the formal elements. Then I added a third story just in case the conversation flagged. A close friend of mine, a professor, had once said that you should always be over-prepared for a class. I photocopied the stories to hand out to the group.

That first night, five women and one man showed up by 7:00. All in jeans, boots, sweatshirts, leather jackets. I stood and greeted each one. I thanked them for coming, and I meant it. The banker from Wharton, the one who'd won the fiction prize, didn't appear.

I shut the door. We sat around the table and talked companionably about who they were, what they were writing, why they were taking a workshop at this point in their lives. At a break in the conversation I told them that I'd prepared an introduction, I wanted to make some general comments about fiction. As the group focused on me, my heart started shuddering with the familiar anxiety. I coughed, cleared my throat, took a deep breath. I d made it through the first few sentences when there was a quiet tap on the door. Nobody moved. Another tap. I cleared my throat again. A thump. The custodian? The door opened, and a man stood at the threshold.

"Sorry I'm late," he said with that smooth British accent.

"Come in, come in." This tall, thin, black-haired man walked slowly toward me. I stood up, put out my hand. He grasped it delicately. He wore full-blown business attire, navy blue suit, red paisley tie, light blue shirt with white collar and cuffs, and gold cufflinks. I took note; the rest of the group took note. Vive la différence.

Now all seven folks were here. We had a class, a minyan—my own first workshop. I was happy to see them; I was scared to see them. We sat there in silence for a minute. I took another deep breath, exhaled, and started in again on the intro. I stammered a bit in the early part. When I looked up at the group, they stared back. I paused, started, and stammered again. Then I caught steam. I caught a breeze. The breeze transformed into a wind. I blew through the introduction.

I checked my watch. Three minutes had passed.

For a moment I was proud to have gotten through it. Then reality set in. Three minutes. Three friggin' minutes! The seven students sat around the table, blank-faced—That's it? What are we gonna do now? Is that all there is?

Sweat began sluicing down my face. My cheeks felt hot, flushed. Someone asked, "You all right? It's not that warm in here."

"I'm all right," I said, "yeah." I grinned. But I felt faint so I stood and walked over to a window and yanked it up. White paint chipped off the frame. "Hey, if I pass out," I joked, "just throw some water on me until I wake up. Whatever you do, don't call an ambulance." No response, still the stony expressions. I came back, sat down, opened my briefcase. Thankfully I had listened to my friend the professor. I began dealing out the three stories I'd brought. To this day, I'm always over-prepared for a class.

The first story was "Water Liars" by Barry Hannah. It's a mostly linear, scene-by-scene, first-person narrative. Easy to follow, humorous, with several interesting themes. I sat there quietly, watching their faces—the down- and up-turned mouths, the crinkled brows. I heard a couple of chuckles.

When they were finished I handed out my sheet on formal elements. I asked which they thought was the most compelling: voice, character, setting, structure . . . ? I waited. No one spoke. I was forced into being the teacher. I talked about the voice and the dramatic action of the story. The banker agreed with me, adding that he liked the quirky language. The *Inquirer* woman identified a martyrdom theme. Two people found the story depressing; they didn't like it. I was momentarily jolted by this because I thought the story was so good. As the discussion rolled on, however, I realized the contrariness was useful. Contrariness generated conversation; after all, plot equals conflict.

People even made a few points that I hadn't considered. I was learning too. The discussion became lively, and I chattered away, expanding on my ideas about fiction. In truth I talked too much that first class. It took many classes before I appreciated the need to shut up.

Before the class broke up I pushed a sign-up sheet across the table, a schedule for when we'd discuss each person's submissions. I asked two volunteers to put their names down for the following class and for others to sign up for subsequent classes. People were confused: Did they sign up for the day their piece was critiqued or for when they sent it out? I explained that they should choose a day for their critique, and that they had to deliver their piece beforehand so everyone had time to read it. (In those days, people had to snail-mail their pages or bring the necessary number of copies a week ahead.) I asked everyone to write constructive comments on the manuscripts, keeping in mind what the author was trying to say. Romnesh, the banker, offered to go first, with an old story he'd written at Penn.

"Don't you have something new?" I said.

"I'd really like to workshop that one."

"Okay."

Two days later a manila envelope arrived with the glossy label of an investment firm. The story inside was creepy, erotic, elegantly written; a compelling narrator, a disturbing situation. There was almost nothing that needed to be changed. Was I imagining it? Could it really be that good? Or maybe I didn't know jack about stories. But—I did know jack. The story was excellent: a couple of misused words, two or three awkward sentences, a few small grammar problems. The guy had written a nearly perfect story.

I thought, What am I doing teaching? What am I gonna teach this guy? He already writes at a higher level than most people I know. Hell, he writes at a higher level than me.

I started to feel jealous of his talent, his gift. I started to think cruelly about him. I could undercut this young prodigy. I could tell him his story was no good. I could defeat this talent that made me feel envious. I mulled it over for a couple of hours. Then he called and asked me, hesitantly, whether I liked the piece. I put him off. Afterward I wondered, He doesn't know how good it is? He's young, inexperienced—maybe he doesn't.

Then I recalled one of my workshop instructors from grad school. I had submitted a piece and he'd torn it apart. I thought he'd been nasty and gone too far. I wanted to kick his ass after class. I wanted to slap that smirk off his face. Instead I told him what I thought of him and his critique, that he was a punk who had cheap-shotted me. He apologized, sort of, then went on to tell me he'd written stories similar to mine and where he published them: all top-tier journals. I realized he was competing with me, and that was one of the reasons for his disdain.

I thought, That's not what a teacher is supposed to do. A teacher is supposed to nurture and promote talent. Even if it's a bigger talent than yours. There must be tons of people with more talent than me. I just have to work harder. I just have to write better. I have to moderate my jealousy. I can't be like that jerk who ripped my work.

Critiquing Romnesh's story became a lesson for me, a crucible, about how to teach. I met him for a drink and told him kiddingly that his story wasn't good, that it needed a lot of polish, but that maybe it could be salvaged. Then I told him the truth: how fine the piece was, how impressed I was by it. His face blossomed.

At the next class I told the group how good I thought the story was. I talked about its honesty and emotional power. I realized at some point that I might be over-praising it and didn't want the group to feel inferior to him, so I softened my enthusiasm.

I asked them what they thought about the story. Some loved it. One made a negative remark and Romnesh spoke up to defend himself. That's when I remembered the workshop custom that an author should remain silent while his story is discussed. This promoted a more honest exchange among classmates, so I asked him to hold back until we'd finished. Some were put off by the darkness and sex. You can't argue preference. I reminded them to focus on what they believed was the author's vision for the piece, to try to see it through his eyes, to appreciate that what he was trying to do was as valid as what they'd be trying to do.

When Romnesh showed it to me later, I saw he'd made a few changes but left most of the story intact. I told him to send it out. Eventually it was published in *Columbia Magazine*. He went on to publish stories in many top journals and win a grant from the Pennsylvania Council on the Arts. He lives in Hong Kong now. He's still a banker, still publishing great stories.

That first workshop started in October and ran for ten weeks. By December a couple of people had dropped out. I found it tough, as a neophyte, to fill two hours with only five people in the discussion.

On the evening of the last class, snow swirled through the brittle winter air. I stood inside the glass doors at the Ethical Society looking out into the bare beauty of Rittenhouse Square, waiting for my students. Two had called to say they couldn't make it because of the weather. Romnesh had a cold, so he wouldn't be there. In the end, nobody showed up. I can see myself standing at the door, staring out into the dark.

2

I'D FAILED. It wasn't the weather; it was me. Nobody showed up because the workshop was shit. It was back to the bricks, looking for employment.

Later that week I picked up the classifieds. There was a teaching job at a small local college. I applied but didn't get it. A vocational school needed someone to teach basic English skills. They turned me down. I noticed a part-time position distributing the *Wall Street Journal*, a glorified paper route. I thought maybe I could work a few hours a week, and attack my novel the rest of the time. At least I'd have some cash, feel partly legit.

The interview was scheduled for 4:00 A.M. I drove a few blocks to a loading dock under a high-rise. It was barely lit and stank of overripe dumpsters. I banged on a steel door but no one answered. I peered around nervously. Maybe I was being set up. Finally the door opened and a guy stood there—long narrow face, bulging eyes, a small startled mouth. He reminded me of a newborn giraffe.

"Welcome to Scumville," he said. Eventually he offered me the job, but I turned it down.

I continued to write, but it was only tinkering. I worried about finding work. My older brother had some connections at a local Ford dealership and suggested I become a car salesman. I shivered. I didn't want another dead-ass job. In the eight years between college and grad school I'd had too many of them. I'd been a house painter, bartender, hotel factotum. For a year and a half I'd slaved for a New York company that set up trade shows. My boss was one pinched-faced, squinty-eyed, pocketchange-jangling fucker. He made Simon

Legree look benevolent. He didn't like me—said I didn't *track* too well, meaning I didn't follow exactly the orders he barked. I spent almost two years trying to make him happy. Finally I tore myself down from the cross.

Adrienne encouraged me to try the workshop again. "It takes time to build momentum," she said. Romnesh said if I held another session, he'd join. If this writer whose story I admired thought the workshop was decent, maybe I hadn't done so badly.

I knew I needed to make some changes. There hadn't been enough people who stayed through the whole ten weeks so I shortened the duration to eight. A few people invariably showed up late and I wanted at least two hours to discuss submissions so I decided to start the class fifteen minutes earlier. And I lowered the price.

I posted flyers again. I re-ordered ads in the local free presses. Then the woman from the first workshop who worked for the *Inquirer* said she'd like to post a flyer on the bulletin board in the newsroom. She liked me, and I think she felt sorry for me. I thought, Why would anyone from the paper want to take a fiction writing class? Didn't they already know enough about writing? Weren't they already making a living writing?

I waited, wondering whether she'd get results. Within a couple weeks, I heard from a few people. They were interested in resurrecting a novel or a short story, one they'd stored in the attic or the closet. And they weren't just stringers. One was the Foreign Editor, one was the City Editor, and another, a well-known reporter. Three heavy-hitters. Two of them signed up. I worried whether I really knew enough to teach them anything. But that was how I'd felt about Romnesh, and by now he'd signed up again; maybe he could help me.

I also worried about whether to accept a nineteen-year-old woman who was much younger than the rest of the group. She'd never graduated from high school, hadn't written much fiction, hadn't taken a workshop. I told her I was concerned because she was young and new—I didn't want her to get hurt or set back by criticism. She told me she could handle it, that she was determined to write well. She said she'd nearly aced the verbal SAT. Her persistence and enthusiasm persuaded me. (Enthusiasm is dope to a teacher.) I said okay. With that, I had ten people in my second workshop.

I thought hard about what I could do to make the first meeting better. For one thing I needed to extend my intro—slow down my speech, maybe add more material. Also I wanted to cut my anxiety (though I realized that could take years).

I thought about how to give my students more help. I recalled that in grad school we got to meet with the instructors individually for a half hour or so, two times a semester. They were supposed to explicate the comments they'd written on our manuscripts and help us synthesize the critiques made by students. These rendezvous were almost always disappointing; much shorter than we'd expected and way too formal—a job requirement that the instructors had to fulfill, not a real interest in a student's work. I wanted to improve on that by offering students an hour outside of class where we could sit down and talk informally about their work, over a cup of coffee at some casual place.

At the start of the first meeting of the second session, I asked everyone to introduce themselves, talk about what they were working on and who they read. I wanted to promote openness and honesty, to begin building camaraderie (though I couldn't have identified it as such at the time), and to encourage the informal atmosphere that I hadn't had in school. This group seemed much livelier than the first: chatty, smiling, friendlier all around.

I spoke briefly about myself, said I'd published a few stories—still feeling embarrassed about my lack of credentials. "Let's get to it," I said and shuffled the pages of my intro, now increased to ten minutes. I began to sweat, my heart pulsing like a frog's belly as I started my presentation. I had added some remarks about the importance of revising, something I hadn't heard much about in school. I said that a lot of people never revised or didn't know how to. I explained that it was much more than copy-editing or changing a few words or moving sentences around. To revise, you really had to unpack a story, which might require rethinking it: shifting the point of view, adding scenes, amplifying and probing characters and emotions—going to the dark places where you didn't want to go. You most likely wouldn't get it right in draft two; it could take twenty drafts before the story was successful. There was a ton of work involved. So much of writing was about the *work*.

I handed out a sign-up sheet and asked everyone to choose two dates when we would discuss their work. I had to explain again that the day you signed up was the day your piece was discussed, *not* the day you sent it out. *Yes*, you had to make your own photocopies. *Yes*, you had to bring those copies to class a week beforehand. *Yes*, you should send copies to the people who were absent that night. *Yes*, I expected everyone to write helpful comments on the manuscripts even if you thought you didn't have enough time or were going to be absent. Then I asked two people to submit work for the following week.

I had a list of addresses, but not everyone was comfortable divulging where they lived. I understood paranoia, and tried to assuage their fears. Some asked if I would mail their submissions to everyone. *No*, I said, you should bring sufficient copies the week before. Some asked, If a person wasn't present and wouldn't disclose his address, how would he get submissions? In that case, would I mail them? *Maybe*, if you give me enough postage.

Over time I found that, occasionally, some members would get confused about the mechanics of the workshop. To me this seemed a resistance to or scorn for the grunt work required to be a writer. The technicalities corrupted people's fantasies about their future lives as famous authors. They should have been thinking that the more people who received and read their stories, the greater chance of someone saying something useful. Again, so much of writing is doing the work, and that includes listening to authority and following the rules when necessary. You have to do everything that pushes you toward mastery.

I announced a maximum of 7,500 words per submission. Thirty pages, 250 words per page. It seemed like the right limit. I think I remembered from grad school that most people felt that this was the approximate length where they wouldn't get tired of reading and writing comments. I recalled that folks sometimes challenged the limit. A novelist would say that their chapter ended a few hundred words beyond it. A short story writer would insist that a certain place was the natural spot for a break in the action. Someone might submit 10,000 words. Despite the complaints, the fact is that even genius can become interminable. Almost anything, if it goes on long enough, can make you holler "Stop!"

I handed around "Water Liars," the Barry Hannah story, and asked everyone to read it. When they were finished I decided to read the story out loud. I wanted to give sound to the words they heard in their heads. Hearing rhythm and tone makes the whole story clearer. Plus we all elide sentences when we read to ourselves, and I wanted them to notice this. Another thing: I liked reading aloud. I liked my voice. People had pointed out it was nearly basso profondo. Others said it had a primal timbre. I imagined I was bringing back the magic of childhood, a time when parents read fairytales aloud.

The words were flowing until I hit the line "Just an older guy with a big hurting bosom." The word "bosom" made me titter (pun noted). I could feel the heat rising on my face. A woman asked, "What's the matter with you?"

"I'm sorry," I said. "I have a hard time with the word."

"What are you, like twelve years old?"

"I-I guess . . ." It was true that underneath my seriousness lurked an adolescent stooge, but that turned out to be a good thing that night. The laughter put the group at ease, and vanquished my first-night jitters.

I finished reading and handed out my sheet on Formal Elements. The conversation had begun.

The following week I asked the two contributors to read aloud. When they resisted I reminded them that I'd done it. I hoped they'd been inoculated by my embarrassment. I told them I wanted everyone to hear their words. I picked two pages or so of a compelling scene in each story. After the first woman read I made some prefatory remarks, talking in a general way. Instinctively, I started with the positive, and that was how I handled critiques from then on. Even if a story wasn't strong I'd still begin with its good points, for example: the vividness of the scene, the engaging voice, the well-paced action, the lyrical lines. Maybe I would point out that the piece had a great premise or that I'd reacted to the emotion—the anger, humor, sadness.

Then I'd raise some fundamental questions: Is the intent clear? Do you know what the story is? Where does energy come roiling off the page? Do you understand the main character and why he does what he does? Are there sufficient consequences for him? Does the story show enough development, or is it about stasis? Does the ending work? What about the beginning? Does the piece take too long to get going?

"Who wants to speak first? . . . Who wants to leap into the breach?" I scanned the room, looking into each person's eyes. Some turned away. Others stared hard back at me. Some grinned ironically. I grinned back. "Uh . . . uh," I stammered, kiddingly. "All right. You." It was usually the person staring and beaming the most.

The nineteen-year-old I'd been worried about submitted a powerful story, full of attitude and wit, much savvier than what many older writers could have produced. I was delighted, but when I asked her to read it she said she couldn't.

"Why not?"

"Because . . . if I do, I'll cry."

My first feeling was that she was being defiant. She just wanted to rebel. "Crying may not be a bad thing," I teased. "Come on. You'll be fine."

She glanced at me, then looked down. She raised a slightly trembling hand to her face, then slowly rubbed it along the ridge of her eyebrows.

"Your story's really good. You sure you don't want to try?"

She didn't look up. Nobody spoke.

Was she too young? Was she was too sensitive? It hadn't occurred to me that someone might cry. Then it hit me: her story was laced with pain. This young woman had been through it.

I coughed into my fist. "Who wants to say something about this pretty darn good story?"

3

Rᴉᴛᴛᴇɴʜᴏᴜsᴇ Sǫᴜᴀʀᴇ was around the corner from our apartment. I loved the Square: in winter when the trees were shaggy with ice; in summer when the bushes were jeweled with dew. And I loved the neighborhood, with its zillion shops and services, everything from banks and bars to fine restaurants and churches.

Now it was spring, a few minutes before my third workshop, and I was headed to class. I was feeling pumped, not anxious—my confidence had risen. I hit the Square and decided to stroll the lanes. Forsythia was in bloom, and copious hot-pink azaleas. The funk of mulch filled the air, and the sweet scent of pot and perfume. An elegant couple sauntered arm-in-arm, then stutter-stepped to avoid a homeless man. A boy toddled after pigeons while a little girl chalked blue funny faces on the brick paths. Dogs chased frisbees and saucy squirrels. Two red-eyed bums slouched on one of the many benches, side-glancing at some pretty girls. At one corner a group of messenger boys and their bikes stood by the chest-high stone balustrades. Across from them, guys hovered around other guys playing chess. They reminded me of myself and my friends back in the day, hanging at the sub shop watching someone play pinball. Guys hanging out; it never changed.

A couple more *Inquirer* reporters had signed up for the third workshop. Dan, the City Editor, a tall, bearded man who looked like Lincoln if Lincoln had ever smiled, extolled RWG to his coworkers. He had a deep, sonorous voice that was gentle and persuasive. And his enthusiasm was persuasive. He was almost squiring people from the newsroom to the workshop.

Dan had big status. Not only was he the City Editor, but he'd also won a Pulitzer Prize. He was a fine writer and a tireless worker. Most everybody loved him, though some thought he pushed them too hard to perfect their stories. He reinforced for me the necessity of hard work and meticulousness. He was a pillar of the workshop in those early days.

All the *Philadelphia Inquirer* people were great. They really wanted to learn how to write fiction. I think they'd been bottled up for years describing events and people, but never their feelings and motivations. They'd been tethered to "the facts"; now they wanted to uncork their imaginations. I also felt we shared a similar mindset: liberal, ironic, egalitarian, unpretentious. Not decked out in fancy clothes, or the all-black uniforms of the faux artistes, but in workaday outfits—jeans, polo shirts, sweaters. And there was another thing I liked about them: they didn't mind being critiqued or edited.

Other folks usually weren't as inured. Other folks could get upset, especially if their work was close to autobiography. Then they were remembering stories, not inventing them. Then they weren't fully parsing the story: determining what the intent was, and how the events and the characters' thoughts and actions might lead to possible insights for them and for the reader. Because such writers saw themselves as part of the action, they were unaware of the network of assumptions they brought to the story. They'd get blindsided by criticism because they were too close to their work. They didn't have enough emotional distance. Writing about yourself and calling it fiction can be like standing naked in front of a mirror. It's impossible to see your back. You could have a rash there, or an ugly mole—it may shock you if somebody points out the mole.

⌒

CURT WAS a former college football player. He was muscled-up and wore shirts open down his chest revealing a thatch of blond hair and a huge crucifix that swung away from his body whenever he leaned over. He was a chiropractor—a *doctor*, he emphasized. When I told him how much the workshop cost he said, "That's no problem. Half an adjustment."

At the first meeting Curt seemed okay. He made little comments about exposition going on too long or word choices he didn't like, but he could also be amusing. By week two he was making occasional snarky remarks or sitting at the table, looking away, sighing. By week three he was declaiming, "This is an example of lazy writing," and, "You really should rethink your whole story." He began to make racist and sexist remarks: "He's a black dude. Of course he likes chicken. He's genetically disposed to it." "Good-looking chicks don't have to do much in bed." People rolled their eyes, twisted in their seats. Sometimes they laughed uncomfortably. So did I, but he was starting to bother me.

For his first submission Curt presented thirty pages of venom. Supposedly fiction (even though the narrator was a chiropractor and his name was Curt), it railed against blacks, Jews, Asians, women, gays, indigents, and the mentally ill. One black character called "Juice" was prominently featured. He was an alcoholic and poor, and the narrator's "best friend." The narrator gave him odd jobs in the office—dumping trash, washing linens, wiping down the adjustment tables. He paid him in booze and a little cash.

Along with the intense, angry tone, there may have been a touch of sardonic humor, but I couldn't be sure. The piece was so over-the-top nasty that I wondered how seriously I should take it.

One thing was certain: the narrator was intolerable. No self-deprecation balanced the hateful attacks, no evidence of an early trauma that might have produced such contempt. He hadn't lost his parents in a car fire, his face wasn't horribly covered with boils—either of which might have made the reader somewhat sympathetic. No, the guy on the page was a mirror image of the guy in the class, now perhaps with his true meanness revealed. There was insufficient distance between the "I" in the text and the observing "I," that is, the author, who should stand above the story, who should know more than the character on the page does. And when you finally got to the end, he'd added a full-page picture of a gorilla, a xeroxed cartoon of a dark furry silverback and a word-balloon: "Don't dis me. You be buggin', fool. I'll bust a cap in your lardy ass." Perhaps he meant this as a rejoinder from the black community.

I was chilled. What kind of crazy motherfucker would do this? Curt seemed to believe the picture was funny. Or was it really his intention to piss everybody off? He seemed to be oblivious to how it would affect them. The group was all white, and I wondered whether he'd have included it if there had been any black members.

I had to figure out what to do. My first impulse was to kick him out, but he seemed like a furious, dangerous man. I worried about repercussions. Then I thought, Shouldn't I accept whatever a person submits? Shouldn't I try to help everyone who signs up? After all, they wanted me to teach them. Heck, I'd been the marginal guy in most every class I took. I'd been suspended from every school I attended. I knew what it was to be a misfit. Shouldn't I give this guy a break?

I told myself I should focus on the writing. I could turn it into a lesson for the group. I could talk about how the piece felt under-fictionalized and how the narrator needed greater psychic distance. Maybe Curt shouldn't have used his real name in the story. Maybe he should rewrite it in third-person point of view, which might give him greater perspective. I also considered whether the story *was* fiction. Maybe I was wrong and the autobiographical feel was a pose; maybe this artifice could become the story's strength. Then I began to fantasize on a grander scale: maybe I could help Curt become a better person—more self-aware, less disdainful—if I pointed out how obnoxious some of his remarks were. And then I wondered how much I was rationalizing. I calmed myself by thinking, Let the group handle this. They'll get at the truth. I won't have to say much.

As I walked to the Ethical Society for the next class, the aftermath of a nor'easter whipped me and bent the trees in the Square. When I got there a few people were already in the room. Curt was among them. His shirt was V'd open, and one shiny brown loafer was pressed up against the table. He was talking affably. "Hey," I said. Everybody smiled, then continued talking. The others arrived. 6:45; it was time.

We had two stories to discuss, and I decided to look at Curt's second. That would maximize the number of minutes we spent on the first and reduce the time we spent on his. We finished the first piece around 8:15, then took a short break. Curt had been quiet during the critique.

When the break was over I slid his story out of my briefcase. As always, I started by mentioning a couple of positive points: the voice was energetic; the material was bold and risky, though I could see how people might be offended. I tried to appear nonjudgmental. I repeated to myself that maybe we were dealing with an invented story. It was a fiction class; this guy had created a character.

Then the group began to tear the piece apart. The City Editor and others jumped on the racial issue. The women were appalled by the narrator's misogyny. One guy identified a sadomasochistic streak, which he claimed to like. Someone else stated that the narrator must really hate himself if he needed to degrade so many people. Then the remarks began to shift into personal attack. There was a side of me that wanted to see Curt get lashed and another that recognized that we had to stay focused on the story. There were things we could learn—and shouldn't I uphold decorum? Finally one brave woman brought up the picture. She said it was bizarre and whoever did it must be nuts. Most people agreed. They smiled, but it was a smile that masked their apprehension. Curt sat there mutely, with an affectionate grin. Occasionally his eyebrows rose or he twiddled his pen and chortled.

The group finished—and he laughed, he roared. He thanked everyone for their comments, said how much he appreciated what had been said. Then he told us how we'd all missed the point. The story was a satire; it was meant to be funny; the monkey photo was supposed to be a joke—who would include it if it weren't? He was sorry if he had insulted anyone, but no way was he racist, and he *loved* women. Then he described how he wanted to put the whole thing into a time capsule. He was going to bury it in Philly and when it was discovered in, say, a thousand years, it would show the city as it was today. Was he being facetious or serious? I couldn't tell. He shook his head and concluded with a sigh, "You all just didn't get it." He leaned back in his chair.

I was surprised by his reaction, and I think the group was too. I expected him to be angry after being criticized. People were still bothered, but were mollified by his response. I decided I wouldn't have to kick him out. Maybe he wasn't that bad. But I hoped, after he'd taken such a pounding and because we didn't "get it," that he wouldn't come back.

The next week Curt didn't show up. I felt relieved. Some people asked where he was. "Don't know," was all I could say. They made some gibes. We had a couple of tender stories to discuss. A half an hour before the end of class there was a knock on the door. "Hello," I called. Then another knock. "Come in. Enter." The door banged open, and Curt strode in accompanied by a tall black man. They didn't say anything, just sat down in two chairs against the wall.

"What's this?" I showed my palms. "What the hell?"

"I brought Juice with me," Curt said. "He's here to tell everyone I ain't no racist."

"Ain't no racist," the man concurred.

I reacted instinctively. "You both gotta leave."

"How come?"

"One, you're late, and two, I don't let anyone audit my class." Thus rules were born. I gave the duo the thumb-out.

They got up reluctantly and marched into the hall, leaving the door open. I followed. The doctor repeated that he'd brought his friend to exonerate him. He fiddled with the crucifix on his chest.

Juice said, "My man ain't no racist. He's a great guy. Do anything for me." With every "s" he sprayed me with a mixture of saliva and hootch.

His breath smelled like whiskey and dead fish. Now I smelled like that too. I was angry at him; I was furious at Curt; also a little embarrassed and afraid. I told Curt, "You can stay. Your friend's gotta go. He can wait in the hallway or outside." The doctor chin-pointed. "Give me a few minutes," he told Juice. The two of us returned to class.

The discussion continued but I didn't really hear it. It's tough to teach when you're distracted. I kept thinking, How am I gonna deal with this lunatic after class? What am I gonna say? It could get ugly.

The class went on about the tender story, but I was hovering above myself, observing myself talk. I looked at my watch, I looked at my watch. Time became suet. Where was 9:00? Finally it came.

The group usually went out for a beer after class. When they asked me if I was coming, I said, "I'll be right with you. Give me a minute." Then I turned to Curt. "Hold up."

I told him this wasn't the right workshop for him and I didn't want him to return. I told him he was nasty to the other members and that made them—and me—uncomfortable. People didn't feel safe, and if they didn't feel safe they wouldn't give wholehearted critiques and they definitely wouldn't want to submit their stories. I asked how he could bring Juice to class. Didn't he think it was a crazy idea? Then I said, "You don't respect the class or me. That might be the most important thing."

By the time I finished I thought we'd be fist-fighting and I didn't think I had a real chance of beating him. I'd been in fights as a kid. I had boxed a little. I could throw a good sucker-punch. But this dude was big, and full of malice.

He stood there, immobile, staring at me, the silence hanging between us. Then his face buckled and his eyes got soggy. He told me how much he liked the class, how he liked everyone, especially me. He apologized for upsetting us and for bringing his pal to class. He was practically begging me to let him stay. He grabbed my right hand and shook it hard. He got down on one knee, mock-groveling (or maybe not), and asked me for another chance. "Doc," I said, "it ain't gonna work. I don't think this is the group for you."

"Please, please think about it," he said.

"Okay." I nodded.

He pulled himself together and went down the stairs.

I got my briefcase, surveyed the room and left. The crew was outside, waiting for me. One guy said, "We were worried about you. We didn't know if you'd be all right up there."

"If you were so worried, why didn't you stay?" I smiled, but I was a little pissed. "I could've used some backup."

"We had your back."

"Yeah, from out here."

"Well . . ." Everyone smiled. "We thought you could handle it."

After that we partied. We knocked back some drinks. And I learned something more about the workshop: It was just my ass against the world. No one was going to sweat the teacher's problems. And why should they? That's not what they were paying for.

Curt never returned. I momentarily considered letting him stay, but he never came back and never called. As a result, everyone was impressed with how I'd handled the situation, first kicking him and Juice out of the room, then kicking the doc out of the group. They thought I'd done well, that I had balls. Maybe, or maybe I was just lucky. With Curt gone, people were more at ease. It was like we had all hunkered down together against a storm. The group united. We worked well together after that.

4

THE WORKSHOP wouldn't have lasted a year without Adrienne's encouragement, Romnesh, the fine writer, signing up again, the woman from the *Inquirer* posting flyers, Dan lauding the workshop to his compadres, and my responding to Curt's presence the way I did. Luck was a factor in helping the group succeed that first year—luck, along with what I started to believe was my intuition and nascent teaching ability. But most important, I think, was the feeling I conveyed. I really cared about the group and felt responsible for everyone. I worked hard to figure out how to strengthen their writing, and wrote extensive comments on their manuscripts. I was committed to doing well and I sincerely cared, and I think students picked up on this dynamic. Plus, they had to be learning *something* from me.

I'd started the workshop as an experiment, so it hadn't occurred to me to create a business model or determine a specific target market. I had no outline or five-year plan. I think if I'd had a model I would have been constricted by it, not so free to take chances and be myself.

Starting the workshop and learning as I went along was like my writing process: I've rarely used an outline. Sometimes they can be helpful in a general way, to structure material, and they're certainly necessary for genre writing, but for imaginative fiction an outline can hinder organic development that always leads to useful surprises. Writers often find themselves thinking, I can't believe my character did *that*.

As I continued to teach, my precepts became clearer. I spoke more truthfully about a piece. I focused more directly on the heart of a story. I stopped splicing into my comments jargon like "This ending seems unearned" and "I don't see the arc" and literary terms like synecdoche, metonymy, hermeneutics, that I'd learned in school but rarely found useful. More important, I began to trust my authority. I felt more at ease letting others speak and arrive at their own conclusions. I didn't need to be the star all the time; I wanted the group to be dynamic. Anyone could come up with the insight that made a story work. I was more comfortable with saying that I didn't understand something somebody said, or that I'd made a mistake. I was pushing myself toward greater authenticity. I was pushing the writers too, ever mindful of trying not to upset anyone—though this can't always be prevented in the intimate environment of a workshop. Criticism is difficult to hear, and a student can easily feel hurt, especially discussing something as personal as a work of fiction.

Almost nothing exposes a writer more, because fiction comes mostly from the unconscious. It's like a dream, but with intentional agency, that's canalized on the page in images, symbols, and emotions. Just as you're often unclear about the meaning of a dream, you often don't see what you reveal in your work. Plots and characters can unmask painful faults. This doesn't happen only to the author who writes close to autobiography, as Curt did. Any student can feel stupid or ashamed when they realize what they've disclosed to a roomful of critics.

To calm their occasional distress I'd meet with members outside of class to talk about their writing. I was rooting for everyone's success, interested in helping them, and in getting to know them. This could have a positive and a negative side. On the one hand, I could privately illuminate issues about their work; on the other, too much personal interaction and friendliness could corrupt the relationship and, in turn, the vitality of the group.

⌒

ONE WOMAN, who'd taken three consecutive workshops, told me that no one had ever given her writing such an in-depth critique. She said I was brilliant, and I was flattered. She was a good writer in a technical sense, but her writing was polite and didn't take chances. It wanted to be darker, edgier. She was keen in the sessions—insightful, and good-hearted toward the others.

One day she phoned me to clarify the group's critique of her story. We talked, and later on got together for coffee. We shared a determination to get the little words right, and an affection for silly jokes. She asked me personal questions that at first put me off because I rarely spoke about myself, but she didn't press it, and as our conversation went on I began to appreciate her interest in me. Then we started talking on the telephone more often—almost every Tuesday morning, after class the night before. She gave me her impressions about what had gone on, the general atmosphere, the tone of the class. She rarely talked negatively about anyone, but when she did I didn't join in. Teachers should never dis their students to other students.

She was single, young, in her early twenties, a little thin but pretty with springy yellow curls and well-padded lips. I was attracted, and I suspected she had a crush on me.

We began meeting occasionally for lunch. At some point she said that if I ever needed a place to write other than my apartment—if it was too noisy, or the electricity was shut off for some reason, or I just wanted a different space—I could always use her house. She had plenty of room.

Adrienne knew about the woman (as she did about many people in the workshop), knew that we talked and met for lunch, but when I mentioned the invitation she was not pleased. I explained that if I did visit her I wouldn't be doing anything except writing, hanging out—no big deal. "Okay." She frowned, and that was it. Then one morning a work crew was jack-hammering outside our building, and I decided to take the woman up on her offer.

I arrived at a brand-new, three-story brick affair, with a parking space next to it—a rarity for downtown Philly. A Bimmer rested comfortably there.

I rang the bell, and she opened the door. Her face was pale, but she was dressed sharp in a black leather skirt and a tight, pleated white blouse, with pearls dangling down. I could see the outline of a lacy bra. Nice. I gave her a big hug and kissed her on both cheeks; she smelled like soap and cinnamon. Behind her were acres of blond wood and chrome.

"Beautiful home you have," I said.

"Thanks. I bought it last year. After my father died." She looked away.

"Sorry about your dad."

"Me too."

We sat at a round glass table in her kitchen, eating bundt cake and swirling our spoons in dark tea. I felt comfortable sitting there, talking to this nice young woman. She sporadically grazed my hand with her fingers, which I tried to ignore. Then she walked up the stairs to her office to work on a fund-raising report. I watched as her behind twitched up the steps. I turned away, and my eyes set on a patch of sunlight on the polished wooden floor.

I took out my notebook and began to write. After a few minutes I paused and gazed at the steps. I imagined going up and putting my hands on her shoulders as she was tap-tapping on the keys, planting a kiss on her sweet-scented neck, leading her into the bedroom, and lifting up that tight white top. I wondered whether I was betraying Adrienne. But we weren't married or engaged, and I hadn't really done anything. Fantasizing wasn't the same as doing.

I pushed the little words around and paused again. It was just imagining. I wasn't seriously thinking about doing anything. At least not today. Maybe if I'd felt more strongly about her and she'd come on stronger—naked under that leather skirt, letting it ride up as she sat, giving me a peek.

I went back to turning the sentences around. Eventually the daytime air turned gray. I called up to her and said I had to go. "So soon?" she called back. She flounced down, frowning. I gave her the strong hug and kissed her again on both cheeks. Without thinking I reached around and squeezed her ass. She didn't move. We stood like that for a couple of beats. "Uhh, sorry." I smiled goofily, then left. I was embarrassed but only mildly. I didn't mention it again, nor did she, and our relationship got closer.

In the workshop I noticed I was focusing a lot of attention on her. If I said something wrong or got into a debate, I'd turn to her, smile, and ask, "What do you think?" She always backed me up. One night, after I'd asked her yet again, I heard a couple of people sigh, saw one woman roll her eyes and shake her head as she glanced at another student. I suddenly realized I was building a mutiny. By concentrating on this one woman I had created the infamous teacher's pet. No one but the teacher and the pet likes that. Everyone wants their portion of acknowledgement and affection. Everyone wants their gold star.

There was definitely a buzz between us. But I recognized at last that I had to keep my distance. A little flirtiness, warmth, extra attention was okay, but only a little—given judiciously. And I shouldn't go further than that outside the group. I'd ruin the group, not to mention my relationship with Adrienne.

The woman continued coming to the workshop. She was unfailingly supportive until a year or so later when she got mad at me after a critique: "You liked absolutely nothing in my story. You had nothing positive to say."

"There *were* a couple of good lines," I teased. In truth I had said some positive things, but I'd grown tired of her cleanly written, tepid stories. "No, really," I added, "I didn't think the story was bad. I just think you could have gone further."

She had a boyfriend at the time. He looked like me, bespectacled, bearded (of course not nearly as handsome). Shortly after our tiff the boyfriend asked her to marry him. She agreed, and they moved to the 'burbs. Then she stopped coming to the workshop.

5

Now that so many people were calling up, even sending letters seeking admission, I could count on conducting a workshop every quarter. My confidence was growing. I began to imagine a future for Rittenhouse Writers' Group. Ideas were exploding in me. Maybe someone from the paper could write an article. Maybe I could set up readings around the city. I knew some folks who'd started a magazine—maybe I could get some of my students into print.

Now I could spend time really vetting people. I wanted the best writers, the smartest and most generous, who really cared about writing and wanted to write better. That was the ideal. The group was heading toward it. The idea of interviewing seemed grandiose, but that's what I did, discreetly, on the phone. I'd ask a few questions: How long have you been writing fiction? Have you ever taken a fiction workshop? Who do you read? Who do you enjoy? Then I'd let them talk while I took note of "the vibe." The vibe was, and still is, critical to me. How does this person make me feel? Will they be a good fit?

One woman said, "I went to Harvard. I've taken several fiction workshops. Tell me why I should take yours." I said, "You shouldn't." In the early days I would've had to put her on the roster.

Most of the time the vibe was right. Maybe ninety percent. But sometimes I wasn't sure. I agonized over this. Usually when a person fell into the gray area and I let them sign up. it turned out to be a problem. For instance, they had sounded too much like a beginner and this translated to their making obtuse comments in class. I'd tell Adrienne about so-and-so and she'd remind me, "Every time you get that feeling, the person doesn't work out." Still, it was important to take chances. When there was an opportunity, I liked to skew the demographic—which was mostly white, middle-class, college-educated. Many smart, articulate, fine writers joined the group. The interviewing process seemed to work. I felt like a lawyer doing voir dire, picking my jury.

I also began fine-tuning the details of the workshop. For instance, at the start of the first class I always asked everyone to introduce themselves, talk about their backgrounds and what they were writing. Some people took this moment to relate past or ongoing traumas, which ranged from the recent death of a loved one to having a hernia at age three. I realized early on that I wasn't leading a group therapy session, at least not explicitly. Now I'd begin the class by joking, "Tell us a little about yourself. Take approximately thirty seconds." After everyone finished I'd speak briefly about myself. I still felt self-conscious about my credentials.

Before I even began my intro the sweat still prickled on my skin. Despite my discomfort I'd expanded it. I talked about how to become a better writer, emphasizing consistency. I suggested that everyone write at least two hours a day, five days a week, working at the same time each day. Back then I didn't realize how daunting this amount of time was for most people. Later I reduced it to at least thirty minutes a day. I encouraged students to monitor themselves on the days they felt stuck and to jot down what they thought they could be doing instead of writing—then to ignore those activities. The truth was I didn't write consistently. My advice was directed as much to myself as it was to the group.

I explained the 7,500-word limit, and how it was just about the only inviolable rule. Sometimes I mentioned that a guy had handed in 7,514, and I'd told him to omit the pesky fourteen. He was bugged but he complied, and kept coming to the workshop.

I continued to hand out a short story to discuss in the first hour of the first class. People were returning again and again, so I kept having to find new stories. I used Breece D'J Pancake's "First Day of Winter," Grace Paley's "A Conversation with My Father," Rick Moody's "Twister," and others. On occasion I arranged for a member to send out a story before the first class, which got people more immediately involved. It also lightened the load of stories in subsequent weeks. Too many pieces in the final classes could become, as one member told me, like a five-car pileup.

I learned not to set too strong an agenda when I introduced a piece because my comments had a big impact on what students said. They tended to pick up on how I felt and follow my lead. So I stayed general and a bit removed because I wanted people to come to their own conclusions. Sometimes I didn't make any introductory remarks. I'd have the group start the conversation, then I'd weigh in later on.

At the start of the discussion I'd ask for volunteers or pick someone. By this time I usually knew at least half of the group because so many people were returning. Now when I chose someone it wasn't because they were smiling, it was because their writing resembled the piece that was up for review, so they'd be apt to identify its strengths and weaknesses. New recruits got a break at first. I'd let them get a feel for their confreres and how the workshop was run. Sometimes they just jumped in, which I thought was cool. If they didn't, when the discussion was winding down I'd turn to them and ask, "What do you think?" That usually inspired them to say something.

As the discussion unfolded I was constantly monitoring it and the workshop atmosphere, especially how the person on the hot seat was feeling. Was he overwhelmed, irritated, upset? Were the same points being made too often? Was a consensus emerging? Or was the group divided on how best to help? Had someone said something hurtful? If so, I'd jump in and try to soften the remark. Who was engaged in the conversation? Who was doodling, yawning, biting their nails?

If people sat back and said nothing I challenged them in a careful way, trying not to appear dictatorial or didactic. I thought everyone should engage in the critique. You never know where the ingredient that really helps will come from, or the words that a writer will finally hear and use for the next draft. Those I prodded sometimes said, "Everyone's already said what I was going to say. I don't know what I can add." I didn't back off: "Is there anything you want to emphasize or reinforce?" I might repeat certain points from my introduction. "Is the intent clear? Is the ending satisfying?" Or, "Tell me about one of your small confusions." These questions usually sparked a response. And, after people's reluctance, it was surprising what they'd contribute.

At the end of the discussion I'd ask submitters whether they had any questions. How could we be helpful? Now they had their moment. Usually they thanked everyone for being so thoughtful and thorough, genuinely appreciative. Then they might say they were unclear about some comments. They'd ask questions and people would make clarifications. We'd work toward a consensus. Sometimes authors would focus on one or two tiny problems in their submissions, which suggested to me that they really didn't understand the criticism or were defending themselves against it.

People sometimes felt they had to defend or explain their pieces. The truth was if the majority of the group didn't understand the work, the authors usually weren't clear about it. They had crafted it around an unclear intent. People sometimes said they had *no* questions, without thanking their colleagues. I might push them and ask, "What's one thing you might consider changing in your next draft?" After that they might open up. Rarely the authors got mad and said they wouldn't change a thing. Then I'd simply respond, "You should take what you need from the remarks, but ultimately it's your work and you determine what to do."

Of course if somebody got upset after their critique I'd talk to them—discreetly—after class. "Let's talk about it in private," I'd say. "We'll figure out what needs to be done."

6

THE WORKSHOP was cutting into my writing. Reading, editing, critiquing, *teaching* was sapping my energy and creativity. At least that's what I thought at first. Then, at some point, I realized that teaching was easier than writing. Almost anything is easier than writing.

Most of my life I've written, in fits and starts. All my life I've loved the magic of the twenty-six little symbols that can conjure a world.

As a kid I wrote poems. In sixth grade I won a gold medal in the Atlantic City poetry contest. A teacher drove me around to school assemblies and trotted me out, in my tiny bow-tie and thick black-framed Henry Kissinger glasses, and I read my verses to all the seat-squirming kids. I wrote stories that I read aloud in front of my classes. My schoolmates applauded; it felt great. In college I wrote stories that shocked my classmates and professors. I liked Edgar Allan Poe and horror films, and I adopted this material and tried to intensify it. I also used a lot of profanity and slang, even when it didn't suit the characters. I liked how my stories affected people, and I loved how I felt, leaning over a legal pad, pencil in hand, inventing frightful scenes.

After college I started writing a novel, a *Bildungsroman* based on my teenage years in Atlantic City and some of the craziness I saw, which had led me to quit high school and eventually get a GED (a "Good Enough Diploma"). Then I got that corporate job in New York, which required a zillion hours a week. When I wasn't working I was partying or sleeping, or sleeping *after* partying. I worked on the novel—intermittently.

Again, writing is hard. Writing a novel, even harder. It requires hubris, plus a marathon runner's commitment. You gotta put in your hours or it ain't gonna happen. Most of the time you're looking for excuses not to write: working, doing chores, exercising, scrolling the Net—all can become bigger priorities.

After quitting the job, I began pinballing around the U.S. trying to figure out what I wanted to do with myself. I traveled to San Francisco, Nashville, New York, Miami. I worked a ton of jobs—everything from ditch-digging to crafting resumes. I took the novel with me and stayed with friends or girlfriends, then returned to Atlantic City where my mother lived, where she always welcomed me back. I fancied myself the *poète maudit*.

A couple of years later I finally finished a first draft, a very bad first draft, which I called *Gettin' Dumb*. The title referred to the stance a half-intelligent guy had to take in order to hang out with the bad guys. I tinkered with the book, but it was discouraging work. I felt dumb most of the time, with little clue how to revise it. Who was I kidding? Me, a writer? No, I had to make money. Part of me wanted a conventional, upscale profession: lawyer, businessman. Another part felt the pressure to write and be heard.

I went to Miami Beach, South Beach to be exact, to be with my girlfriend of many years whom I was supposed to marry, and wound up settling there. I was twenty-eight. South Beach at the time was a dissolute neighborhood split between young Cubans and elderly Jews. Versace and Madonna hadn't arrived yet to make it seem cool.

I kept messing with the novel, even wrote a couple of stories and sent them out, but they got turned down. I continued to look for employment. After a million rejections—my BA in English no help— I landed a job at the renowned Fontainebleau Hotel. But it wasn't a desk clerk, bell-hop, car jockey gig where I could interact with the chi-chi clientele. No, I was offered a position putting vinyl straps on metal chaise lounge frames. The finished chairs would eventually support the well-oiled, sun-bathing bodies up on the pool deck. The man who hired me—handsome, bronzed, with his black hair slicked back and glistening like a wet seal's—took me down in the freight elevator to the bowels of the hotel. The space was literally a shit-stinking, dimly lit, pipe-dripping, mesothelioma-laden trash-and-dust filled cavern, fifty yards long and twenty-five yards wide, with chaise lounge frames stacked high against a lesioned wall. In the middle of this expanse sat a large wooden barrel. The man pointed to it and we walked over. Inside were hundreds of three-foot-long white straps and one industrial strength blow-dryer. "Let me show you how we do it," he said. He marched off and grabbed a frame, came back, set it down, pulled out a strap, plugged in the blow-dryer and proceeded to yank and stretch the band, simultaneously heating it, in order to hook it from one side of the frame to the other. "Whew," he said, after he finished. He wiped sweat from his forehead. "Four dollars a chair. See you in a few."

First I nearly burned off one hand; that blow-dryer radiated blazing heat. Next I ruined multiple straps by over-cooking and melting them into useless fettuccini. It took me an hour of pulling, straining, almost liquefying about fifty straps to finish one chair. When I was done I was so tired I lay down on it and fell asleep. Maybe I dreamed about a better life. I awoke to the rattling wheels of canvas carts. A line of maids, perhaps just off the boat from Haiti or Cuba, were pushing them along the periphery of my dungeon. The carts were piled high with dirty sheets and towels. The women stared at me, shrugged, and shook their heads.

I was beginning to think it wasn't hip to sink this low. Still, it was a heckuva lot easier than writing.

Eventually I quit the hotel and got myself hired as a clerk in a bookstore—something an English degree *is* useful for—and it was there that I read an article in *Vanity Fair* about Gordon Lish. "Captain Fiction," it called him. He was a blunt, no-nonsense guru who taught at Columbia University and had built the careers of many authors. The article inspired me and made me want to go to grad school. By this time I'd realized my relationship with my girlfriend wouldn't sustain me. I felt like I was losing myself. A Bob Dylan line kept playing in my head: "Please don't let on that you knew me when / I was hungry and it was your world." I loved her and I believed she loved me, but we were having furious fights about marriage and money. Every few days I was either packing my bags or she was throwing me out. I retreated to the cheap dank Art Deco hotels nearby. Places like the

Bentley and Hotel Majestic where I'd listen to old folks coughing up end-of-the-world mucosa, young couples fucking, men masturbating hysterically, and dudes in huge Chevys gunning their engines just outside my room.

I couldn't reconcile with my girlfriend, and the bookstore job was, well . . . a *job*. One day in April I slouched out of Miami and hopped a train back home to Atlantic City. I was girlfriend-less, jobless, busted-out broke, thirty years old and living with my mom. "Stay as long as you want," she said, which was both comforting and demoralizing. The big dark cloud fell over me. I never was so depressed. One of my friends said, "You're so messed up even *I* can't hang out with you." My twenty-year-old nephew came for a visit; we got into an argument and he said flatly, "Why should I listen to you? You're a loser." I didn't smack him. Instead I felt a crushing sadness.

My mother pushed me to call my brother about finding work. He managed the assets of a rich family and had lots of connections in the business world. One day I called. He said he might be able to get me an interview with a couple of brokerage firms. "You could be a broker," he said. "You know how to talk. You know a little about numbers. You're from Atlantic City. Everyone from Atlantic City knows how to sell. And you could make a good living." He paused. "One guy I know makes a million dollars a year, and he's an idiot."

"Great," I said. "Get me an interview." My ass was broke. This sounded fabulous.

He set me up with two firms in Philadelphia. One required me to take a three-hour psychological test. The results: I'd never succeed as a salesman. The other gave me an hour-long exam that was designed to simulate the real-world conditions of being a broker. I was given a pad of paper and a list of people to call—all of whom were actors pretending to be clients or potential ones—and told to sell them stocks, whether I convinced them into buying a break-out IPO or that their portfolios were hemorrhaging and it was time to purchase shares in more profitable companies. I employed all my bullshitting and storytelling skills, especially when the "clients" were screaming at me for losing their money. The crazy thing was, I aced the test. One of the VPs said he'd never seen a better score. The firm wanted me, but first I had to meet with the higher-ups and other brokers to see if I fit in and was a bona fide team player. The process could take several weeks.

This unexpected success reinvigorated me. I began writing again. It felt great sitting at the old nicked-up dining room table with my sharpened pencils lined up like darts, my legal pads, dictionary, and thesaurus, making shit up, feeling like a kid again. The magic I often felt putting in my hours—like I was doing what was right, what I was supposed to be doing—sometimes finding those moments when I made the grand connections and discoveries: I discovered something inside me that had always been there but I just hadn't known it.

I worked on my novel and sketched a couple of short stories. My mother occasionally toddled in, and I shooed her away. "I'm doing big things here, Ma. You gotta leave me alone." I don't know if she believed me. I'm not sure if I believed myself.

I continued making my way up the interview ladder at the firm. I started running on the boardwalk five days a week. Then, as I felt better about myself, I decided it was time to start looking for women. It had been way too long since I'd had that good thing.

I began going out to clubs, but I was really nervous. I'd rarely gone out to pick up women. I'd had a few long-term girlfriends, so I never really found myself "on the hunt." Plus I'm shy, and not amazingly good-looking. I had no rap. When I approached the opposite sex they basically told me to split. One time I asked a woman with a beautiful round face capped by black-lacquered bangs, "How would you like to make love to a genius?"

"I got your genius right here." She grabbed her own ass. "Beat it, fuckface."

A close friend of mine dated a woman I liked. She was smart and sweet, with a dark Semitic beauty. They broke up. I phoned and asked him whether he would mind if I asked her out. "It would be my pleasure if the two of you got together," he said, and sounded like he meant it. If his tone had been different, I never would've called her. That's when Adrienne and I started dating.

7

I HAD MOVED IN with Adrienne a few months before I started the workshop. Now, two years later, our relationship seemed solid. We loved each other, worked well together on the day-to-day, shared similar values. I'd been pondering the big question for a while. During a break between workshops I talked it over with my best friend, Dean, whom I'd known since second grade. He said I'd never find a better girl. I talked it over with my mother, and she was both happy and a little melancholy that her youngest son wanted to marry. I asked her for the elaborate ring that one of her beaux had given her. She plopped into my palm a three-carat, glimmering round-cut diamond surrounded by tiers of tiny diamonds. It looked like a miniature chandelier.

The ring was so elaborate I wondered if it was real. I described it to Romnesh. He said he knew something about diamonds, had brought several back from India for his wife. By this time I'd been socializing with him outside the workshop and learned that he knew a lot—about writing, business, arcane things like antique shawls and kilim rugs. Maybe he even knew about precious gems.

We met at a corner of Rittenhouse Square at 5:00, when people were bustling home. It was a bright, sun-heavy day in May. Too bright, Romnesh declared, to get a good look at the stone. "We need shade."

We crossed over to a small storefront that had a red-and-white candy-striped awning. Standing under it, facing away from the sun and the throng, he pulled a loupe from his suit jacket pocket.

"Whoa, where did you get that?" I asked. Who, other than a jeweler, owned a loupe?

Romnesh ignored my skepticism. "Let me see the ring."

"Here? You wanna look at it *here*?" I glanced around. A cavalcade of people hurtled by. Car horns blared at a van with a Jersey license plate that hadn't turned the corner the instant the light turned green.

"C'mon. It'll be all right."

Cautiously I handed him the ring.

"Jeez," he said. He sounded impressed. He twisted it back and forth under the eyepiece. "I think it's real—may even be worth something."

"What kind of *something*?"

"Maybe six, eight thousand."

"Really?" I felt a frisson of excitement.

"Could be," he said. "Of course, I might be wrong." But he was usually right, and I wanted to believe him.

That night I hardly slept.

The next morning I went to a jewelry store around the corner and asked the saleswoman if she had a nice box for an engagement ring. "Hold on," she said. "I'll be right back." She glided into a back room, spoke to someone, and returned with a small gray container.

"How much?" I asked.

"Good luck." She winked.

Adrienne came home late that afternoon. She said she'd had a long day, did I want to go out to dinner? She looked tired, her eyes bleary. But she was lovely as always, her thin dark face bordered by waves of black hair.

"Sure, let's go out. But first I have a question." She dropped her satchel on the coffee table. "Let's get married," I said.

"What?"

"Let's get married."

I pulled the box out of my jeans pocket and handed it to her.

"What's that?" Her smile shot east to west.

She hesitated, looking down at the box, then at me. Her smile shrank a bit. She opened the container and stared at the flashy ring. Her mouth tightened up.

"What?" I asked. My heart began sputtering.

"Is this some kind of joke?" she said.

"No. W-Why do you say that?"

"Where'd you get this from, a crackerjack box?"

I felt the blood tinting my cheeks. "My mother gave it to me."

"Your mother. Is it real?"

"She gave it to me . . . I think it's real."

"Hmm." She took it out of the box, twirled it around in her palm, held it up to the sunlight streaming through the window. Reds, yellows, and greens prismed out. Then she put it on her finger—a little loose, but almost a fit. "Kinda large, isn't it?" The smile returned.

"But it looks great on you," I said.

She stared at it some more. When she looked up she must have read heartache on my face.

Then she kissed me. "Yes, I'll marry you." She laughed.

I think it was me, more than the diamonds. But I still wasn't sure if the ring was real. I trudged into Bailey Banks & Biddle to get it appraised. After they told me how much it was really worth I strutted out. I felt like I should buy a good cigar and rent a limo to drive me home, with my valuable ring for the beautiful woman who'd be mine.

8

A FRIEND INTRODUCED me to Diana, a professor of English at the University of Pennsylvania. She had keen brown eyes and soft, chin-length brown hair. She was talkative, smart, serious, but friendly. She was a novelist who'd grown up in Philly and now taught a fiction workshop for graduate and undergraduate students.

We met for lunch and we hit it off. She said she'd heard good things about Rittenhouse Writers' Group and me, and that there was a spot open for a workshop instructor in the Continuing Education Division. She knew the director and could put in a good word. Was I interested? I gave her a what-kinda-question-is-that look.

She offered to write a letter of recommendation to the director. Then I should set up an interview. She wrote a fabulous letter, noting my years leading RWG and that I was an alumnus of Penn and Columbia. When I called, the director sounded genial and asked me to send my resume and two more recommendations. I asked Romnesh (also a Penn alum) to write one, and the *Inquirer* editor who was head of the Foreign Desk. Both were staunch RWGers.

One afternoon I met the director at her office. She was a reed-like woman in a loose navy blue pantsuit, with a lopsided smile, big white teeth, and shiny blond hair. The place was windowless and spotless. A ghost whiff of Lysol floated through the air. On her desk stood a neat stack of manila folders beside two framed photos of toothy children. A print of Philly skyscrapers reaching up into a cloudless sky hung on one wall. On another were diplomas encased in gleaming glass.

We sat down and I told her about the workshop, how I'd started it four years before, about some of the accomplished people who'd attended, and how much I loved to teach.

"When did you get your teaching degree?" she asked.

"I don't have one," I said.

"Really?" She turned away and began picking at a clear-polished fingernail. "You have a strange accent. Where are you from?"

"Atlantic City," I said proudly.

"People actually live there?" She laughed.

I'd heard this line before and had a ready rejoinder. "Didn't believe it myself. I used to live in Vegas but decided to move to Atlantic City."

"Seriously?"

I grinned. "No, I'm kidding."

The phone rang. She let it ring a few times, then, signaling with a finger that she'd just be a minute, she picked up the receiver. "Uh-huh, uh-huh. . . . Let me call you right back."

She refocused on me. "Do you have any questions you'd like to ask?"

"Umm, do you think I'm qualified for the job? I mean, will I get the job and, if so, when would I start?"

"I'll have to get back to you. I'll call and let you know. And," she paused, "there are a couple more applicants."

"Really? I didn't know." I tasted burnt coffee at the back of my throat.

"I'll call in a few days." She stood. My time was up. She plucked a thread from her shiny blue jacket and, after a couple of tries, managed to flick it away. She smiled brightly. "Nice to meet you," she said and walked me out.

A week later I hadn't heard anything. I got the bad vibe. I wanted to call; I wanted to wait a bit more. Then confusion morphed into a comforting anger. I wanted to tell the director to shove the damn job. Find somebody else—I don't need you. Who do you think you are, making me wait? Who gives a shit about teaching at Penn?

Adrienne advised me to relax. Probably there was nothing wrong; the woman was busy. These things take time. (Adrienne, the optimist.)

After another couple of days I called Diana. "I haven't heard anything. You think there's a problem?"

She was surprised. "It does seem you should have heard by now. I'll call her."

A few minutes later she called back. "Ahem," she cleared her throat. "I don't know how to tell you this, but she feels that because of the way you speak you won't be able to communicate with students."

"What? What do you mean 'the way I speak'?"

"She mentioned something about Atlantic City."

"Atlantic City? . . . That just sounds crazy." I was clenching a pencil between my thumb and index finger, enjoying the pressure until it snapped in half. "Did you tell her I've been teaching for years? That I've been running my own workshop and people keep coming back? I must be doing something right."

"Of course I told her."

"So what am I supposed to do?"

"I think you have to confront her. If you want the job you're going to have to call and tell her you *can* communicate."

"Ain't taking no elocution lessons for Penn. . . . Okay, I'll think about it. Thanks." I hung up.

I didn't want to confront her. If she didn't want to hire me, screw her, screw 'em all. I was fuming at her, Diana, the whole miserable university. As I said before, I liked my voice. People complimented me on it. Some said I sounded like a truck driver or a gangster, a gruff accent that put me somewhere between Jersey and the Bronx—but that was no insult: the voice, hah, was a contrast to my staggering intelligence. Yet now it was hurting me in the ivied halls.

Diana said if I wanted the job I had to call. I thought, I'll do it and she won't pick up; she probably hates me. I felt the paranoia percolating again, braided with the fear of rejection. But I realized that a job at Penn was a step up. It would strengthen my legitimacy. I dialed the number.

The director answered and we set up another meeting.

In her office once again, she explained, "I come from a small town just like you. I can talk exactly like you." She put her elbows on her desk. "But I do it after five o'clock."

"What . . . ?" I think I was more stunned than insulted. I even giggled. What weird kind of discrimination was this? I'm thinking back now, as I write, about the workshop instructor from grad school who'd torched my story: there were a lot of people like him who disavowed their working-class roots and pretended to be intellectuals, members of the elite. They didn't want to be reminded whence they'd come, by people like me who had a similar background. The professors I'd gotten along with best were the real bluebloods, educated at places like Oxford and Princeton. They never seemed threatened by what I said or wrote. They liked my stories about louche, down-and-out characters.

After the director's bald honest statement, and after I reacted in a grinning laissez-faire way, our relationship shifted and we began to get along. We'd both been raised in honky-tonk towns that imagined they were something more. Her diction level switched into post-five-o'clock jive. Reiterate became *ditto*, women became *chicks*, arrested became *snagged*. She cursed. We laughed. At some level we were kin. She twisted her neat blond hair and gave me a wide smile. "You're hired," she said. She stood and squeezed my hand.

9

So I was going to run a workshop at Penn. Could I really teach there? Could I bring them the fire?

To make it easier I decided to pattern the Penn workshop on RWG: the same stories by established writers for issues of craft, two or three students submitting work each week, same inviolable word count. The framework could be similar, but I couldn't set the price. Penn would do that in accordance with its other writing classes, and an eight-week session would be much cheaper than RWG. So I shortened the duration to five weeks, and the class time to two hours. This would also ease my transition and cut less into my own writing.

I had to write a bio and a description of the class for the catalogue, which would be mailed throughout the region. Thousands of people would hear about the Penn workshop as well as Rittenhouse Writers' Group.

My assigned classroom was in Bennett Hall, home of the English Department, where I'd taken many of my undergrad classes sixteen years earlier. It's got the standard red brick, ivy-draped exterior, heavy oak front doors, and polished granite hallways. I was excited to return in my new capacity.

My first workshops there were nearly as shaky as they'd been when I started RWG. Despite nailing down the course structure I still felt the anxiety, and still wished I could control it better. The workshops took place in the evening, and other classes used the room during the day. After navigating the gleaming halls I'd arrive to find a startling mess of *Daily Pennsylvanian* newspapers, soda cans, sticky soda stains on the floor, and notebook pages on the seats and desks.

The kids were slobs. I was back to being the janitor before I could be the teacher.

Another problem was the scheduling glitches. Sometimes I'd show up and the classroom door would be locked, my students milling around outside like pigeons in the Square. I'd try to find an actual janitor to unlock the door, but sometimes I wound up running around frantically before finding a room I could get into. Other times I'd find a class already in session. Through the window in the door I'd see the teacher gesticulating. I'd wait a couple of minutes then tap on the window. She'd look at me, then away. Another tap, then I'd turn the knob delicately and open the door.

"Excuse me, sorry for interrupting, but I'm supposed to have a class here now."

"Nobody told me." Her eyes would narrow.

"Well, umm, when do you think you'll be done?"

"Not for another half hour. Now please let me get back to my class."

Again I'd dash around looking for a room. The whole time my students were like, What the fuck?

Other nights the class would be engaged in carefully dissecting the emotional core of a story when a teacher would appear and say the room was his. Then I'd have to convince *him* to find another place. Later I'd complain to the director. She'd try to help, make a few calls—but the university was one monster bureaucracy. By the time the right person got the message I would have been waiting weeks for a reliable space. There seemed to be little the director could do, or perhaps wanted to do. Plus, after 5:00 was *her* time.

Early on, my Penn workshops attracted some odd characters. One guy submitted what I thought might be a suicide note. He wrote something like: John can't take it anymore. He's sick about all the mistakes he's made. He got shitcanned from the carpenters' union and has been out of work for ten months. His wife rags on him because he doesn't have any money. Last week his daughter yelled Fuck You at him and ran out of the house and stayed at her boyfriend's. Fifteen years old. Everything he does turns to shit. He thinks about shooting himself but doesn't have a gun. Maybe then they'd care. He does have some pills and a plastic bag to put over his head. It gets to a point where it just makes sense . . .

How do you critique this? I wondered. What if I upset him? Then again, maybe it was a *fictional* suicide note, perhaps part of a longer work. Or maybe I was rationalizing to make myself feel better.

In class, I started the discussion about his piece with something affirmative: I said how convincing I thought it was. I tiptoed through my remarks and asked other people to speak, but few did, and what they said was superficial. The whole time the writer sat with his chin on his chest, eyes squinting, arms clutching himself. I had to say something at least marginally sincere that reflected the group's thoughts and mine, so I said at one point that the piece seemed under-fictionalized. He didn't react. A young woman looked up at the ceiling and inhaled deeply. A short time later I dismissed the class.

The next week the guy didn't appear. I wondered about him but didn't check on him, since it wasn't unusual for people to skip class the week after their critique. Then he didn't show the next week.

That was the last class of the session. Afterward I considered calling the office about him. But I hesitated. I was afraid to find out that he'd harmed himself, and I also didn't want to raise doubts about my teaching. On the other hand I felt I'd spoken delicately about his piece, and it bothered me that he hadn't taken me or the class seriously. The more I thought about him, the more I thought he'd probably be okay. He'd spoken little in the weeks leading up to his submission, but what he said had been constructive. He did seem odd, but self-assured too. In the end I decided he'd be all right.

There was another guy, a young doctor—a short, clean-cut man who wrote a story about Snow Black. He portrayed her as a junkie and a whore. She lived in a brothel. She had sex with all the dwarfs, one after another, except, I think, Grumpy. One sentence described her sliding a spike into her arm: "She loved to see the blood boiling in the cylinder." The author thought his story was hilarious and, much like Curt, couldn't understand why people were upset, why they found it offensive and misogynistic. And this guy was a gynecologist. The class couldn't stand him; neither could I, but I had to deal with this maniac because it was almost impossible to kick someone out of Penn Continuing Ed unless they directly threatened a classmate or me. The higher-ups worried that they'd get sued. Thankfully it was only a five-week class.

In another workshop I gave an inspired explication of Paley's "A Conversation with My Father." I spoke about the story's nonlinear structure and how it elevated a well-done sentimental story from pity to pathos. I talked about the narrator's bantering with her dying father, how she invented a story and continuously embellished it to keep him intrigued, and alive. Paley's piece addressed the great glory of storytelling. When I finished I asked if anyone had questions.

One portly man with a carefully groomed pencil-thin mustache raised his hand and said, "I have one."

"Great."

"Uhh, what are these tiny bugs on the floor?" He pointed downward and slid his chair back.

"What? What did you say?" I asked.

"These bugs . . . are they ants or worms or something?"

I stared at the floor but couldn't see anything. After a bit I saw some tiny thread-like undulating creatures. "I-I don't know what they are. Is that your only question?"

"For now." He continued staring at the floor.

Another moment sticks in my mind about a woman whose writing changed because of something unexpected. Before the first class she sent out a piece, rich with glittering, rhapsodic language. It involved a mother, a father, and their mentally challenged young son vacationing on an island when the boy disappears. The parents are understandably freaked out.

The language was beautiful, but it demanded your attention at the expense of the unfolding story; it created a fog around the story. The mother described how much she loved her son—he was a blessing, a gift to her and her husband. The unmitigated goodness of the son was so overdone it generated distrust in the reader. The mother never attested to the anger she might feel, at least momentarily, that the child disappeared. She said she had sacrificed for her boy, but the cost of the sacrifice—she'd given up a career—was so emphatically tamped down you felt the mother was hiding something. And her husband hadn't sacrificed much. Any anger she might have felt toward the boy or herself seemed to be displaced onto the feckless husband.

The writer came to class smiling, upbeat, chatty. When it was time for her critique I began gently, like always—salubrious remarks to create the right atmosphere, leading, I hoped, to a sense of safety and trust in the workshop. I spoke about the strengths in the story: the seriousness of a child vanishing; along with the beauty of her prose. I read out a few lines that were real gems. I said the language reminded me of T. C. Boyle. The author beamed with an eye-crinkling smile. People agreed; they loved her metaphors, and they were horrified by the disappearance of the boy. Then I carefully amplified my remarks about the language: it *was* beautiful, even poetic, but sometimes poetic language could obscure a story. The narrative could be subsumed or trivialized by it.

I asked if the story was clear enough, and if the mother's thoughts, comments, and reactions were clear. I wondered aloud whether the mother might have dreams for herself. Had she concealed her self-interest? Might she be angry over the child vanishing, and for all the time she'd spent caring for him? If so, was this emotion adequately displayed in the story? Was the mother convincing as a character? Could she be proclaiming her sacrifice, her martyrdom, or could she be unaware that she was doing so? The piece was surely about the son, but wasn't it about the mother too?

Some people agreed with me, and at some point during the discussion the author stopped smiling. At first she stared at me, and then her face crumpled and she began to cry. I felt bad for her and guilty. I had overstepped. And this was the first class of a new workshop, where I was supposed to set the right tone. People probably felt that I was being a prick. Maybe I was. Maybe I am.

I told the class, "Let's take a break." The woman continued crying softly. I stood and opened the door and, as students flowed into the hall, one woman gave me a withering look. I paused in the doorway and asked the writer to come out. She shifted her chair around so her back was to me. "Zoe," I said, "come out, I want to talk." She just sat there, she didn't move. "Zoe," I repeated, "come on out, *please.*" She sniffled and shook her head. Now irritation was creeping into my guilt. She pulled a tissue from her sleeve and began dabbing her eyes, then blew her nose—a loud honking sound that seemed intentional, meant to draw more attention to her distress, and which amplified my feeling of embarrassment. Still she refused to come out.

After the break I soldiered on. We had another piece to review. Zoe turned her chair around, but wouldn't look at me. She did make some brief comments about the other story.

I didn't think she'd return to the workshop, but she did. She barely spoke to me but gave good feedback to her classmates. She was smart and could dissect other people's work. She sent out another piece for the final class, another mother and child story, one that was much savvier. The mother was more attuned to her own complex emotions. The language was still poetic in places, but appropriately so, when, for example, a character was ruminating, and the diction level was modulated when the action and dialogue demanded it. It was a much better piece. I was happy for Zoe and surprised by the turn-around.

Afterward I congratulated her. "You really nailed it," I said. "What happened? How did you make the change?"

"I wanted to show you I could write," she said, "and wanted to tell you, Screw You."

⌣

I DIDN'T REALIZE back then just how important it was to teach a Penn workshop. For one thing, it gave me status. People outside academia thought I was an Ivy League professor. People in RWG felt I had more bona fides. My students at Penn called me "Professor" and "Doctor." I usually disabused them. "I'm an instructor," I'd say. "Maybe a writing facilitator. But I still think I may be able to get you to where you want to go. I can sherpa you perhaps halfway up the mountain. Then you have to summit on your own." Their faces became an arrangement of downward-pointing arrowheads. Oddly, "Professor" and "Doctor" had been two of my nicknames growing up in Atlantic City, sometimes in a pejorative way, as emblems of intellect and elitism. Again, you couldn't appear too smart if you wanted to run with the cool dudes. Letting on that you were smart could get you ostracized, or worse. Unless you were skilled at playing "the dozens"—reeling off insults about people's mothers. I was great at that, and careful not to go too far. But most of the time I acted dumb, just another knucklehead blathering about sex, sports, fighting, with the bravado of a street kid headed towards a criminal future.

Now I was Rahn the Penn writing instructor. I noticed on my pay stubs that I'd been elevated to the position of "lecturer." But the truth was I was a freelance teacher conducting a workshop as part of the university's outreach to the community. Anyone could sign up, unless they were too young or had gotten into trouble in another Continuing Ed class by not paying a bill or menacing somebody. For RWG, I screened potential newcomers. If people called up and said they were new to writing fiction or I was ambivalent about letting them in I asked them to join the workshop at Penn. I fancied that it was much harder to get into RWG.

Because Penn was so widely known there was a greater mix of people. The diversity of age, race, and class challenged me. There were many more men in my Penn class. I got a few alumni, some students who'd dropped out of college and were biding their time exploring something new, old folks who wanted to tell their life stories and thought that by changing people's names they were writing fiction.

There was also a broad range of writing ability. Many people were beginners or just hobby-writers. I couldn't take the group quite as seriously as RWG. Nonetheless I was always over-prepared and I never dumbed anything down because I wanted to give my best for the best—I strove to keep the discussion geared to the most committed people. But I didn't feel quite so much pressure because my ego wasn't so much on the line. My soul wasn't wrapped up in it the way it was in my own workshop.

Occasionally I'd get a fine writer. When I did I asked them to join Rittenhouse Writers' Group.

10

Into the mix at the Penn workshop arrived an elegant, soft-spoken woman named Diane. Behind her glasses her eyes expressed intensity and kindness. You saw it the moment you met her.

She was working on a novel about an older couple who find a baby in a box on their stoop. The key event occurred close to the beginning, but not in the first chapter. Chapter one limned a party on a porch, during which the porch collapses and several people are injured. Diane kept writing it over and over. It always felt baggy, a bit overwrought, or as if she were practicing (which maybe she was, at least unconsciously). Yet you heard an exceptional voice and sensed a great storytelling ability. She spent months re-writing that first chapter despite my suggestion that she could jettison it and start somewhere else. When she finally transcended that compulsion to perfect something that didn't need perfecting—at least not in a first draft—the book took off. The story and characters soared. In the end she omitted that chapter. By this time she was a member of RWG.

Diane worked for the Forestry Service, forty hours a week. Monday through Friday she got up at 4:00 A.M. to make a pot of coffee and write for a couple of hours before she fixed breakfast for her two kids and husband. Then she spent the rest of the day at her job. On weekends she followed the same morning routine and spent the rest of the day writing. Nobody worked harder than she did. She set the standard for all of us.

One night at a workshop party attended by Diane and her husband, Greg, he pulled me aside and asked, "James, do you really think Di has something here? Tell me the truth 'cause she's considering giving up her job."

"Greg, she's really good," I said, "I think you're gonna be all right."

In truth I thought she was wonderfully talented, but I couldn't predict whether a publisher would buy her book, or how committed she *really* was to making her project successful. How would she handle the unavoidable problems that come with writing a novel—formulating the structure and logic, imagining new scenes, enhancing others, ripping out whole sections when necessary even if they're well written, keeping a reader engaged? How would she handle the ever-present self-doubt, and encountering her own limitations? And later, if she finished a satisfying draft and it was time to market the book, how would she manage the inevitable rejections? How could I know? But I believed in her.

By this time many group members had published short fiction and a few had won Pennsylvania Council on the Arts fiction grants. I thought my students deserved even more recognition, and I wanted everyone to know about RWG.

Then a hip new bookstore, Borders, opened up in downtown Philly. All the putative literati and fly bohemians hung out there, the thin, ashen-faced, black-garbed aspiring intellectuals who sat cross-legged on the floor reading paperbacks. The store was doing a bang-up business. Every other week famous authors showed up to pitch their latest books. I saw Joyce Carol Oates, Russell Banks, Tim O'Brien. Celebrities appeared with their wild stories and autobiographies. One evening John Douglas, the FBI profiler, did a presentation. He told mesmerizing tales about Charles Manson and Ted Bundy. Peter O'Toole was scheduled to read one day. He strolled in smoking a cigarette held in a gold cigarette holder. The event coordinator informed him that corporate policy didn't allow smoking in the store. In that case, the actor said, he wouldn't read. The woman changed her mind when she saw the line of people waiting outside, halfway to the Walt Whitman Bridge.

I called the store manager and asked if RWG could do a reading. He said he'd heard about the group, was friends with one of our members, and that he liked to support local talent. I picked stories that I thought were the best the group had produced so far, and asked five people to read. They'd get fifteen minutes each. For advertising I tacked up flyers around the city and mailed others to former RWGers. "Run with the Hunted" was the headline, a Bukowski title I'd always liked.

I knew I'd suffer from the familiar anxiety at the lectern. I also knew that I sucked at speaking extemporaneously, so I wrote yet another intro—a sketch of the group and how I'd started it *to further the importance of fiction writing in Philadelphia*. I typed that out, and jotted down on index cards a brief bio of each reader. If I read from notes I'd be okay. Then I printed up a more expansive page about RWG and another about the readers and stapled them together. Adrienne and I brought them to the bookstore and laid them out on the chairs. We also wheeled in a shopping cart filled with jugs of wine, plastic cups and napkins, as an attempt to give the evening a semblance of poshness.

The crowd streamed in, maybe a hundred people—fucking huge for a reading. I picked up the microphone and, channeling Richard Pryor, ad-libbed a couple of lines before we got started. "Heckuva audience. Hope I'm funny." The mic squealed. No one laughed. Swiftly I turned to my notes.

The readers and the audience were plagued by the noise from the nearby cafe: the *whirr* of the coffee grinder; the banging of the cash drawer as it opened and closed. The PA system erupted intermittently with a voice touting a bestseller that everyone should buy. After the first three readers, we lost half the crowd. Too much noise or too many minutes of narrative, I thought. My stomach started to churn. Those who stayed to the end said they loved the event and congratulated all the presenters, who sparkled in response. Adrienne and I gathered up the wine, which almost no one had drunk, except for a couple of winos, and tottered home. All and all, it was a good night, which encouraged me to hold more readings.

Several months later, Diane, Romnesh, and a woman named Sheila read. By now I had streamlined the event: three readers and absolutely no more than fifteen minutes for each one. Shorter was sometimes better than longer. I wanted people to leave feeling that they wanted to stay. I tried to choreograph the *narrative* of the evening, deciding what emotion the audience would leave with. The last impression of a story, novel, movie is the most important. The last emotion is what you take home. Adrienne and I also brought better wine.

An audience of a hundred and fifty filled the chairs and stood in the aisles. Many folks had bought books at RWG readings. When I asked the manager to mute the ambient noise from the cafe and the PA, he nodded. "Sure. No problem."

All the presenters knocked out the audience. Romnesh offered another creepy, erotic tale. Diane read a chapter where a man recalls his mother being whipped. As her voice and emotion took hold, the tale became a freight train barreling down the track. Sheila recounted a death scene where she imagined a daughter and mother buried in their coffins, reaching through the dank wood to hold each other's hand. Half the listeners were crying afterward. When the performance was over, I didn't get out of my seat. I sat with the emotion, not just ending the silence and breaking the spell. I wanted everyone to sit with the emotion. Writing should move people; art should move people. These folks were undone by three unknown writers who were as good as anyone around.

Diane continued coming to the workshop and working steadily on her novel. She finished a first draft and began painstakingly writing a second. It was exciting to see the book evolve. A character that had started out as a single sentence developed into a fully formed participant. The narrative themes began to cohere. Diane's writing kept getting better and better. (The second draft is often where a book really starts to coalesce—but first you have to finish that initial draft.) The workshop was doing its job too, with insightful comments and support. We all couldn't wait to see the next installment. Some people were even reading the entire book in addition to the excerpts Diane submitted. The whole process made me feel good.

After a year or so she completed another draft. Then she did deep revisions. In the workshop she met a woman who knew an agent in New York. She asked if the woman would contact the agent; not long after that the agent asked to see the manuscript. About a week later I got a call from Diane.

"James," she said, "you sitting down?"

From her tone I didn't know what to expect. "Hold on," I said. I walked into the bedroom, lay down and pressed a pillow behind my head. I picked up the second receiver and asked Adrienne to hang up the first.

"I just heard from the agent."

"Yeah."

"She's been shopping the book around."

"Great."

"And she just got an offer."

"Really? An offer? That's fabulous. Can I ask you discreetly, and you don't have to tell me . . . umm . . . how much is the offer for?"

"You ready?" she said. "You sitting down?"

"Yeah."

"A HUNDRED THOUSAND DOLLARS!" she cried.

"What?" I leaped up. "A hundred thousand dollars? Did you say a fucking hundred thousand dollars?"

"I did."

"Oh shit, oh Jesus, that's great!"

"I know!"

"*Crazy!*"

"It *is* crazy, James. But one thing I want to ask you . . ."

"Sure, anything."

"Can you please keep it quiet for a couple weeks, until I see the contract, until I know it's real."

"No problem," I said. "I'm skilled that way. Diane—I'm really happy for you."

11

At the same time that these good things were happening for RWG, a family problem was emerging for me. Ma was showing signs of dementia. She was repeating herself a lot, and constantly misplacing her keys and purse. She had begun to do odd things like cutting out voluminous amounts of coupons and balling up hundreds of rubber bands. She lived alone in the house where I grew up in Atlantic City, and she was becoming paranoid that people were watching the house. She was fearful of driving. My supremely confident, independent mother, who'd stood by me through all the trouble I got into after my dad died when I was eight, was beginning to falter. I'd drive down to see her every couple of weeks, and when I mentioned her strange actions she said she recognized them too, but couldn't stop herself.

"What's the matter with me?" she'd ask. "What's happening?"

"Nothing's happening," I'd say. "You're just getting older. You're doing different things." I'd chuckle. At first it seemed amusing rather than alarming. I didn't take it seriously. But I didn't know then what was really happening to her—or I didn't want to know. Looking back now, my laughter and teasing were defenses against my fear.

Her condition worsened. She was *really* losing her short-term memory. "What's happening?" she kept asking. "Something's the matter with my mind. I used to be so smart and now I'm dumb. I'm sorry." She'd sniff. She'd have tears in her eyes. It shook me.

Adrienne and I took her to neurologists. They couldn't identify the exact problem. They variously diagnosed Alzheimer's, mini-strokes, organic brain syndrome. We realized she could no longer live alone. Still, she was cognizant enough to insist that she didn't want anyone

living with her, nor did she want to live with anyone else. She wasn't
going to give up her independence.

We considered pushing her to stay with us. But we knew that we
couldn't take care of her properly. We lived in a one-bedroom apartment and worked two jobs. I talked to my two brothers and my sister,
but they wouldn't take her in. They had their own problems—real or
fabricated, I wasn't sure. Ma had an insurance policy that covered
home health care. She qualified due to her mental state. We found an
agency that provided home health aides.

My mother didn't want them. We didn't want them either. Who
wants strangers in the house? And who wants to recognize that their
loved one needs this kind of help?—and you have to take action even
though they don't want it. You feel terrible that you're adding to their
distress. Then again, you're providing safety and care.

With the hiring of home health aides I hoped for the best. I knew
they had a tough job. They worked twelve-hour shifts. They got paid
little and had to care for someone who probably wouldn't get any better. I wondered how they would tolerate Ma's behavior and her repetitions—how much of her conversation could they endure? How
much TV could they watch, how much could they talk on the phone,
before these distractions devolved into boredom? Then what—they'd
go to sleep or bring their friends over, neglecting Ma?

The first person who showed up was stout and partly toothless,
with red blotchy skin. She perspired a lot and kept scratching herself inside her dress. She talked about herself in the third person.
She turned to Ma and said, "Molly'll take care of you. Molly loves
old people." Later, she asked, "You're having a good time with Molly,
aren't you?" "You like everything that Molly cooks, don't you?"

"Y-Y-Yes," my mother stammered, looking at me misty-eyed.

Whenever I sat down with Ma, Molly was there. She didn't give
us any room. She seemed afraid that we would talk about her.

Then one day I drove down to the house to visit. Molly took me
into the kitchen.

"I have something to tell you," she whispered.

"What?"

"The shower downstairs is broken and I had to give your mother a bath and all I could find was the mop bucket." She pointed to a gray plastic container next to the refrigerator. "But I cleaned it out good, washed it out with Pine-Sol a couple times, and gave your mom a bath with it. Hope you don't mind."

I looked at the bucket again, then noticed a mop covered with black grime, leaning against the wall. "The same bucket you use to clean the kitchen floor with?" I asked.

"Yes." She grinned.

"Not good," I said.

I phoned the agency and told them I needed someone else. It took two weeks before they could find a replacement

The situation mostly declined from there. I learned quickly that the aides were some of the most inefficient people you could meet. They didn't show up on time or they didn't show up at all. I was constantly calling the agency to get one to the house or to replace one. And they were treacherous. I'd moved out Ma's jewelry and other valuables before they arrived, yet they found things to steal. They took clothes, food, dishes, petty cash. I wondered if the agency really vetted these folks. Did they really do background checks? The aides also managed to ruin and damage things: they left windows open during rainstorms so the wallpaper got soaked; broke washing machines, dryers, most every appliance; toilets and sinks were forever clogged.

There was always a problem. The aides were always calling me or I'd discover some unexpected calamity after I drove down. Sometimes they took Ma back to their house or apartment and left her there while they did errands. I'd phone for hours wondering where everyone was or if Ma had fallen, blacked out or died and why none of the aides was there. My guilt morphed into an intense apprehension where I fantasized all the terrible things that could happen. I tried to change agencies, but it was the only one in the area that provided round-the-clock live-in help. Rarely did we actually get that coverage.

A few of the aides were honest and competent. The good ones I asked to work for me privately. I said I'd pay them more than the agency did. But they usually said no, or if they did take the job, they'd quit after a few weeks. The job was tough, as I said before: long hours, insufficient pay. But probably the biggest drawback was Ma herself. She wasn't improving. How long can you abide helping someone who doesn't improve? I'd contemplated this question myself, regarding some of my students.

Adrienne was almost as upset about the situation as I was. But it was *my* mother. Although our careers were going well, our domestic life suffered. We often fought about the time I spent dealing with her.

I'd show up at the workshop after some havoc in Atlantic City and have to shove the bad shit aside, suppress it, compartmentalize it, so I could do my job. My students didn't want to hear my problems; they weren't paying for that. I always felt that no matter how difficult things got for me personally, I could do my job. I'd try to deliver my best. There was my livelihood and there was my personal life, and at some level I felt that my livelihood was more important. The workshop was mine, something I'd created and loved. I was fortunate enough to make money from it. I could almost control it. My problems melted away when I was teaching.

The bright spot in our domestic life was Adrienne's sister's little girls, McCall and Marlyn. One was a cheery, twinkly-eyed seven year old, the other an energized toddler. We saw them on the weekends when we were caring for my mother. Their parents owned a store that wasn't doing well. They couldn't afford a babysitter, and they took the kids to the shop—where they were stuck all day and didn't get much attention. Adrienne also began to suspect that there were deeper problems in the family. She dug her nieces, so she would pick them up and give them a break from the store and their parents' struggles.

Adrienne spirited them to shops in and around Atlantic City and bought them little-girl things—scrunchies, barrettes, glittery nail polish, candies. Then they would come to my mother's house. They watched TV, played games, ran up and down the stairs. My mother sat quietly on the couch. I think she enjoyed their vitality.

12

In 1994, the Pennsylvania Council on the Arts awarded nine fiction fellowships state-wide; four went to members of RWG. Each person received five thousand dollars.

In 1996, Diane's novel, *Tumbling*, appeared. Reviewers raved and it became a bestseller. She embarked on a ten-city book tour. During the Q&As she would talk about Rittenhouse Writers' Group and how it contributed to her success. I didn't ask her to do this. I was thrilled. She was interviewed on Philly public radio and referred to the important influence of the workshop and me. When the interviewer asked how other interested writers could contact RWG, Diane gave out my number on the air. For hours after that my phone didn't stop ringing.

Lauren Cowen, another member, published a nonfiction book titled *Daughters and Mothers*, which celebrated this special relationship with essays by Lauren and striking photos of women of all ages and backgrounds. Diane and her daughter were included. Lauren's book also became a bestseller; and she also mentioned RWG.

Reporters from the *Inquirer* and *Philadelphia Magazine* began calling. I was uncomfortable talking to them—maybe "distrustful" is a better word. On the one hand I wanted everyone to know about the group. On the other I worried about what they might write. I remembered my days working for the trade show company in New York and how my boss had warned us not to talk to reporters. The boss said most everyone liked talking about themselves and their work; reporters knew this and conned you by saying they'd write something positive. Then they'd twist your words and you'd come out looking like a fool or, worse, a rat. Conflict, not harmony and peace, drives plot, and it also sells papers.

But laudatory press would be great, and why shouldn't the group be showcased? They'd achieved much success. If only I could control what the reporters wrote. At the same time I felt the old nervousness—I didn't deserve to be in the spotlight; people would find out I was an impostor. Finally a different thought broke through: the members of RWG would be the focus, not me. I was there to serve my students; I was there to help them. That bolstered my confidence. It gave me the necessary distance to withstand public scrutiny. Once I found this strategy, I returned to it whenever I felt pressure to perform.

I told the reporters that I'd be happy to answer their questions, but maybe they'd like to hear from students. The reporters liked the idea so I called a few folks who I knew loved the group and who'd gotten a story published or had won a fellowship. Everyone I approached was happy to talk. Great, I told them. Whatever you want to say is fine. I have faith. Tell them what you want. That's how the articles were written: others opined while I remained in the background. When the pieces came out the group shone.

Another journalist wanted to film the workshop, or at least to sit in and take notes during the critiques. I was concerned about this too; it could be too invasive. Letting a reporter audit might even be worse than having Curt's drunken friend, Juice, sit in. Remembering that episode made me flinch. Publicity was great, but wouldn't an outsider corrupt the group's intimacy or diminish the magic? I talked to a few members. Some were actually excited; others thought the act of filming or even note-taking would give a false picture since everybody would be self-conscious.

In the end I decided once again that *no one* should audit, but I told the reporter that he could have a photographer take pictures at the beginning or end of class. Now I worried that he'd abandon the article. If that's what happened, *say lavee*; it was more important to protect the group. He said he still wanted to write the piece, and one night a photographer came in, set up his lights and white screens, and snapped several shots. Again we got lucky and the piece made the group look strong.

I never had to pay for advertising after that. Everybody wanted to be part of RWG.

So many people called that I decided to expand to a second night. Now I was teaching on Tuesday as well as Monday night, for a total of thirty students. With RWG, the Penn workshop, and a three-week-long literature class I'd started there called "Eight Great Short Stories," I was running around like a maniac. I wasn't getting much writing done. I kept putting it off thinking, I'll get to it, I'll get to it. Maybe next month. Let me get used to my new schedule. Again—almost nothing is harder than writing.

MONDAY NIGHTS I reserved for long-time members. They were serious, dedicated writers concentrating almost exclusively on literary fiction. The new Tuesday group gave me a chance to sign up people I wasn't so sure of—those who seemed interesting but gave me a slightly hinky vibe when they called; students from Penn who were sharp but fairly new to fiction; and a few writers of genre stories. They turned out to be a wilder, looser bunch than the Monday crew. ·

Let me tell you about some of the Tuesday-nighters. Mike was a hardcore South Philly guy: bartender, former casino worker. He wrote about tough, ballsy, dissolute characters. He used lines like, "'Fuck me with my socks on,' she said. 'I wanna feel like a school girl.'"

He wrote about bartending, Atlantic City, the mob, in muscular *and* lyrical prose. He was intense. When people critiqued his stories, his face flashed red and a huge vein bulged out across his brow. Another guy, Fred, looked like he was a member of the Pagans motorcycle gang. He had eyebrows like half-circles of black shag carpet. Pupils that lasered holes into you. I asked him if he'd been a biker, and he just grinned at me like a jack-o'-lantern. After I got to know him he seemed more like a hippie. He worked as a maintenance man at an all-girls private school. He built props for school plays and mowed the grounds on a John Deere. He used to come to the workshop smelling of sweat and churned earth. He wrote sensuous, colloquial deconstructions of old myths.

One night Fred and Mike got into an argument about a story, which devolved into a "who's smarter" competition. One recited a line from *Hamlet* and the other provided the next line. Back and forth it went; it was a verbal boxing match. Their knowledge was amazing, and humbling. When they finished the scene the rest of us were tongue-tied. To ease the friction I resorted to my usual tactic of cracking a lame joke: "Maybe they should make a beer called Shakes Beer!" I pulled at my chin with my thumb and index finger. "Now, can we all please get back to the original story?"

In another class Mike got pissed at a preppie type who was critiquing his story. The guy knew nothing of the street and was less than self-aware. Mike asked at one point, "Are you *telling* me how I should write?" In his grandiosity the guy continued on. He reminded me of some of the jerks in graduate school. They used words like "epiphanic" and "adjectival," but didn't know the words that would back somebody off. Mike barked, "What the fuck you mean?" The vein on his forehead was ready to pop.

The kid went on obliviously, "What I'm saying is, what I'm saying—"

"What the FUCK are you saying?" Mike leaned forward, banging his fists on the table. I was sitting next to him. He was a second away from leaping across the table and beating the living hell out of the boy.

"Yo man," I whispered. "He doesn't know what he's saying." I had my hand on his back. I gently rubbed circles on his denim jacket. "It's a workshop," I murmured. "Just a writing workshop. A fiction writing workshop. No big deal. He doesn't know what he's saying," I repeated. "You don't have to get upset, ain't no big deal." Mike glanced at me, snarl-mouthed. He huffed a couple of deep breaths, blew them out, and began to relax. "I think we all get it." I stared at the kid. "Let's push on." He shut up . . . finally. He didn't know how close he'd come to getting his ass beat.

Another guy, with a torso like a weightlifter, wrote a story about local fishermen casting from a jetty who drown an Asian man who's *netting* fish near them. They toss him off the rocks into a boiling sea. The plan to kill him and the graphic details of the murder seemed so real, so personal, that many of us wondered if he'd actually done it. We hoped, of course, that he was merely adept at writing realism. His second story described a man on a ferry to Nova Scotia who slaughters all the passengers and crew. Murder appeared to be the author's bailiwick. The group commented about how brutal and sinister the tale was, like the first one. The guy didn't say much, deflecting the comments with witticisms. After class, when the rest of us went out for drinks, he declined to come along. He said he was tired and wanted to get home.

I was worried about him. The anger expressed in his work was stoppered in the class, and I wondered how he handled the tension. While he imagined killing people, I thought maybe what he really wanted to do was kill himself. We know the close connection between these opposites, and how one can quickly shift into the other, as in Germany before WWII, when the would-be suicides became murderers. Someone in the group asked me if the guy had served in Vietnam. "I don't think so," I said. "Well, he might as well have," she replied.

I recalled the questionably fictional suicide note from a couple of years before. I hadn't acted then. Maybe that heightened my concern.

We partied a bit after class. Then I went home and called him: no answer, and no answering machine. Adrienne asked if I was all right. Had everything gone all right? Sort of, I said. We went to sleep, but I woke up about 3:00 A.M. and despite hesitations called him again. The phone rang and rang. I called at nine the next day. In the afternoon I finally reached him.

"Where've you been?" I asked. "I've been calling for hours. You all right? I'm worried about you."

"How come?"

"You seemed upset last night when you left. Was the criticism all right? Are *you* all right?"

"I'm fine, I'm fine. The criticism was great. Really helpful. I was up all night rewriting the story. I want to show you the revision when I'm done."

I was relieved, though I didn't really want to read his story again. At some point you can't take any more horror. I remember reading

Blood Meridian by Cormac McCarthy. The language soared, but the subject matter was so brutal that I quit halfway through. Sitting on the couch in my apartment that afternoon while we talked, I watched one squirrel chase another along the edge of a tarred roof. They jumped onto some tree branches, then darted down the trunk. I was the one trying to get away.

"Umm, no problem." I sighed. "See you Tuesday."

The guy wasn't freaked out, not even upset. I relied on my ability to understand people, but this was a complete misreading. It wasn't the first time; still, it disturbed me to realize I'd worried all night about the guy's mental state. Why? Was it hubris to believe what happened in the writers' group could be crucial to someone? Or paranoia, a predisposition to imagine the worst? I needed to try harder to keep my feelings in check so my thinking would be clearer. And to be more tolerant of my mistakes.

The Tuesday night participants wrote many fine stories. Some were inventive narratives built around the events of everyday life: spouses fighting with each other, children clashing with their parents. One or two stories took on the feel of fairytales. Others were set firmly on the dark side.

One guy wrote about wearing nipple clamps, which set off the metal detector alarm at airports.

A woman wrote a story about pole-dancing and flaming dildos.

Another wrote about smoke jumpers, the elite firefighters who put out wildfires. That was Gwen, a tough cookie herself. She didn't tolerate shit from anybody. One night during a critique of another student's story I brought up its subtle incest theme, framing it in terms of an Oedipal drama. Gwen cracked up.

"Oedipal? There's nothing Oedipal here. The girl doesn't give a damn about her father. It's just a battle between her and the father's girlfriend. Has nothing to do with her wanting to screw her father. I don't know what story you think you read, but this isn't it."

I started backpedaling. She probably knew more than I did about the Oedipus complex, and my status as the teacher wouldn't help me prevail.

I liked Gwen and her writing a lot, but now she was mocking me. I felt like a jackass in front of my group. After class, on the sidewalk across from the building, I asked who wanted to go out for a drink. Usually we went to the same bar every week. Gwen suggested a different one she wanted to try. I was propped up against the lamppost like it was an auxiliary spine.

"Yeah, let's try a new place," somebody said.

"C'mon—we're tired of going to the same place every week."

I hesitated.

"You coming with us?" Gwen asked. She studied her watch. She hitched up her shoulder bag.

"Yeah." I reluctantly followed along, trying my best to shelve my low spirits.

During the week that followed, I worried about the next class. I felt that I'd lost some authority and the group might be looking to Gwen for answers. Who would be the leader, she or I? A real-life Oedipal power struggle could unfold. But in the next class she didn't mention the episode. The group still turned to me for my judgment. One thing I realized: You better know your stuff or you could get blasted by someone who knows more.

13

A YOUNG MAN who joined the group, thin with sharp cheek-bones, reminded me of the liquid-metal villain in *Terminator* 2. He blinked a lot when he spoke, as if sending messages with his eyelids. He wrote a story about a guy who stalked the city streets at night in search of stray dogs and, when he found one, coaxed it to him with a piece of meat, then shattered its skull with a claw hammer. It was horrifying, but even worse it read like autobiography: a first-person narrator who spoke and looked like the author, set in Philly, close to where the author lived. I read the story late one night and got the chills. I read it again the next day and got chills again. One line went something like, He longed to see the ghost of the puppy leap out of the dead dog's eyes.

The group discussed the story. All of us were distressed. But there was artfulness in the piece, especially in the details—the blood, bone, and fur and the death shrieks of the unsuspecting animals. After-ward a couple of the women members told me they wouldn't stay in the workshop if he remained. He had the "creep" factor; they were afraid. I didn't tell them I was nervous as well. Instead I told them to hold on, that I'd talk to him.

I called and asked him to meet me for lunch. He was happy to get together. My intention was to determine how crazy or dangerous he really was, and whether I could keep him in the group or should make him leave.

We met at a quiet tavern and discussed his job and his writerly ambitions. He twitched, and blinked with those signal-lamp eyes. I brought the conversation around to his story, hinting at how disturb-ing the group found it. He was excessively apologetic. (He reminded me of Curt.) His next submission, he said, would be a lot gentler.

"Send it to me beforehand," I said. "Maybe I can give you a couple of general suggestions before you send it out to everybody." I wanted to screen it first, see how gentle it really was.

"Great," he replied.

I felt better after we spoke. He was weird but didn't seem dangerous. He mailed me the story, which wasn't violent at all. In fact it ended with a sunrise beginning to purple a mountain. I decided he could stay, that he and the group would be all right. I told the women who'd been anxious that they shouldn't be afraid. I also decided that I wouldn't send him the usual notice about the next workshop. That was a tactic I sometimes used to get people out of the group. If they didn't get a letter they might call me, or not. If they called, it would often be after the class had filled up, or at least that's what I said.

He didn't call. A few months later I got a note saying he'd applied to a top-tier MFA program and had been accepted.

I KNEW that if I wanted to get good, genuinely creative writers in the workshop I had to take some risks, and it was inevitable that some students would make me nervous and self-conscious. When you feel that way you can't do your best job; you have to learn how to handle it.

There are the intensely angry students. They may use jokes to mask their rancor, but they constantly say negative things to others about their writing. Some give off a scary S&M vibe. I've seen three or four of them over the years.

There are the perpetual cynics, who can't connect to others without sneering slightly.

The dogmatists constantly recite the rules they've culled from how-to books: "You gotta hook 'em from the first line." "You gotta show, not tell." Good writers know there are mostly no rules, or rules can be broken, challenged, reinvented. Great writers make up their own rules.

There are students who argue constantly with their confreres and me. They may insult me. I don't mind a couple of insults or gibes; heck, I mess with people. I never intentionally insult them, but I do tease and challenge them. And I don't mind their teasing or challenging me. But if it becomes a constant battle with someone, or a competition about who knows more, or an issue of who's in charge—then the person has to go. There can't be two leaders of a workshop.

The flip side is that you can't give too much positive attention to one person, constantly agreeing, acknowledging how much they know about fiction, or implying that the class should listen to what they say. It's okay for a while but there's a danger. If you've schooled them over the years, if they start publishing a lot and come to believe they're your peer, your equal, even your superior—then you have that same predicament: who's leading the workshop?

One might emerge as a kind of sergeant-at-arms, which is slightly different from the teacher's pet. This person you like but don't have a buzz for. You may really like them. You may have done exactly what you're supposed to do, sharpening their writing and critical skills, helping them to love writing and to be more self-aware. In some way, though, the process inflates them too much and creates a countervailing force in the group. It may be a good thing for that individual, but it's no longer beneficial for the group. And it's your fault.

It happens rarely. When it does I'm never happy about sitting down with the person (usually a woman because the group has more women), sipping coffee with my friend, my ace, my ally, and telling her that she may have outgrown the group, and me. Her mouth may arrow down and she may pause for a second, gather herself, and say, "Are you asking me to leave?" I'll demur. "That's not exactly what I'm saying."

She may go on to say that she's been having similar feelings. She doesn't want to compromise our friendship, but lately she's felt stymied in the group. She loves the group and appreciates all we've done for her. "Thanks," she says. "I really mean it. But you're right. Maybe it's time for me to move on." It's the old breakup story where each person tries to shoulder more of the blame. But the truth is both of us feel badly and sense it's the end of something significant. It's probably for the best, but we can't be sure. Afterwards we may or may not continue to be friends.

Is it possible to salvage your sergeant-at-arms? Perhaps. But you have to be profoundly aware of her status and your feelings towards her—which range from appreciation to anger. Perhaps you can modulate your attention towards her, perhaps you don't turn to her so much for her insights (which are similar to the ones you've been thinking of or have forgotten about—heck, you've taught her well), or you don't smile and ask her to wrap up the discussion. Perhaps then you can hold on to her, and everyone will be rewarded.

Last, there is the workshop scapegoat. The scapegoat writes genre stuff, or about wide-eyed children with loving parents, attending sun-drenched, mosquito-free picnics. Maybe one of the children wants to wander down to the creek alone, and the parents forbid him, and he starts to cry. That's about it, that's all that happens. He cries and they give him a wedge of cake. He pouts and rejects it, then gives in. The family is intact once again. A good writer could make an interesting morality story about this event, but not the workshop scapegoat, who's unencumbered by nuance.

"Do all stories have to be grim?" the scapegoat wants to know. "What about happy things? Why is everything so serious?" "The world is harsh," someone might say. I might add, "Fiction likes crazy, fucked up people doing fucked up things. Murders, suicides, deceptions, betrayals, revenge, weird sexual practices. Normal people who make big mistakes, forced to go beyond their usual limits. Fiction likes tragedy. It likes comedy and wondrous happiness too, and all the gradations in between. Fiction loves love, but people have to go through shit to get and keep it. Fiction flourishes in onerous settings: combat zones, penitentiaries, mental hospitals, surreal worlds, and contentious domestic environments."

Scapegoats like *facts*. They're wed to them. They like to point out where you've erred. They don't realize that a good imagination will get you close to the truth, and exactitude should be left for a later draft. They also crave blueprints. "What are the rules? Tell me what I should do."

They make generalizing statements that everyone already knows as if they're elucidating Kant: "The protagonist should eat or she'll . . .

lose weight." "If he turns off the water he won't have . . . a leak." Tautologies dressed up as illuminations.

These folks bring the group together for a while. They have power in their beleaguered, victimized standing. They don't know it, but the instructor should be aware of it. When others ask, "Why is she in the group? Her writing never changes. She's been writing the same crap for years. I can't read it any more." I say, "Maybe she can't do any better. Or doesn't want to. But she's all right." The scapegoat is usually nice, after all.

Eventually the group begins to project their own writerly problems onto the person. Usually it looks like anger or aggression, but it conceals feelings of guilt, shame, and doubt as to whether they're writing as well as they should. Their reaction parallels the story of the biblical goat, around whose neck the villagers tied lists of their own sins and which was sacrificed, either slaughtered or sent into the desert to die. God would be appeased and the villagers absolved—at least until the next plague or drought.

Scapegoats are okay until they become a weight on the group or me. I'm usually the last person who wants them to leave. They're nice and have been paying me a long time to attend, with never any quibbles about the money. At some point I begin to feel I might be leading them on, less than sincere about their work getting better, or mad at myself for their writing not improving. So, at some point, they have to go—sent out into the desert, sacrificed. It sounds cold, but it has to be done. The question is always, What's best for the group?

14

MORE AND MORE RWGers were getting published. Several novels came out: *The Undiscovered Country* by Samantha Gillison, *Frontera Street* by Tanya Barrientos, and Diane's second novel, *Tempest Rising*. Samantha won a Guggenheim. More members were appearing in quality journals and receiving grants from the Pennsylvania Council on the Arts and fellowships from foundations like Leeway and Pew. The group was generating a lot of success, and I made sure members realized they'd contributed to it. I wanted everyone to take pride in knowing that at some point they'd said something that improved their colleagues' writing.

Sometimes I felt as if I were hosting two parties every week, Monday and Tuesday nights. Sometimes, in the restaurant after class, I sat quietly watching as students drank their beer or wine. I liked to see them laughing and carrying on. It gave me joy to see what I'd created. I'd say to myself, I'm getting *paid* to do this?

I liked it when people got together, became friends, read each other's work outside of class. Discreetly, I encouraged people to do that. Maybe even wanted them to hook up. Maybe I saw it as another feature of RWG: learn to write better *and* fall in love. I liked to see a blossoming romance. I felt like the proud papa and the matchmaker combined. One couple who'd met in the group wound up getting married. The *Inquirer* wrote a few lines about them, saying it was another first for the Rittenhouse Writers' Group.

There were students who came to me and told me about their affections. Sometimes they seemed to be seeking my blessing. I was *el papa*, the big daddy (or mommy). One young guy—a modest, sensitive type who'd recently been dumped by his girlfriend whom he claimed to continue to love—was mixing pleasures with two women in the workshop. They were friends but only one knew that the guy was screwing the other. One of them told me about it. I listened, and kept it to myself. People love good stories, and we're attracted to gossip. It shows kinship to join in, but a teacher has to be scrupulous. People pay big money to those who keep secrets: lawyers, doctors, accountants, shrinks—all professionals. Teachers should guard the secrets of their students the same way.

I heard all kinds of gossip—who liked whose writing; who thought it sucked; who, everyone said, got treated too kindly or constantly got thrashed. It's okay to agree with positive remarks but not to amplify them because the student who proffered them may feel demeaned. It wasn't hard for me to see the positive side because I was rooting for everyone's success. Still there were a couple of dilettantes, dabblers, who weren't willing to put in the work. I rarely told them so, and never agreed with anyone who identified those traits. You can listen to a student badmouth another in your presence, but you have to cut it short. I tried to emphasize what's good about someone; at the very least, I wanted to be noncommittal. Never add your voice to trash. The disparaged group member will hear about it, feel hurt, quit, tell others what was said. Everybody will lose trust in you, and trust, in the sensitive, potentially bruising environment of a writers' group, is an absolute necessity.

Sometimes people idealized me. I became the father figure who knew everything, who didn't make mistakes. I recognized that they were projecting onto me some unconscious wish that I would guide and love them the way their parents once did—or perhaps never did—and that now they could be re-parented. They could return to a fantasized vision of a loving childhood. They could get back home, back to the Garden.

When you're offered the chance, it's tempting to collude with your idealizer. I learned to be careful. Sometimes a student, female or male, would develop an erotic fantasy. I had figuratively neutered myself a long time ago. My unwillingness to say much about my private life—plus the fact that I was married, safe, ostensibly unattainable—may have contributed to an attraction. "I'm mono-gaymous," I was fond of saying. Yet I was also a sexual guy. I flirted a little, made goofy, pubes-cent-boy jokes. I was aware that I was messing with people. I wasn't quite aware that I was also channeling an interpersonal dynamic, per-haps an honesty, that cultivated greater closeness in the group.

15

Back in 1985 when I lived in Miami with my girlfriend, I didn't write much, and I didn't start to work seriously again until after I returned to Atlantic City, moved in with my mother, fell into *une dépression majeur*, then got an unexpected lift when I scored amazingly well on that test, the one that simulated the real-life job of being a stockbroker. All the applicants were given the exam by the firm where I was trying to get hired. They said they'd probably take me, but I had to meet with the executives and other brokers first. I guess most of them were on vacation because the process went on and on.

At my fourth interview, a vice president sat me in a beige conference room and brought in several potential colleagues. They told me anecdotes about their lives in retail and the road they'd traveled to get there. One guy said he'd been a forklift driver and that, while hoisting the pallets up and down one day, he saw the obvious connection to market volatility. "Brokering was a calling," he added. Another guy said he'd always been gabby and, as a kid, had made lots of money in his neighborhood hustling boxes of cookies and greeting cards. The more I heard the more I perspired. Sweat seeped from my armpits and broke out around my neck. My tie was a garrote. They asked me why I wanted to be a broker, and I gave an impressively uninspired answer. "I like talking to people, and I want to help them out financially." I forgot to say that I wanted to make money. The crew nodded perfunctorily and then it was over. They headed back to their desks while the VP ushered me out. "We'll let you know, James. Have a nice day."

I felt as if, after all that time and effort, I'd blown it. It took me a few days to recover. My disappointment shifted into quiet anger, a much more comforting emotion. Did I really want to be a broker? Did I really want to hang out with those guys?

I went back to writing and attacked the page. Hours each day I scribbled on the foolscap. Then one afternoon I wrote a story about a man and woman fucking. I scrawled a blow-by-blow scenario. It was a revenge piece directed toward my ex-lover, and the world. The language was blunt, the emotion unstoppered. I sent it off to an editor I'd known since childhood who worked for a men's magazine in New York. Around the same time I began investigating MFA programs. If the broker thing didn't fly, maybe I'd go to grad school. I mailed out a couple of applications.

A few weeks later the editor called. She said she loved my story and wanted to publish it. She exclaimed that I had "out-Bukowski-ed Bukowski."

Your first story acceptance is a marvelous thing. (Yeah, it was porn—but still I was ecstatic.) The rejections melt away like snowflakes on glass. After the phone call I plugged in a cassette of Rick James's "Give It To Me Baby." I boogied around my room. I went sailing down the street like I'd just hit the Pick-Six. I was buzzing like I'd swallowed a fistful of Adderall. *Swank* wanted to publish my story!

After a week or so I visited my friend at her office. The place was posh, all mahogany and Berber carpeting, not seedy, which was what I'd expected. Clearly the magazine was making money. Before being shown in, I had to wait in the anteroom for her to finish talking to Chocolate Thunder or Animal X, some huge porn star with a crazy name. When she came out she greeted me warmly and told me again how great my piece was. She introduced me to the other editors who were so friendly and conventional you'd think you were at a recruitment picnic for a church. They all repeated how impressed they were by my work. They wanted more stories. They even handed me a loupe and asked if I'd like to review the latest thumbnail photos for the upcoming issue. I declined blushingly, but I did leaf through their collection of beaver and big-cock shots. I fantasized I could be the next Bukowski or Henry Miller. I felt as if I'd finally arrived at the place where I fit in.

A short time afterward, I got accepted to Columbia.

Was I meant to write porn—or something nobler?

And the brokerage job was still a possibility. Every week I'd call the veep and ask if the firm had made a decision. Every week he said they were still considering it. I was losing interest. I wanted to go to grad school, but it was expensive. My mother said she'd mortgage the house if that's what I wanted to do. My sweet mother. After several weeks the veep told me the company was possibly going to open an office in the Atlantic City area, and if they did I'd get the job. That's when I stopped calling.

In January I enrolled at Columbia. In February I received an envelope from *Swank*. I tore it open, and the official acceptance letter fell out along with a check for three hundred dollars. I began jumping like a quarter in a tambourine. I whirled around the living room.

When I went to class that same day a student was running around the classroom screaming, "I can't believe it! I can't believe it!" She'd also had her first story acceptance—from the *New Yorker*. People grinned and told her how great the news was and how happy they were for her. I congratulated her too, but didn't really mean it. I suspect many of us were envious. Her success undermined my happiness, but only a little. I still felt proud, and that I was a real writer, a money-making writer. But I didn't tell many of my classmates the news.

As time went on, while still in grad school, I became a very minor smut-meister. I hawked stories to *Kink, Sex Acts, Couples Today*. Every few weeks I'd write a salty piece, send it to an editor, and it would be accepted. A month later I'd see the story in print—under my pseudonym. I wanted to use my real name but decided not to. What would the other students think if they saw it? Some of them probably read this stuff. Maybe my professors did too. Plus, it was the era of Ed Meese and the Moral Majority. They could put me on the bad list, come after my ass.

There I was ensconced in a highly touted MFA program, and I was writing porn, and I was good at it. To this day, when students ask how to write a good sex scene, it cracks me up. How can you *not* write a good sex scene? As with all fine writing, you have to deliver your heart to the page, that is, your deep emotion and sincerity. Porn, along with the work I had to submit for school, was pushing me to write more and more, and teaching me how to construct and deconstruct stories. I took more risks with the salacious pieces, experimenting with structure and form, intensifying the subject matter. I worked hard on those stories (pun intended). I took them seriously, as I do all writing. You have to be sincere in what you write, you have to find emotional connection with your material. A smart reader will always know when you're bullshitting. And, at least when it comes to writing, I'm not a bullshitter.

Though I didn't hear about this until I'd nearly completed my degree, the best writer in the program was making a living crafting 150-page gay smut novels. He wrote one every three weeks and got fifteen hundred dollars for it. He told people that writing them was how he'd learned to write. I don't know if I believe that, but he was a heckuva writer. He was the only person in the program whose submissions read like published material. You'd actually forget you were reading typed pages.

I didn't tell many classmates about my successes in the porn business. I didn't tell anyone years later at Rittenhouse Writers' Group, either. I didn't think I could build the group using that part of my past; I wanted the group to be serious, high-minded. But because I had so few credits, I did list *Couples Today* as one of my publications, believing that nobody would figure out it wasn't a psychology journal.

Like every other student in the Columbia program, my goal (at least at the beginning of my career) was to publish in literary magazines. I stopped fiddling with the novel and began writing literary stories. I wanted to see my name in a respected journal, and once I began teaching I wanted the confidence that publishing in such a journal would bring.

I submitted stories. I got tons of rejections. They bounced off me like dum-dum bullets—which means they didn't bounce off. They were all the more painful because Romnesh was sending stories out too, and it seemed as if every one that crossed an editor's desk was accepted. Other people from RWG began to get their stories picked up, and so did a few folks from my grad school class. But not me, the vaunted sagacious instructor. No, not the illustrious workshop facilitator. I was envious of everyone else's success. Of course I was happy for Romnesh and the other RWGers. It was great for them, and for the group. But I felt like a fraud. Maybe I should just teach, I thought, and jettison the writing. Maybe I could become a great fiction teacher, despite never really publishing anything. Maybe I could be the best fiction teacher in Greater Philadelphia, or in downtown Philadelphia, or in Rittenhouse Square. At the same time I kept writing and concealed my feelings of inferiority.

About two years after I started the group I finally got an acceptance. It was from a Philly-area magazine called *American Writing.* I didn't know anyone there, but I felt as if I did after they called and told me they loved my story. It occurred to me briefly that the fact I was local might have influenced the decision, but I shouted down that negative voice.

My reaction to the acceptance was equal to when I first heard from *Swank.* Adrienne and I dined and drank at a fancy steakhouse. Later we bounced around our apartment like bonobos.

The magazine said they were going to have a reading. Did I want to participate? Of course I did. I'd get the word out about RWG and me. Trumpet the good news. This would be the beginning of my legitimate writing career.

The reading went great; a hundred people attended. I received kudos for my story. People from the audience inquired about joining RWG. I began writing more stories and sending them out. It was two years before I got another acceptance.

16

By 1999 my mother's mental and physical health had deterio-
rated significantly. Now when Adrienne and I drove down to check
on her, the house, and the aides, she could barely remember who we
were and who she was, let alone anyone else. Sometimes I was her
father or grandfather. Or her boyfriend. I'd sit on the couch with my
arm around her and she'd start batting her eyelids at me. "Ma," I'd
laugh, "you gotta stop." She wouldn't reply, just stare at me with her
misty blue eyes. Her coquettishness was comic *and* tragic. But I was
mostly past the point of sorrow. There was nothing I could do to stop
her decline. What I could provide were loving moments. I felt she
could sense how much I cared, and that meant a lot to me.

Again our nieces provided Adrienne and me with respite. We'd
see Ma for a couple of hours, then go and pick them up. We had a
good time together, even though they were going through some shit
themselves. Their parents were always fighting about money now.
We, and others, had given them some, but it didn't seem to improve
the situation. They bounced checks, neglected bills, or put the cash
towards partying away their problems. The kids suffered the fall-
out. Our older niece, McCall, eight at the time, knew something was
wrong but couldn't quite grasp it. Marlyn, three, had problems with
asthma and was often frenzied from lack of attention and discipline.
We did our best to cheer them up.

One afternoon when we visited my mother, the aides told me she
could hardly swallow. They said she was pocketing food, meaning
she stored it squirrel-like in her cheeks. I didn't quite believe them,
or want to. Later I watched her chew and then extract the food from

her mouth—raisins from raisin bran, nuts from butter pecan ice cream—and use it to decorate the rims of her bowls. "Ma, what are you doing?" I asked.

She had almost no short-term memory, sores on her feet, rattles in her lungs, cellulitis, and incontinence. Our family doctor said we should put her in the hospital. My cousin, a surgeon, agreed. They both said she'd be safer there, get better care. Then, after they got her stabilized we should get her into a nursing home.

I resisted. I felt the hospital and "home" would be way stations before the final stop. Maybe, I thought, we could have nurses around the clock and keep her in the house. Maybe her health problems would magically disappear. But we couldn't afford the nurses, and the truth was, Ma was in bad shape. Finally I agreed to let her go. I felt like someone had sawed through my ribs.

The morning she left the house it was nearly impossible to get her out of bed, almost as if she knew something bad was happening. Finally the aide got her up, cleaned, and dressed. Then we had to get her from her bedroom to the living room. She slumped along, dragging one foot, holding onto our arms. "Come on," I coached. "You can do it, you can do it." It was distressing, getting her to move. At one point I tugged her to get her through a door. "Come on already. Jesus," I said. Anger bubbled up inside me. But it was my mother. How could I be angry at her? How could I be angry on this particular day? It had to be the damn aide that was provoking me, with her sing-song voice and how she kept calling Ma "Sweetie." Didn't she know my mother was a powerhouse once?

Medics from the ambulance toted a gurney up the front steps onto the porch and rolled it into the house. Ma smiled at them; I think she liked their uniforms. They took hold of her, gently but firmly, and lifted her onto it. "Ohh, ohh," she moaned in a hopeless effort to stop them. They put a pillow under her head, squared some blankets over her, and yanked up the rails. The aide asked me if there was anything else she could do. "No, nothing," I said.

"Goodbye, Sweetie," she said to Ma, giving her an air-kiss alongside her cheek. I watched her amble out the door and fade down the steps.

I helped the medics roll Ma to the ambulance. After they had maneuvered the gurney, and her, inside, she stared blank-faced up in the air. "Ma," I said, "you're gonna be all right. You're just going to the hospital. You're gonna feel better."

Under a blue dome of sky the ambulance cruised down the street. The air was cool and fresh with a touch of wood smoke in it, and I knew that winter would be coming on fast now. I walked back up the steps and idled on the porch. The wood needed to be sanded and repainted. The whole family home needed TLC; I'd neglected it to use the money on Ma's care. One day I'd fix it. Not today.

I gazed out at the street. Everything had a glittery, surreal appearance—the whiteness of the homes, the sunlight burnishing the trees, a neighbor throwing a football to his kids. Everything and everyone seemed to gaze back at me. I rubbed away tears with the heel of my hand.

A short time later I drove to the hospital. In a mauve-colored room she lay under stark white sheets. She looked like a tiny doll lying there. I came in, leaned over the guard rail, and kissed her on the cheek. "How you doing?" I said. "You doing all right?" She just stared. Her white hair seemed scribbled on top of her head.

"I'm sorry, Ma," I said. I paused. "Do you know where you are?" She took in some air through her teeth.

"In a hospital," she whispered. I couldn't believe she knew. A few minutes went by and I think she said, "Jimmy."

Three days later they moved her to a nursing home.

Three weeks later she died there.

17

The FIRST WORKSHOPS after my mother's death started in early January of 2000. I'd hoped Ma would make it to the millennium, but then I was always hoping she'd make it to the next celebration—a grandkid's birthday party, my birthday, *her* birthday. I was always bargaining with the Reaper. I was upset over her death, but not devastated; she'd been sick a long time. I threw myself into the workshops. I appreciated my students' condolences, but kept my feelings and thoughts mostly private.

Students had always asked me what was going on in my life. "What's your writing schedule like?" "How's your book coming along?" I doled out a little, but not much. Then I'd shift the conversation back to their work. If they noticed that I was deflecting their questions, I'd say I didn't like talking about myself. The truth was I didn't think much of myself. Any success—writing, teaching—underneath I felt I didn't deserve it. Praise was something I couldn't accept. At a deep level I felt I was bad, guilty, deserving of punishment and blame, like a criminal—but what crime had I committed? These feelings generated my reticence, but also a big fantasy life, which led me to write, and to a desire for my words to be heard.

New RWGers would ask where my stories had appeared, and I'd tell them there were a few places. They'd say, "I tried to find them online, but couldn't."

"They're there. Or maybe the journals are out of print."

"Are you writing under a different name?" they'd ask suspiciously.

"Could be." Then I'd flash on the porn, and grin. By this time I'd published stories and some nonfiction pieces in other literary and local magazines. Nothing huge, of national import.

A by-product of my secretiveness was that I created an aura about myself, an air of tragic mystery that attracted people. It wasn't intentional, but it helped solidify the workshop. Downplaying my achievements and keeping quiet about my private life suggested that there was more to me than there appeared. Intellectually, I recognized that I'd taught for years at Penn and RWG and many of my students had been published, so I had to be doing something right. Maybe I couldn't appreciate success, but others could. They knew something good was happening.

Sometime after my mother's death I hit a midlife crisis. I couldn't afford the red Porsche and wasn't looking for an affair. Instead I decided to do something physical. I took up boxing.

As a kid I had sparred, my best friend's father had been a world-class fighter, and I loved watching the sport. I knew there must be deeper reasons, but I didn't want to explore them. I just wanted to beat the hell out of somebody, or have somebody beat the hell out of me.

Several times a week I went to two gyms where trainers I'd hired taught me to jump rope like a fighter, shadow box, and pound the heavy bag. I bought training gloves, boxing gloves, hand wraps, head gear, and a plastic mouthpiece, which I had to boil to soften up and mold to my teeth so it fit in my mouth. I burned the shit out of my mouth when I first put it in. You *had* to wear a mouthpiece. There was no way you wouldn't get hit in the face, and you didn't want to shatter your teeth or your jaw.

After a couple of months I was sparring and coming home regularly with sore hands, sore wrists, chipped teeth (despite the mouthpiece), a bloody nose, an aching back and neck. Adrienne asked, "What's the matter with you? Why, why, are you doing this?"

"I love it," I said. I felt badass.

One gym in particular was superb. It was a medium-sized cinder block building with whitewashed walls and high, bright lights. I loved pushing open the heavy steel door and entering the hot humid funk tinged with the wafting scent of damp leather. I loved hearing the bells blare out the rounds. I loved the guys nodding "Yo" to me when I walked by while they wheeled through their routines. I loved the chatter, and listening to the coaches motivate their fighters in the ring. "Double up on the left hook. That's it. Let your hands go. Don't back up, you're making him brave." I loved wrapping my hands, carefully crisscrossing the tape over my knuckles and wrists, then strapping on the gloves. Most of all I loved the intimacy of duking it out with someone in a physical rather than an intellectual way. In that moment when I eyed my opponent across the ring, waiting for the bell, my heart slammed against my ribs, and I'd go from ordinary reality into crazy combat mode. I got what I wanted: I beat guys and they beat me.

It doesn't get any more intimate than fighting. All the emotions are in play—fear, courage, anger, even affection. The pain mixed with adrenaline sears memories into the brain. I saw the connection to what I aspired to in my writing, and what I wanted to inspire in the RWGers—getting to the truth, the core desires and fears. "Writin' is fightin'," the author Ishmael Reed said. I loved the raw truth of boxing.

One of my trainers was a former light heavyweight pro who looked like Nick Nolte before the DUI and the wild-hair mug shot. He brought his own timer to the gym. He worked the hell out of me, shadow-boxing and sparring. Sweat sprayed from me like I was a sprinkler, and I could barely catch my breath. It was amazing how wasted I felt after only two or three rounds. I could barely move; I "left it all in the gym," as they say. It would take me months to build up enough endurance to fight three three-minute rounds.

One day I heard the bell ending the round, then a second later, it seemed, it rang again. I checked the timer, which was set on thirty-second intervals. But I was supposed to get minute-long breaks. Nick had adjusted it to burn me out fast so he could leave early. I called him on his hustle and he apologized, saying he was only trying to build up my stamina. "Yeah, right." I shook my head. "That sounds good," I said sarcastically. I liked him and didn't fire him though I knew he had conned me. I thought, I'll get his ass in the ring, I'll fuck him up. But the guy had fought Mike Tyson in the Olympic trials. He had a professional record of seventeen wins, three losses, with most wins by knockout. He could kill me—literally. Clearly, there wasn't much I could do against him. We sat around and jawed about boxing or whatever. I paid him fifty dollars for the hour, then split. I let several weeks go by before hitting his gym again, but eventually I scheduled more sessions. I liked him even though he was a bullshitter.

He nicknamed me James "You Betta" Rahn. I dug it, though I wasn't sure if he meant other fighters should run away from me or I should run from them. One day, he hit me viciously with a left hook to a floating rib, one of the lower ribs not anchored to the sternum. I yowled and fell on the canvas, clutching my side. The pain was spectacular. It felt like he had shoved a shiv in my back. I couldn't get up. "Motherfucker," I screamed, "I'll kill you." He started laughing. He stood across from me with his arms resting on the ropes, and he howled. Then he taunted me, "James is gonna kill me, James is gonna kill me. Oh I'm afraid. I'm really afraid." Then, more seriously, "Isn't this what you wanted? To be a real boxer, a tough guy. Well you got it now, baby. Get up. Get up!"

It was ten minutes before I could stand. When I was finally upright I chased him around the ring, swinging wildly. He was dying laughing. I was furious. "You're an asshole, you know that? And you're killing your meal ticket, you dumb motherfucker."

Driving home that day, I turned the radio to the local hip-hop station. Every song made perfect sense to me. I blasted the music and pounded rhythms on the steering wheel like I was a young G, a bad black dude, a soldier of the street, instead of a middle-aged white guy who was mourning his mother. Back in my neighborhood, out on the street, I looked for a confrontation. I couldn't beat Nick, but I wanted to test my abilities on a civilian who wasn't a professional boxer. I wanted to hurt somebody the way I'd been hurt.

I did tell the workshop members that I'd started boxing. Some thought I was nuts; some were impressed. Ishmael Reed backed me up. "Writin' is fightin'," I told them.

18

Every year the University of Pennsylvania held a Writers' Conference. Every year I taught a one-day version of my workshop there. Mornings I talked about craft; afternoons we discussed work that had been submitted.

One year the director asked if I wanted to create and teach another class in addition to the workshop. By then I had a strong following, and I think the university figured they could use my reputation to attract students. I developed a seminar that I called "Fearless Fiction." I was inspired partly by my experience with boxing, where I had to work through and control my nerves in the ring, and partly by something I'd come to understand about many students—fear held them back from writing with authenticity, from making the statement that only they could make.

A lot of failed writing seemed to result from a disinclination to take subjects and characters the emotional distance they needed to go, especially when the characters approached a crisis. Emotional timidity shortchanged imagination. Consciously or unconsciously writers felt their audience might identify them as, say, racist or misogynist or misandrist; or, conversely, too weak, tenderhearted, sappy. Often authors resisted investing a character with "negative" qualities when they sensed their own private self-image could be damaged; self-knowledge can be painful. Any number of fears tempt writers toward compromise. I came up with some binaries: fear of failing vs. fear of succeeding; fear of being known vs. the desire to be known; fear of being seen as hateful vs. the need to camouflage oneself with politeness and restraint; fear of rejection vs. a desire for acclaim.

Another thing I realized over the years was that I could point out these drawbacks but writers often wouldn't listen. I'd give them what I thought were the most profound insights, and they'd turn away, even get mad at me. Some of the time I could be wrong, but most times I was pretty sure I was right. It was my job, I thought, to bring their work to this level. I pictured students standing on a cliff above a chasm. I wanted them to leap to the other side, but most wouldn't, or couldn't. They continued to write stories, oblivious to the flaws. Some were engaging, but a sharp reader could see the dishonesty— as if the stories were vast shimmering lakes, miles wide but only two feet deep. Eventually I realized that there was a quite rigid limit to what some students could absorb emotionally.

A few students did leap across the chasm. They confronted their fears about their dark side, and afterward wrote with authenticity. And they never wrote another bad story. The stories may not always have been successful—maybe the ending didn't work or the material just wasn't big enough. But it was never less than a quality job, always professional, never amateurish, always well thought out and with a clear intent.

⌒

ONE WOMAN wrote a story about an American couple who fly down to Mexico to adopt a little girl. They see her for the first time at an orphanage. The child seems slow, with slightly crossed eyes, and has a pocked complexion and a small jagged scar along one cheek. Her thin cotton dress reeks of fried food. The wife thinks she's ugly, but the husband likes her. He says, "We came all this way, jumped through all these hoops, and you wanted a kid, bugged me incessantly, we did the IVF boogie for two years, and this kid's okay, she seems very sweet, we have to take her with us."

"I'm not sure," the woman says.

There's much discussion between the man, the woman, and the matron who runs the orphanage. At the end of the story the couple is riding in a taxi on the way to the airport without the child, and they're not talking. They're staring out at the mountains and the sere brown land, and the sense is that their marriage is over.

The story was almost successful. It wasn't quite clear whether the description of the distasteful little girl indicated the wife's feelings or the narrator's. More distance was needed between them, and the reader needed to have a better sense whether to trust the woman's perceptions. Would she have rejected *any* child? The group liked the story, despite its inherent sadness—except for one woman in the workshop who was well respected. She didn't make many comments, but when she did, they were almost unfailingly correct. That night she was voluble. How could the woman do this to the child? She didn't believe a woman yearning for motherhood would be so callous, certainly not *this* woman. The story needed a lot more work, and even then she wondered if it could be saved. Everyone was surprised by her intensity, and the author was hurt.

I knew something that most of the others didn't: the critic was in the process of adopting a child herself, a South American boy, and she was struggling with all the details and paperwork and background checks that would determine whether she'd be permitted to get him or not. It seemed to me that she'd let her usual objectivity get subverted. That happens to all us. We all have our blind spots, especially when our current difficulties are mirrored in a story.

After class I spoke to the writer, and she was enormously upset over what the critic had said; she wanted her approval. She also mentioned that she knew a little about the woman's desire to adopt a child. Now she didn't know if she wanted to revise her story. She regretted that she had revealed her conflicted feelings about motherhood. Maybe, she said, she should just chuck the story.

"Am I a bad person?" she wanted to know.

"No," I said, "you're talking about a reality that contradicts the myth that every woman wants a child. It's a good thing, getting to your core emotions; not an easy thing to do, not easy to absorb. And pushing against the unspoken truths of a culture is something a writer *should* do."

I told her how strong I thought the story was, and how important it was for her writerly maturation. I pointed out that adoption was the critic's nightmare, the source of her overreaction. "Don't be afraid to write your truth," I said. "How many times have I told people?—you have to make the statement that only you can make. In your writing, discover what you really feel, then step back so you can see it better, but don't turn away."

The author told me that she always felt one hundred percent that she could trust me to tell her the truth. She listened and revised the piece, adding more insight into the feelings of the would-be mother. She embraced her ambivalence about her own feelings and wrote the story, pushing her own voice even harder. She was one of those who never wrote another bad story.

I think all of us writers suffer fears. The trick is to be as aware and as self-accepting as possible, so you can find ways to work through them. I have difficulty writing directly about my father's death, but if I use a secondary character I can bring it into fiction. You need to be open to and aware of the obstacles; then maybe you can use them to refine and deepen your art.

For my Fearless Fiction seminar, I asked the Penn General Studies office to mail out beforehand three stories for discussion, "A Distant Episode" by Paul Bowles, "Lawns" by Mona Simpson, and "People Like That Are the Only People Here" by Lorrie Moore. I also gathered some excerpts by former students (omitting their names) with which I could illustrate where writers were fearful, avoiding something that had twanged their emotions, and what they did to avoid the discomfort. A discerning reader could see sudden shifts in points-of-view, flashbacks substituting for characters confronting each other, abrupt changes in tense and tone. I thought of strategies to help students at these crucial moments. One was to write expansively, intentionally over-explaining the drama; later the author could pare it back.

I noticed on the attendance sheet for the first Fearless Fiction class the name of a famous local writer, Alice Schell. I didn't know her personally, but I'd read somewhere that she'd won a Pew fellowship, a fifty-thousand-dollar award presented annually for excellence in literature. I also knew that she'd been published a few times in *Story Magazine* (a preeminent literary magazine), and one piece had received a Pushcart Prize. I was excited that she'd signed up for my class, and a bit intimidated

That day as I called out names from the sheet, I waited to see who she was. In due course a tiny, stylish, bespectacled woman grinned and raised her hand—a small, shy, upward flutter. Maybe because I felt honored that she was there, and maybe because I felt intimidated and wanted to defuse the sensation, I told everyone that we had a great writer in our midst. I pointed to Alice. People turned to look at her. I think she blushed. I realized I probably shouldn't have said anything, and hoped that she wasn't embarrassed, or mad.

As the seminar went on, I found she was bright, funny, and unassuming. She packed a lot of wisdom into that tiny frame. She pointed to things about the three published stories I'd selected that I hadn't realized. Where I was concerned about the psychological and emotional, she opened up the discussion to the existential issues.

I had forgotten the simple truth that fearless stories embrace matters of life and death.

PART TWO

⌒⌒

19

In February of 2006 I turned fifty-one. I was enduring another midlife crisis (maybe my third). It was especially intense because my father died at fifty-two. I was feeling my mortality more than ever.

On a Monday night a couple of weeks after my birthday, Adrienne got a phone call from our older niece, McCall. She, her sister, and their mother had been evicted from their apartment. Her mother had ridden on the bus with them to the Rescue Mission in Atlantic City, but then she'd disappeared and McCall didn't know what to do. (By this time the girls' parents had divorced and their father was AWOL.) She was cold and scared, and there were creepy men lurking.

Adrienne was freaked. I wasn't immediately drawn in by the drama. It was a Monday night, and I was almost out the door to the workshop. In retrospect I probably could've been more sensitive.

She opened the coat closet. "I have to drive down there and get them. NOW. I can't leave them there."

"What about their father, their grandmother? Where are *they*?"

"They're useless—you know that."

"Want me to go with you? I'll call off the class."

"No, stay here. I'll call you when I'm done," and she fired down to Atlantic City.

At the workshop I did my best to shore up my distress, but I kept hearing the winter wind screeching outside.

When class was over I told the group reluctantly I wasn't going out with them.

"You all right?" somebody said.

"Yeah." I trudged back to the apartment. No one was there.

A short time later I heard them get off the elevator. I opened the door to my frazzled wife and two dazed, trank-eyed, bedraggled children. *Urchins*, I thought, like in a Dickens novel. Angry bug bites circled their ankles, rashes raced up and around their necks. Their clothes gave off a river-bottom rankness. They clutched large plastic bags and small pea-green duffels containing everything they owned—more stinky clothes, toothbrushes, combs, and gray teddy bears with the fluff gone out of them.

Adrienne got the kids showered and scrubbed, threw some of their clothes into the washer, and made dinner. We sat at the small dining room table and I watched Marlyn, the younger girl, stuff roll after roll into her mouth. McCall barely touched her food and hardly lifted her eyes to look at us.

In our bedroom later that night I asked my wife, "How long are they gonna be staying?"

"This is it, I think. They have no other place to go."

"So we're gonna be taking care of two kids in this apartment?"

"What else can we do?"

"You mean, what else can *you* do? I don't know if I'm hanging around for this." It felt like years that I'd been dealing with this crap.

I didn't say any of this with heat. It was just that my whole cosmogony was shaken. I saw my mostly solitary life of writing, editing, communicating with students, coming to an end.

"We have to take them in. They have no place else to go," she repeated. There were tears in her eyes. She wanted me to feel the same.

I dug the kids—but was I supposed to take care of them, maybe raise them? Hell, I wasn't sure if I could raise myself. Even when we'd tried to have kids back in the day, I was never really sure that I wanted any. Maybe the fact that we hadn't hit the kid-jackpot was a sign that we weren't supposed to be parents.

"Three months," I said. "I'll try it for three months. After that I don't know."

"We have to take care of them. They're family," she said.

Your family, I thought. Not mine.

⌒

I WAS never keen on family. I didn't like most of my own, couldn't talk to or identify with almost any of them. Not a creative one in the bunch. And my early years mostly sucked.

The stork dropped me on my mother when she was forty-two. She'd already raised three kids; she didn't need a fourth squalling baby, eleven years after the last one. Her mother had died suddenly the year before, and Ma—making the best of it in a fantastical way, I suppose—believed I'd be her reincarnation. She was convinced she'd have a girl. When the doctor told her it was a boy she said, "That can't be my baby. I had a girl. I already have enough boys." I grew up hearing this story. She laughed when she told it, but I didn't find it funny. From the beginning she made it clear to me that she didn't want to be bothered, my father didn't want to be bothered, and if I made too much noise I could give him another heart attack.

Ma ruled. Dad worked and didn't say much when he was home. I do have a couple of pleasant memories of him—meeting him at his office and going to lunch with his buddies; driving with him to the country club where he golfed; hanging out at the bar there sipping Cokes and eating pretzels, watching TV, while I imagine, he shuffled around the greens. Then, when I was eight he died of a heart attack. I'd already been programmed to think it was my fault. The year afterward is almost a blank. I do remember my mother forcing me to go to synagogue each week. It felt punitive, like there was a big light shining on me for what I'd done and everybody was watching. I knew the Kaddish before anyone else my age. I still carry the vestiges of guilt over Dad's death, like I'm shouldering a corpse.

After the nieces arrived I considered taking off, becoming fugitive. For weeks I didn't get any writing done. Rittenhouse Writers' Group became a burden.

There were so many things to do for the girls: find doctors and schools for them, deal with the Department of Youth and Family

Services, and most difficult of all, carefully consider the ramifications of taking them in. They weren't in great shape, psychologically and emotionally. The older niece barely spoke. The younger one would suddenly roll her eyes and start twitching like she'd been plugged into an electrical outlet. Like ours, their world had been turned upside down. They must have been wondering whether they really wanted to be living with their aunt and uncle. Why couldn't they live with their mom? When would they be going home? I reflected on what it must feel like to have two living parents who weren't in prison or rehab, yet had no place for you—the guilt and shame they must feel. What would they tell their friends and the new kids they would meet? Through it all, of course, they still wanted their mom. We knew because we'd ask them general questions about her, but they disclosed nothing. They longed for her even though she'd shattered their lives.

She hardly ever called to speak to them. She rarely kicked in money, and when she did it was a pittance. We wondered about our legal rights and liabilities. Who exactly was responsible if the girls got hurt or seriously sick? What could we do if their mother or father came up and snatched them? We worried constantly about it—that their mother would appear and spirit the girls away to yet another hovel. Adrienne ran back and forth between work and making all the arrangements that had to be put in place for the girls to thrive. She was the angel. I was involved but ancillary, still boggled by the situation, still reluctant to be the uncle-daddy.

It was propitious when the efficiency apartment next door became vacant. We asked the landlord if we could rent it, knock down part of the wall, and install a door to connect it to our place. He agreed.

One weekend when the girls were visiting their grandmother we did just that. The maintenance guys cut a hole, hung a door, cleaned out the adjacent room, painted the walls, and put in new carpet. We added beds and lots of frilly things; strung some festive pink and purple balloons; put up prints of the girls' favorite rappers, Pretty Ricky and 50 Cent.

Adrienne drove down to get the girls, and when the threesome returned I was waiting in the living room. She and I pointed to the white door with the gold doorknob that was now embedded in the living room wall.

"Check it out," I said.

"What is it?" McCall asked, dropping her backpack. She scrunched her eyes as if expecting another problem.

"A door that leads to a magic room." I smiled.

They both seemed scared, suspicious, confused.

"Maybe some fairies came down and put it in," Adrienne suggested.

The girls moved to the door and tentatively opened it. They peered in. Suddenly they began to squeal. They went in, then came out of the room laughing, dancing. That was a moment of true joy for all of us.

They got their own room, and we (mostly I) got some breathing space. But now the girls had become entrenched. I continued to wonder how the family situation would resolve—for me, for all of us. Would their mother suddenly reclaim them and continue to buffet them around? Could Adrienne and I be their guardians? Could we, should we, get custody over them? We were riding a roller coaster to an unknown terminus on a track that might be busted up ahead.

20

THE WORKSHOP was how I made my living. I didn't make it from writing. I freelanced a little for *Atlantic City Magazine* and had a couple articles in *Philadelphia Magazine*, but I'd long since given up the porn gig. I was a teacher who wrote, not a writer who taught.

After my nieces came to stay, I let into the Monday workshop a couple of folks who'd given me a "gray area" vibe. My chaotic domestic situation distracted me, and I was concerned about money. My nieces didn't miss many meals.

An older woman named Carol had called and told me she'd published two novels, was struggling with the third, and had traveled extensively. She'd left South Africa at the end of apartheid, worried that conditions could be perilous for whites. She'd never taken a writing workshop before; did I think she was a fit for RWG? Yeah, I said, despite the arrogance in her voice. I was seduced by the fact that she'd traveled the world and was already published.

Sabrina called around the same time. I was caught up in something or other, so I just asked for her address and told her I'd send information.

At the first class, Carol introduced herself and went on much longer than those who'd gone before her. She enumerated her books, her travels, and the famous writers she knew—J. M. Coetzee, Nadine Gordimer. I had to cut her off.

Sabrina spoke briefly but seemed incredibly antsy. She was still wearing her coat and hat.

"Are you all right?" I asked.

"Why?" she said. She sat there, quivering.

"Why don't you take your jacket off, relax?"

"I'm cold." She sniffed. "Is that a problem?"

She made just one comment about that night's submissions: "If it were a car and it got towed he should leave it in the lot."

Carol was more garrulous and more abrasive. Regarding a story's plot she once said, "So a girl goes out into the bushes and defecates. Is that it? Is that all that happens?" In fact the story was far more complicated. Another time she eviscerated someone over their punctuation. "Either you don't know the rules, or you're just damn lazy. Maybe you should get yourself a high school grammar book."

"Let's keep the discussion a little more general," I said. Her disdain bothered me. Her hair was stuck-up too, an auburn swirl that smelled tart from hairspray.

A young guy was due to submit the following week. He called beforehand and said he was afraid of Carol, that she'd shred his story.

"You'll be fine," I told him. "Want me to speak to her?"

"No," he said. "She might get madder."

I was concerned; I could see Carol becoming a weight on the group. I decided to call her and talk about her attitude—give her my spiel about "iron fist in the velvet glove." When we spoke she was contrite, and said she wanted to be a good workshop member.

At the next class, when I asked her what she thought about the guy's piece, she said, "It's one of the most impressive stories I've ever read. I wouldn't change a thing. He should send it out immediately, as is. It's great."

He beamed. The rest of us weren't as sanguine. The story was pretty good, but had its problems. When Carol was challenged about a particular scene, she dismissed the question. "I already said the story was great. What more can I say?" The guy loved her after this.

Sabrina was quieter but I came to see her as a viper under a rock. She was a part-time limo driver, part-time psychotherapist. Therapists in the workshop could be dogmatic, paradigm-infused pains in the ass who believed they knew everything about human nature and were prone to diagnosing fictional characters. Most cared more about the answer than the exploration. The answer is much easier to tolerate than ambiguity, and it shuts down discussion internally and externally.

Being a driver, Sabrina often showed up late and agitated. Before class she'd speed around for a half hour trying to find a free parking space. She'd usually wind up parked illegally outside the building and every few minutes she'd race out the door to make sure she hadn't gotten a ticket. To make the dash quicker she kept her coat on. She also wore a knitted cap and chewed on the curls that snaked out from under it. She never took off either garment. "Relax," I told her, time and again.

The week after Carol went into extravagant-praise mode, she and Sabrina ganged up on a woman who was a good writer and a long-standing member of the group. I should have seen it coming. The woman was quiet and self-effacing, perhaps a perfect target for the two. They said they didn't care about her silly coed novel, that it was trite. So what if the protagonist falls in love with a professor, then a priest, and ends up banging him in the apse. They'd *never* read a book like this unless they had to because they were in a workshop.

I told them we were there to help the author. I didn't care what their reading preferences were. "What can you say to help this writer?"

They sat mutely.

The author got puddle-eyed. I stopped the discussion, but I hadn't stopped it soon enough. The woman seemed stupefied by the negativity, as if someone had hit her in the head with a mallet. After class I tried to soothe her, but she said goodbye and left.

That night when I got home Adrienne asked me, "How'd it go?"

"It sucked," I said.

"What happened?"

I told her and added that I should've never let those two in.

"You know, when you get that bad feeling—"

I cut her off. "If it wasn't for them"—I nodded toward the nieces' bedroom—"this never would've happened."

We got into a huge fight. I was furious at Adrienne, myself, everyone. Later, after a couple of shots of vodka, I sat slouched in the big easy chair and thought some more about the class. Why and how had I let them torment the woman? I was off balance because of my new family situation, but I knew it was more than that. I wondered if, at some level, I agreed with the duo's noisome remarks. Had I said similar things to the writer in other workshops? Had I suspected she didn't listen to me? I'd told her that people would be more interested in a narrative about a conflicted, love-struck coed if it was filtered more strongly through her own sensibility. She wrote smart, clean, thought-out prose, but perhaps, over time, it became tiresome to me. She hadn't changed it very much. I felt stupid. I'd failed, wasted my time telling her my opinion. At the moment Carol and Sabrina were attacking her maybe I'd converted my sense of failure into a small cruel pleasure at watching the poor woman get flamed. Maybe. Or maybe I just hadn't paid enough attention.

Nonetheless this duo had crossed the line into asshole-dom. They'd heard my mantra about positivity, but they hadn't listened. They were chronically disposed to being wounding and cynical, with little desire to help a classmate. They were mean-spirited and had insulted a nice person, a fine writer who'd taken many workshops. Maybe she didn't write about galvanic, existential topics, but an everyday story could be as great as the finest combat tale.

I began to consider ejecting Carol and Sabrina. I agonized over it. Would it ruin the class? Would I look like an ogre? This was the first time I'd been faced with possibly kicking out two people at once. It came down to how they were affecting the group and me, the leader. Thankfully over the years I hadn't been faced with many of these decisions. As I had before, to confirm my own perceptions I phoned a couple of group members to get a sense of how they'd experienced the discussion. They said things had gotten uncomfortable. I apologized. I also called the woman who'd been hurt and apologized to her.

Carol and Sabrina seemed to be fueling each other's offensive behavior. Carol wouldn't be attending the following week because she was having knee surgery. I'd catch a break (pun noted); I could put off deciding whether to eject her. Then I thought, she'll be back in two weeks. I'll still have the problem. That's when I made the decision.

In the past when I'd made these calls, I'd always tried to sugarcoat the situation and put the blame on me. Standard break-up procedure. I phoned and told Carol I was sorry but I wasn't sure the group was right for her. There were others that might suit her better. I asked whether she had a problem with the workshop or me. She said I was fine, then started badmouthing others.

"They're decent folks," I said. Though I'd asked the question, I wasn't going to let her demean anyone. "It's a good group. Let's not talk about anyone else. Let's talk about you and me. Maybe the chemistry's not there between us," I suggested. "It has nothing to do with you as a writer. You're a good writer. I just don't think this is the workshop for you."

"Are you telling me I shouldn't come back?" she asked.

"Umm . . . well, yeah, I think that's best for all of us."

"I can't believe you're telling me this," she shouted.

"I'm sorry," I repeated, meaning it. I didn't say it with sarcasm, didn't bite down on a smirk.

She yelled something at her husband, then slammed down the receiver.

Now I was aggravated, which pushed me to call Sabrina. She seemed indifferent. She asked how much money she'd get back. "Your two submissions have already been discussed. There're only three classes left. I don't think you should get any money back." *Click*.

Afterwards I felt better, and I think the rest of the group did too. The atmosphere improved. We began to work well together. The woman who'd endured the tough critique returned for two classes. After that she never came back.

21

ADRIENNE AND I had to make so many decisions regarding the girls, psychological, legal, and mundane. Regular parental stuff regarding schoolwork and chores, and questions particular to them, like how to deal with their silence about the past. Should we get them to shrinks? Should we talk to them directly about their mother and how she'd bounced them around after the divorce, from one father figure to the next, from one home to another? They were spending a lot of time in their room with the blinds drawn, alone together. They were also spending a lot of time in our bedroom under the covers in the dark, watching horror movies. They loved the gory, serial murder crap—Jason, Chuckie, Freddy—the bloodier the better. What did that mean? I thought they might have watched those flicks with their mother, but at the same time a darker issue was suggested: Why were they energized by watching people get hurt? What had they seen or been through that would make them identify with the torturer or the tortured? What were they bunkering themselves against, hidden in the dark, huddled under blankets? After a movie they'd plunge into the kitchen and load up on cookies, ice cream, chocolate syrup. It seemed like a reconnection with their past, an unconscious attempt to resurrect what they knew—most of it grim, but ending with a dollop of comfort.

Of course they were seeking stability and security, but I didn't want them embracing the rituals of the past. And at eight and thirteen years old, I thought they should probably be more separate from each other. It seemed they were twins or that they shared the same brain. Shouldn't they act differently now that they were here? It made sense and it didn't, after what they'd been through. When they left for school in the morning, the younger one would set up a tableau on her bed—three stuffed bears propped against her pillow, one big bear in the middle with a little one on each side.

There was the problem of dealing with their mother. Early on I decided I wouldn't see her, but I never said anything negative about her to the girls. Adrienne dealt with her. We'd both decided it was better for the girls to see her than not, so Adrienne drove them down to Atlantic City every couple of weeks. Their mother would meet them on the boardwalk in front of a casino. Adrienne couldn't stand it, her sister's bumminess—the cigarette tang and mildew exuding from her clothes. She hated her sister's bullshit and manipulation, the giddy way she greeted the girls—*mommy's little babies*, she'd say, whom she loved so much, *higher than the highest mountain and deeper than the deepest sea*. The trio would trundle off together, holding hands, united again in familial bliss. When Adrienne picked up the girls a couple of hours later there were more coos, I love you's, and big hugs from their mother before the kids scrambled into the car with bags full of old clothes, stuffed animals, candy and donuts, and one or two weird novelties from the casino. At first Marlyn and McCall would be upbeat in the car, but eventually they'd get quiet. When they arrived at the apartment they'd say hi to me, then rush into their room and shut the door. It must've torn them up to leave their mother, but they never said a word about it. Adrienne kept asking them questions, but the girls were clams. We wanted more communication from them. I guess they felt they were betraying their mother, and if she found out maybe she wouldn't want them back. She may even have planted that idea in their heads. Their behavior made sense, but it was still upsetting. They were boggled and so were we.

I wanted to build a level of trust. When they first arrived they were shut down, but I wanted them to feel comfortable expressing whatever was on their mind. It seemed essential to me, the foundation of our connection to them as well as the road to—what? Recovery? Feeling like they mattered? Feeling better about themselves? I told them they could always talk to me, that my door was always open and if they told me a secret I wouldn't tell anyone else.

I didn't want to represent another bad man. They'd seen so many in their lives, starting with their layabout, dumb-ass father and the various guys their mother hooked up with. (My best friend, who lived in A.C., told me she'd been hanging with low-lifes and degenerates.) I also deliberately established boundaries: I never entered their room without knocking and getting an okay from them, never walked around the apartment in my underwear. I was afraid from the first that they might have seen some bad sexual shit—I hated to contemplate anything worse. They seemed ashamed and were extremely modest in how they dressed and spoke, as if they were trying to distance themselves from something.

Thankfully I had women friends from the workshop with daughters roughly the same age. I'd call and they'd help me figure out what to say and what not to say, how to discipline them, whether they were acting in an age-appropriate way, how to deal with their feelings about us versus their mother. Then there was normal parenting stuff like talking to their teachers, and their problems with other kids. I didn't know what to do. Adrienne wasn't sure either.

I learned from my friends that there was no set way to raise kids. Ultimately it came down to common-sense-ing our way through, making decisions based on what we knew and felt about the girls and about ourselves. No matter what we did, though, I worried.

One day, McCall came down with a bad cold. Or was it the flu? I was the de facto doctor in the house because, having doctors in my family, I knew a few things. But should I give her aspirin, acetaminophen, nasal spray, or what? Was she allergic to anything? I asked her; she didn't know. Should we take her to a real doctor? I wanted to give her NyQuil, but knew her father had a history of asthma and the label said that a doctor should be consulted before using it if there was a breathing problem. Adrienne and I conferred. I said I thought she'd be all right. I asked McCall if she minded me giving her medicine. She coughed, snorted, and said, "Whatever you want to do." It was weird that the kid was so trusting. I felt a strange sense of power that was almost sadistic. I could give her anything—she'd take it because I was the adult and I should know what's right. Right? This primitive feeling came over me for a minute, and suddenly I pictured

myself as a child, daring a weaker boy who didn't know any better
to jump from one rooftop to another, or to leap from the bridge into
the dark eddying bay to find out whether there were any rocks at the
bottom. It was years since I'd had that thought, of having so much
power over someone. Now a sense of my huge responsibility came
over me. I gave McCall a small dose of the green liquid and watched
her for a few minutes, stressing over whether she'd have a seizure or
stop breathing. Her eyes were soupy, her nose a red bulb.

"How do you feel?" I asked.

"Tired," she said.

"Maybe you should sleep on the couch or in the other bedroom so
your sister doesn't get sick."

"I wanna sleep in my own bed."

I hesitated. "Okay." Now, I thought, we're gonna have two sick
children. But it would probably comfort my niece to sleep near her
sister. Maybe it was better that they were together, sick or not.

She trudged to her bedroom. After a few minutes I went to their
door and hovered, listening. I knocked, and after a moment I heard
my younger niece mutter drowsily, "Come in." I opened the door and
saw her with her eyes closed, her sister in the bed next to her snoring softly.

For a moment I felt relieved, but of course I worried through the
night.

The kids and their issues interfered with my relationship with Adrienne. When they fought, should I always take her side? Adrienne
was incensed with her sister—with her irresponsibility, her lack
of employment, the guys she hung out with, her drug- and alcohol-
fueled mind. My wife could barely control herself. When her anger
burst out, should I intervene? It was a release from the chronic anger
and worry; when a pot is bubbling over, you have to take the lid off. I
felt similarly, but not at the same level. I had a degree of pity for my
sister-in-law. I'd said from the start that we shouldn't badmouth her,
that it would only hurt the girls and might make them withdraw further. And I had my own anger to staunch, not just at the mother, but
at Adrienne too, at myself, and the kids as well. Why was I stuck in

this situation? Why was I forced to make so many tough decisions? Why didn't I just take off?

There was our marriage and our sex life too. The kids' proximity presented obvious problems. My anger made me less romantic. Sex had lost some of its verve. Adrienne struggled with this too. We talked about it, but didn't *act* much. These feelings and thoughts had to be dealt with or overcome, or we could end up in the desert, *coitus sacrificus*, like the scapegoat.

After the anger came guilt. Adrienne was an angel; she'd taken on so much. I was a drag. Why couldn't I be nicer? Surely I wanted things to be easier for my wife. I wanted her to be happy. I wanted *us* to be happy. I wanted to go back to what we'd had before the girls arrived. But our world had changed; now we were shackled, had less money. I wondered, Had I ever truly wanted kids? My parents didn't want me, so why would *I* want children? The pattern would repeat. To break the cycle I'd have to constantly assess what had been done to me, how I'd been victimized—easier to stay blinkered and keep repeating the past, the horse dashing mindlessly around the track. But I was a thinking, truth-seeking man who challenged the status quo in my work, my writing, and my life; I believed in change and flexibility. Didn't I?

My buddies said I could stay or leave and both would be understandable. My best friend, Dean, said, "You were always a stand-up guy. You know what to do. Take care of the girls. They need you." My sister knew the girls, liked them, had always been nice to them. She said she'd support me in whatever I did. Some people didn't want to give me advice, or balked when I tried to discuss my altered life. Fuck them. In the end I decided I needed professional help. Between my new identity as paterfamilias and approaching the age when my old man died, I felt like my ass was pressed up against eternity.

22

I was still trying to get writing done, still running two RWG workshops and one at Penn, reading and editing nine pieces each week. Compared to what was happening in my life the stuff I read seemed so mundane. I felt I was sacrificing too much of myself. I could feel my life draining away as if someone had shunted an IV into my arm and was siphoning my blood drop by drop. I saw myself strapped to a gurney while some mad scientist in a white lab coat slowly leeched the life from me. I could see the blood dripping into the beaker.

Half the people in the workshop were seeing a shrink. They'd told me. I'd worked hard to establish a rep for never breaking confidences; my students knew they could trust me so I also knew what medications they took, everything from Prozac and Zoloft to Klonopin and Seroquel. They wanted me to know in case they flipped out during class. Thankfully that hadn't happened. But I couldn't ask any of them for a referral because it would compromise our relationship.

One of my good friends was a therapist. He suggested I contact a guy I'd met with many years ago, back when I was thirty and going through it. I'd forgotten about him. He was a Jungian analyst with a real-world approach; he'd been good for me, helpful. I called. He'd moved out of town but gave me a couple of local names. They were Jungians like him, into collective unconscious stuff—heroes, goddesses, symbols, and dreams (they were great at analyzing dreams). There was a magical, exciting quality to it.

I went to see one of the names. On her front door was a knocker, a yellow sliver-of-a-new-moon with a serious face and red puckered lips. Next to it was a doorbell. I pushed it and was about to raise the knocker when she opened the door. There stood a thin, angular woman, wearing horn-rimmed glasses. We introduced, clasped hands, mentioned our mutual friend.

She motioned me into her square, spare tidy home. She said her office was in the basement and asked me to remove my shoes before going down. Was I entering a mosque, a shrine, a sanctum, a sacred space? Of course. But I worried my socks might have holes in them. And were they clean and pleasant smelling, or mismatched?

We marched down the stairs into a bunker-like room. *Ohmmm* music floated through the air. Figurines and statuary sentineled the place: heroes, heroines, pinch-faced moons. What was it about shrinks' offices that they always had these little figures? I'd seen a few in my life, and they all displayed odd objects. Most shrinks pretended to be neutral, aloof. They didn't want to disclose much about themselves, fearing the relationship could be contaminated. But all around there was information; their unconscious emerged no matter what (as did the client's). It couldn't be stopped. All the objects I saw were symbols revealing who she was.

She sat down in a ladder-back chair. She pointed to another one opposite hers. I sat, observed more: Miró prints, several certificates and diplomas; one said she had studied at Jung's home base in Zurich. She gazed at me and steepled her fingers. They were bony, like long white sticks. No plumpness on them or on her. I didn't see any round figures in the room except a nymph with an urn trickling water into a shell. There were no squashy chairs or cushiony sofas, no objects with wheels, no ovoid containers. I wanted more *round*—everything here was square.

And there was nothing out of place or messy looking. Shouldn't there have been a little more chaos? Something that admitted to life's disorder. That excessive order, the square edges and linearity, turned me off. It spoke of rigidity, lack of creativity or play.

She turned her head and light glinted off her glasses. The set of her eyes felt sharp, unsympathetic. And she perched there clutching herself tightly, holding herself like she was afraid I'd attack her. Maybe I thought of attacking her. Or was she projecting that onto me?

I inquired about her diplomas and how many years she'd been a therapist.

"Why are you asking me this?" she said. "Why does it matter?" She crossed and uncrossed her legs, rocking in her chair.

Why is she so defensive? I thought.

She ventured a few exploratory questions, then asked me to commit to one session a week for a year, saying that's how long it would take to make any progress.

"That long?" I said. "Really? I gotta think about it." In truth I'd already made my decision.

"You think about it and give me a call."

I met with three other therapists after that. It took me months and a lot of money to find the right one. I realized it's essential to do a thorough investigation. This person will be carrying your internal world.

You know you're with a good therapist when you stop assessing their degrees, their background, how many years they've been seeing patients. You just know they know their stuff. The biggest factor may be this: You get along.

This guy was a stocky Jackie Mason type, seventy-ish, and an old-school Freudian analyst. He came across to me as a wise, compassionate father figure. When I mentioned that I was approaching the age when my father had died, he understood why I was anxious. There was a name for it, he said, anniversary syndrome. When I told him about the nieces and my fear that I was ill-equipped to raise them, he offered that there might be positive aspects to our relationship that I might not see now. Later on, say, after six months, my life would be different—it could be better. Of course I didn't believe him at the time.

But as the weeks rolled on, the home situation got easier. Once Adrienne and I had enrolled the kids in schools, lined up their health care, figured out appropriate meal times; once we'd established the hours when I'd be left alone to write and to prepare for RWG—in short, once we re-established *order*—things improved. Despite the chronic uncertainty of how long the girls would stay with us, we were starting to have fun with them. Going on mystery adventures in the car; listening to them recount their dramas at school, which inspired the recollection of our own adolescent dramas; watching goofy movies with them or listening to their raucous hip-hop songs; seeing how our comments could really impact their lives; seeing how poised they'd become when talking with our friends. They were learning from us and we were learning from them. We were learning what it meant to be a family. It was better than I had thought it would be.

I noticed I liked hanging out with the girls occasionally. I listened to their chatter about songs and boys. I told them crazy stories from my own erratic past, trying half-heartedly to temper them, but still inflamed with the impulse to tell them the truth. If Adrienne was around she'd sometimes censure my riffs. They're girls, she'd say, you can't tell them that. This after I'd told them about an article I'd read about a man who'd fallen in love with a dolphin. "What's so bad," I said, "about inter-species sex?"

I sensed that I'd been hurt in a way that was similar to the girls, not by weird comments but by unloving ones, from a mother who didn't want me from the moment I popped out and a father who was absent most of the time. I sensed that I had endured a similar past. They sensed it too. They opened up to me a little more than to their aunt.

One night, early on, Marlyn, the younger niece, got upset and said she was going to kill herself. She was going to jump out of the dining room window (we lived on the twelfth floor). "Go ahead," I blurted. "You think that worries me? I think about killing myself every day."

"James!" Adrienne shouted. "What's the matter with you?"

I had to ask myself: Did I really think about suicide every day? Do I? Did I really want my niece to hurl herself out the window? I think I was responding to how she tried to manipulate us by instilling guilt (she was good at this), by projecting her feelings of guilt *into* us. Perhaps it was a necessary survival skill, expelling the bad she felt about herself. But I knew the game well and could play it. I told her, "Every trick or scheme you think you can run on me I've already done or already know. There's not a thing you know at this point in your life that I don't know, and I'm not putting up with any crap." Her mouth gaped open. She looked huh-what. She backed away from the window and ran out of the room.

Later, I told my shrink about it. "You said what?" He arched his eyebrows. He smiled, then his face changed into a tight grim expression. "I can't believe you said that to her. What happened after that?"

"Hasn't talked about killing herself anymore. At least not to me."

Without a joke, though, I realized I had to be careful about what I said to the girls.

McCall was much calmer than her sister and much less histrionic. She was dutiful, quiet, not so demonstrative. But underneath I felt there was a volcano.

As a by-product of the girls' arrival and my entrance into Shrink-ville, it became easier to talk about myself. Since my analyst could handle my assertions, fantasies, secrets, my pitiful weaknesses and mistakes—my *confessions*—and it seemed that he still liked me (he laughed a lot, especially when I talked about sex), I felt more comfortable with myself. And I felt I had to be open and honest with the girls. I was adulting-up, accepting more responsibility, realizing more my own agency and power. I was even writing more, working on a bunch of short stories, and still hoping to finish my novel at some point. Nonetheless, at times my life felt like the nightmare of maturity. I wanted to huddle under the covers like my nieces, curl up against the wall and suck my thumb.

Folks in the workshop noticed a difference in me, especially ones returning after a hiatus.

"You've changed."

"How so?"

"You seem calmer, less anxious. I think those girls have really had an effect on you."

"Nah . . ."

"It's true."

"Really?

"Definitely."

"For the better?"

"Yes, for the better."

"But there's one thing," I would add.

"What's that?"

"Now there's never enough peanut butter in the house."

Curiously, I felt good talking to the workshop crew about the girls. I appreciated their recognition that I was changing, maybe even doing a good job. I was joining a community I'd always disparaged—parents. Anyone could have a kid, I'd thought, so most everyone did—and I usually ran the other way from what most people did. When people talked about the achievements and problems of their kids, it sounded so commonplace, so boring. And please don't show me any pictures. I'd never considered before how hard it was to raise a child, and the joy that might come from it. Now I was talking excitedly about the girls, though I hadn't yet made the leap to calling them *my girls*. It was a new conversation for me, and I liked it. I enjoyed this new feeling of belonging. I sensed that I'd always been fearful about having children, that a voice was always telling me that children were no good. I realize now whose voice that was.

23

My analyst was one wise dude. He gave me advice, which most analysts are unwilling to do. In the beginning I didn't believe him. I'll feel positive about the girls in six months? Please. But he was right, and that astonished me. When I anticipated the worst, and felt pre-rejection anger, he'd ask, "Haven't you felt this way before, then later on it worked out? This will probably go your way too." He was almost always right. It was amazing that he knew these things and could predict what would happen in my life better than I could. And it was amazing that I'd actually changed, that people could see I'd changed. It was way beyond my expectations of what would happen when I paid somebody to listen while I talked, and it was exciting.

I wanted to be like him. Then I'd be less confused about what to do about the girls, or about problems in the workshop, or about my own feelings, which jangled me at times. Freud's theories (as well as my analyst's life experience) led him to wisdom, so I began to read Freud's work.

There I discovered that aspects of the Oedipus complex explained a situation I often encountered in the workshop. I was the teacher, but some of my students saw me as a father figure. They idealized me, imagining I had far more power and knowledge than I really did. They'd project their wishes and needs onto me: for knowledge and guidance; for affection and nurturing; for protection and safety. What they believed they lacked would find a home in their image of me. There was the woman who'd had a crush on me: her father had died, then she'd met me and begun to see me as somebody much better than I was. Wasn't she re-enacting the child's Oedipal situation, wanting her father's love?

Sometimes a student's idealization collapsed. Like the woman with the crush, who got upset and then quit after I criticized one of her stories, students sometimes became angry with me when they started to see me realistically. A group member told me he met a former RWGer who exclaimed, "I know James Rahn. James Rahn's a horror." (The ironic upside was that the remark had made him want to sign up.)

I'd always fantasized that the workshop was like a tribe, and spoke nostalgically to my students about their ancestors—the writers who once graced the big seminar table and then went on to publish great stories and books. But if I was the parental figure, in keeping with the Oedipal construct, then we were a family with my students in the role of children. That idea certainly fit when I considered the competition that I sometimes felt within the group, though I tried hard to diminish it, wanting students to take pride in each other's success. But it was a kind of sibling rivalry—students squabbling with each other, vying for my attention, wanting to be the favorite child, even when they didn't idealize me. I had to become more aware of these competitive feelings. The trick was to figure out what each student wanted and to give it to them—within limits—in a caring way. I didn't have to like everybody equally, but they had to know I cared and that I treated them all fairly. This applied to the group and to my new family as well.

I decided I wanted to learn more so I applied to the psychotherapy training program at the Psychoanalytic Center of Philadelphia, where my analyst was a member. The training program turned out to be a terrific education. My instructors were some of the best analysts and psychotherapists in the region. They confirmed and articulated what I had experienced, about group interactions and character, in life and on the page. It was there that I read a paper by Hans Loewald that was a reinterpretation of Freud's work. Contradicting Freud, he said that the Oedipal conflict is never really mastered, that the desire for parental love along with the desire to separate from parents is a lifelong struggle. When there's a conclusion (usually unconscious) that the parent can never be permanently won, then a person will either incorporate this understanding into adult behavior or continue to enact the idealization-devaluation scenario.

Another dynamic that occurred again and again in the workshop played out this way:

Marie writes stories in which the protagonists, we're told, are caregivers, sacrificers, people concerned about their loved ones, but who underneath care mostly about themselves. She doesn't realize there's much under the surface, but I do. Most readers won't either; there's too much shiny veneer. Her work brings to mind Zoe's story about the boy who disappeared. The truth is that in the story she's actually presented her own narcissism as well as her attempts to appear unselfish. I get annoyed by what I see as her unconsciousness, her failure as a writer to go deeper. I want to point out the contradiction. But at the same time I suspect she won't get it, or won't believe me, because she's too defended against her hostile feelings towards others. When I talk about her work, I'll be talking about something that occurs within her that's slightly removed from her awareness, and she won't like it.

I know beforehand that there could be a problem—that I could hurt Marie, embarrass her. I know I should temper my feelings because I like her, she comes to the workshop regularly, extolls the group and me to others, and she pays me to attend. So why do I have to say anything about her protagonist's falseness? Why is there a hot hand at the back of my neck pushing me to speak, to unmask her dishonesty? I ask myself such questions yet, at some point, I go to class and deliver a tap or the hammer-blow and Marie gets upset. I get upset too, and mad at myself for doing this yet again.

The same scenario repeats when I read a guy's story where the narrator says he loves women, but most of the dramatic scenes portray the opposite. Again I'm compelled to deliver the truth—that his misogyny is dressed up as love and compassion. (Not until after I began my psychoanalytic studies did I realize it could be my own dissimulation reflected there, or my own unwillingness to examine my unsavory side. I'd like to think, though, that most of the time I was reacting to a sense of falseness in the work.) Again I might feel that the author won't hear it, but I have to say it, even though he might get mad. I'd like to think that maybe if he continues to come to the workshop he may one day believe that what I've told him is right.

Why do I feel a certain compulsion, even a mission, to make the truth clear to the author? Freud's theory of Repetition Compulsion gave me the distance and the tools to unlock these dramas. He observed that people unconsciously repeat distressing, often traumatic situations, and thereby re-experience negative feelings about themselves. All of us do it, partly to master those negative feelings. I began to think of my past, of my mother and the authority she had over me when I was a child, and how she claimed to be a mother with a capital M. when in fact she didn't care much about me—how I yearned for her to care. It wasn't until after my father died that she told me, "I'm your mother who loves you more than anything. Nobody loves you more than me." She got much nicer after he died. By then the damage had been done.

I came to see this as my repetition compulsion, as well as my students'. Some need to portray themselves as someone different, better than who they are, and I need to inform them of the truth. Knowing the theory didn't completely eliminate the repetitions, but it helped. I was able to practice more discernment in what exactly I said, when I said it, and to whom.

Make friends with your dark feelings and thoughts, so you can deploy them consciously and thus more skillfully in your writing. I tell this to my students, and I repeat it to myself.

24

At the Psychoanalytic Center I was the guy on the academic track, as opposed to the clinical one. I was the guy with the asterisk by his name on the attendance sheet. Alas, the eternal asterisk. I fairly loved the training program. I say "fairly" because love is a worrisome word to me and usually needs a modifier. As I've said, the program was a great education, perhaps the best I ever had, and I've been through some pretty darn good schools. But the caveat here was the danger that the academician—me—could get bitten by the clinician bug. Each week of attending classes without clinical material to share became a small torment. I wanted to see the theory and abstractions in action. I wanted to be where the rubber met the road. I wanted to know what it felt like to face actual patients.

I wondered whether writing and storytelling could help patients make sense of their inner chaos. Certainly a journal or diary can help organize one's thoughts. But imaginative writing is different. It can be both an act of control and a release. In a first draft you let your thoughts go where they want to. Not too far or for too long, because imagination can become too free-wheeling, with associations spooling out endlessly like hyperlinks. It has to be canalized at some point. In subsequent drafts, writers must be more reflective about their narratives, must distance themselves in order to identify themes and intent around which to craft their pieces. When they get stuck they move back to imagination, become expansive again, then return to conscious craft. Writers' minds should move like pendulums, back and forth between the unconscious and consciousness.

I was fortunate enough to know folks at the Center who connected me to the psychiatric director at a local hospital. He gave me the name of the director of volunteer services. I met with her, told her my background, and explained that I approached writing analytically. I thought about characters on the page in a psychodynamic way, always looking for deeper motives and conflicts. I pushed students to explore the dark places their writing took them to.

She told me that wasn't what she wanted. She believed writing by hospital patients should be used therapeutically, not analytically. Perhaps people couldn't tolerate the criticism; perhaps they didn't want to revisit dark places. I felt deflated. This wasn't how I taught my workshops; this wasn't what I was learning at the Center. But I backed off because I wanted the clinical experience. Of course I'd use writing therapeutically, I said. I understood exactly what she wanted. Fortunately I managed to convince her. She decided to put me with the mood-disorder patients, some of whom had recently tried to kill themselves.

After a year and a half of attending the training program I was finally going to have some real-world experience. I would introduce writing as an activity in an hour-long group therapy session. The group was coordinated by a nice, savvy occupational therapist named Tracy. It was her group, and she'd monitor everything that went on. I was the volunteer "hired-gun."

Tracy and I met to establish a framework. We'd give a writing prompt, the participants would write for fifteen minutes, then they'd read aloud and we'd all discuss what they'd written. I'd make some comments about how to sharpen their writing. We'd look for experiences shared by the whole group.

The first day I was nervous. I'm always nervous before a new class, but this was different because I wanted to really embrace the experience. I also wanted to be helpful, and I didn't want to embarrass myself after so much analytic theory. I felt . . . uncertain. Then I remembered something an instructor from the Center once said: Tolerate your uncertainty; sit with your disturbing emotions. He'd meant it in reference to dealing with patients, but I knew it was also true with writing. Hadn't I been preaching this emotional stance since I started RWG? And uncertainty—that was always in play. The feeling of being stupid, not knowing where to go with the narrative. E. L.

Doctorow said, about writing fiction, "It's like driving a car at night: you never see further than your headlights, but you can make the whole trip that way."

There were eight people in a common room when Tracy and I arrived. Everybody seemed downcast, gloomy. One man looked furious. The gloomy mood hit me—my first clinical countertransference. Of course, I thought, these are the mood-disorder folks, teary-eyed, anxious, angry, depressed.

Tracy gave me a warm introduction. I smiled and spoke briefly about myself. Then I described our prearranged topic—Write about a memory, a "moment-of-being" (à la Virginia Woolf), a moment when you suddenly understood something differently, something that perhaps a parent or friend had tried to convey to you for years. A change, an insight. Make it a positive change. Put some emotion into it. The people sat in a semi-circle facing me and looked nonplussed. I repeated what I'd said, then added jokingly, "Nobody fails this assignment. Everybody passes or gets an A. Write whatever you want. I don't care. Just make it sincere."

They began to write. Most people. A few just stared into the winter sky.

The windows looked out onto a broad avenue and an American flag on a flagpole pulsing in the breeze. Windows also faced the main corridor. The walls were putty-hued, hospital drab. While my new group bent over their papers I studied the room's accoutrements. There was a TV, an exercise bike, an upright piano, a big clock on the wall; scattered on a round table were jigsaw puzzle pieces and piles of New Yorker magazines; a sarcophagus-like closet stood in a corner.

I felt the heat in the room as I sat there waiting. I listened to the shuddering, humming radiator. The clock ticked behind me, and I wanted to know the time. "Sit with the uncertainty and the disturbing emotions." Finally I turned around. Only ten minutes had passed. I waited a while longer, then asked everyone to stop writing. I suggested that someone read aloud. They hesitated. I could feel the sweat gathering under my arms. I wiped the side of my face on my shoulder. I pushed harder for someone to read or speak about their memories.

A couple of people read exquisite, intimate, heartfelt memories, filled with lyrical language (after fifteen minutes of work!). One young woman talked about how her father had finally told her he loved her after he'd been a junkie for twenty years. Another woman spoke about how she'd found the right meds so that she no longer "heard" voices. Some people didn't read, though I tried to get everyone involved; I called on everyone. Almost all participated. The mood changed from gloom to excitement.

For the next few weeks I gave short exercises, not based on memories, which might upset people, but directed toward some positive idea or emotion. All I got were descriptions of lovely beach scenes—shiny, glittery, sun-washed sand—and nothing much to discuss afterward. "That's nice," I'd say. "That's really beautiful. Maybe if you decide to rewrite your piece you can add some more sensory details: the cries of the gulls, the smells in the air." What more could I say?

The director wanted my prompts to evoke "therapeutic" feelings, but the results felt saccharine, unreal. I wanted to unlock greater emotion. I wanted to balance the positive with the negative, the light with the dark, though the emphasis could be on the light. Much like what I espoused at RWG.

I asked Tracy if I could make a change. She considered it, then nodded. "Let's try it." So I began to use different prompts, for example: Write about a person viewing the ocean after something wonderful has happened, then contrast it with a description of the ocean after something tragic has happened. Don't mention the precipitating event. Let the details and how the person feels suggest it. With this oppositional approach, people wrote longer. The discussions afterwards became more honest, vigorous. Tracy told me she was amazed at how much the patients were opening up. She said that people revealed things in their writing that they'd never talked about publicly.

Then I started reading brief stories to the group, always with a certain theme: a father-son disconnection, some argument between a mother and daughter. I think reading stories aloud can have a calming, nostalgic effect. I talked about the resiliency of the characters in the story. Afterward I'd ask everybody to write whatever the stories inspired in them. Again I was impressed by the honesty of the writing. I commented on how courageous the participants were to present such poignant, intimate events. I had many thoughts, though I didn't analyze them. Instead I spoke about how people can carry their problems a long time, and it can take a long time to work them through.

Mood-changes rolled through the group in waves. One person started crying, several people started crying. One person read an anecdote about his parents teaching him how to tie his shoes; his parents started fighting and left the room, so he laced his own shoes. He said, "I learned that I could do things for myself. I didn't need my parents to solve my problems." Everyone was suddenly upbeat, smiling.

I made mistakes in my efforts to help this group. When I was ironic and challenging, some patients got upset. I had to back off, or Tracy bailed me out. It was a good thing we got along; it wouldn't have worked otherwise. Some stories I read aloud distressed a few of the patients. Then I would amplify the positive. One time I read a piece called "The Flowers" by Alice Walker. It's about a little girl skipping through the woods who unexpectedly discovers some human bones and a length of frayed rope. I talked about how bold the little girl was, and how this revelation would help carry her to her future. One guy shouted, "Bullshit!" He was partly right. Another person disagreed and said, "That was a great story that James read; dark, yes, but I'm tired of having things sugarcoated. That's how I ended up in here. Everyone was always sugarcoating something." The majority agreed. The group rallied behind me.

I found that I wasn't very different from the patients I worked with. Only a thin line divided us. My toes were just about touching that line. I knew that anyone could be broken by life, a couple of bad events in a year and anyone could be shattered. The group probably picked up my sentiments, and that helped make our meetings successful. I think they knew I sincerely wanted to be there with them.

At the hospital I saw how hurt people were. There were people on the ward with acute problems—a young mother whose child had recently died; an investor who'd lost his money and couldn't stop thinking about it. My training at the Center led me to believe that the chronic sufferers were usually undone by a parent's lack of love, or their perception of it, and hated themselves yet still wanted that parent's love.

The psychoanalyst W. R. Fairbairn suggested that a bad object is better than no object at all. In the literature "object" equals "parent." At the hospital I met a man who, at the age of six, accidentally knocked his brother out an open window and killed him. I listened to a woman who was enduring the first anniversary of her son's murder. All I could think at that moment was, *Wow.* This was beyond my experience, and I wanted to change the subject, move on to another person and hear his or her story. But I remembered my training, and sat with the emotion.

Then I told them that revealing the past in their writing was another step in their recovery. I emphasized how courageous they were, which wasn't very analytical of me. But what could I truly say to them in the brief time I was there? I had to be careful not to unsettle people, leaving them upset over the weekend or just before they were discharged. What I did say was how much I appreciated their allowing me to hear such intimate stories.

I thought about how deep some patients' work was, after writing for such a short time. They didn't bullshit, they got right to it. Of course they had pressing existential concerns. But don't we all?

I brought some of my experience to RWG. I urged folks to work harder to identify the story they were born to write, and *write* it, almost as if a gun were put to their head. I said, "Procrastination is for people who think they're immortal."

25

AFTER GRADUATING from the psychotherapy training program I decided to open a private practice just for writers, to address whatever was preventing them from writing their truest stories. Because of my teaching experience and my knowledge of psychotherapy I felt I could help, though I didn't quite see myself as a therapist. With some reluctance I gave up my volunteer job at the hospital. Tracy and the nurses said they were sorry to see me go.

I got business cards printed that read "Psychoanalytically-informed consultations for writers." I hoped it didn't sound too grandiose. I built a website that incorporated both RWG and my new practice, and people began emailing and calling.

A therapist friend who had an office in a high-rise building in central Philly allowed me to lease it on an hourly basis. People from the workshop as well as the general community began meeting with me. All suffered from some form of writer's block. I knew a bunch of exercises to knock it down: Write thirty minutes a day, five days a week; start each day by adding a couple of words to what you wrote the previous day. I gave clients prompts like the ones I'd used at the hospital, to write a memory or event filled with feeling, where you realized something afterward. Then I'd read the piece and we'd talk about its strengths and problems. I'd point out, for instance, where two characters were arguing and the anger, and therefore the drama, felt short-changed. I repeated that many writers were afraid to reveal their angry side. I pushed them to be more aggressive. I said things like, "You can be a mannerly, genteel lady in the real world, but in your writing you can be a hellcat." I'd smile. "You shouldn't miss that opportunity." I identified places in the text where there were seemingly unintended shifts in tone and points of view, suggesting that the narrator felt uncomfortable with the material. Writing is the dream on the page and the dream never lies.

As an editor, when I found word repetitions I'd ask people for synonyms, but now as a therapist I wondered if these particular words symbolized something deeper, and if the sounds of the words signified anything. I'd ask clients to say the words aloud to see what thoughts, images, feelings might be triggered. Sometimes they'd unlock hidden memories and they'd be excited and moved by what they recalled. In conversation I'd hear subtle switches in pronouns, changes from "I" to "you," for instance, which suggested a distancing from painful thoughts. I'd point these out too. My clients and I worked together to figure things out. Exploration and answers were co-constructed.

Not only did I listen carefully but I watched people's facial expressions, eye shifts, body movements, hand gestures—to try to determine when their words collided with their emotions. One's concept of oneself is so wrapped up in one's writing; I offered clarifications and interpretations cautiously. As in the workshop I constantly monitored whether I was upsetting someone or overwhelming them with too much information.

The exercises were effective for the short term, but then clients would hit a bump and be stymied again. Writer's block, I began to realize, went much deeper than the symptom. It represented profound unconscious, refractory conflicts that weren't sufficiently touched by the exercises I prescribed. These conflicts seemed to be based on fear, the fear of addressing disturbing emotional issues, connected to confronting and transmuting some parental attachment.

I began searching for a way to effect longer-lasting results. I wanted to help people make an inner structural change so that they could produce creatively without freezing up when they encountered the bad feelings again. My mentors at the Center helped me with this. They reminded me that change can take a long time. The essential thing was to be a good and constant force in my clients' lives.

One man was stuck halfway through his novel. He couldn't get past a scene where a bomb explodes and kills a bunch of children.

We explored why he'd written it and what it could mean to him—the idea that a childhood had ended suddenly, traumatically. I gave him the emotional memory prompt. The following week he handed me a piece about a mother giving birth to a son, then dying a short time after. We talked about it as a piece of writing, and tears filled his eyes, yet he didn't seem to recognize the guilt and shame I suspected he was feeling. I thanked him for writing such an honest, powerful piece, and suggested that he start writing random scenes for his novel occurring *after* the impasse with the bomb, perhaps adding new characters—not worrying about where they or the scenes fitted. I hoped that producing something new would re-energize him.

We began meeting weekly. His pages flowed, with wild idiosyncratic characters and events, told from various points of view. Things ran smoothly until he hit some problems in his life, with work and with one of his kids. He stopped writing. I didn't worry about it; there was always regression in a therapeutic relationship. We talked about his current troubles. Weeks went by, and his family problems abated. We talked about his book, but he still wasn't writing. When I brought that up he'd shift the conversation to superficial occurrences: He'd had a fight with his wife; one of his employees had quit. Each week our dialogue moved further away from his writing and devolved into quotidian I-had-a-porkchop-for-dinner chat. I kept trying to steer him back to the book.

We had hit a wall, and I didn't know what to do. Maybe, I thought, I should just let him go on with his nonsense; it was a necessary reprieve from the rigors of the novel, and eventually we'd return to more in-depth things. Maybe I should keep my mouth shut so I wouldn't upset him and he'd continue to come weekly, maintaining his treatment, our therapeutic relationship, and (honestly) paying me.

I sat there week after week like a jackass, watching him as he squeezed the flesh on his belly, listening to him complain, listening to him crack gum, then occasionally his cell phone would ring and he'd mouth, "Sorry, I gotta answer this." I could barely stay awake. I pictured the cliche of a man—me—with his eyelids propped open with toothpicks. Whatever had deadened in my client had been projected into me. I gave up talking about his book. After two years, he terminated. I had almost no qualms about his leaving. I wondered if I could have/should have done more to help him. In truth I didn't know quite what to do.

Another client had started a novel about a semi-famous ancestor of hers. He'd traveled around the world and made some scientific discoveries. My client wrote various scenes about him but couldn't bring him to life. She'd get him to some exotic backwater town, but he never encountered any danger, never fought with anyone, never had any strange thoughts or any sexual adventures. In short he didn't do very much—or rather my client's emotions thwarted her imagination. The problem was that she idealized him. I told her so, and that he was a character begging for nonfiction, not for fiction.

I asked her to write pages about herself and her interest in him. She agreed and sent them to me. The parts about her sang with honesty and originality. I suggested that she focus the story more on herself; maybe her true desire was to put herself center stage. But she said that wasn't it. For months she continued to come to me with scenes presenting her relative as the main character. For months I pointed out gently how she'd failed to round him out. I grew bored, impatient, felt I was at another impasse. Also I noticed that she'd started to idealize me, but I didn't explore this with her. I stayed at the writing level. Then she cancelled a couple of appointments and, during this interlude, emailed me what she said was a new start to her book. When I read the chapters I was surprised to find I'd seen them all before except for a few small edits.

She scheduled another session to talk about her work, and there I told her truthfully that she still faced the same problem, that her idealization of her ancestor was keeping her from moving forward. She got upset and left—another unsuccessful intervention by me. I called her later, and she told me she was distraught over what I'd said. Momentarily I felt badly, but that was about it. She never returned for another session.

What did I realize from these two clients? That perhaps I wasn't the most compassionate person. That I was much more the writing teacher rather than the psychotherapist. I could sit with clients one-on-one for a certain amount of time, several months maybe, but to talk with them for years about their writer's block—that was something I couldn't do.

26

As FOR ME, I've never suffered from the long gaze at the blank page. I've always written stories, essays, articles—but I wanted to complete a book, my book, and I wasn't doing it. I procrastinated, like so many others. One inner voice told me, Next month you'll hunker down and really get to it. Next year you'll finish it. Another asked, Does the world really need a book by James Rahn? Do you really want to write a book? Maybe you're just in love with the idea. Self-doubt and the dream battled each other. Was I blocked? You're damn right I was.

I'd counseled so many people in the workshop and in my practice, but I couldn't get *my* writing done. It was as if I'd come full circle, back to when I first started Rittenhouse Writers' Group, when I wasn't writing as much as I told my students they should. *You gotta put in your hours,* I exhorted them. But I wasn't putting in mine.

I was determined to break through the block. My analyst helped me with his insights about my fear of failure as well as my fear of success. He talked about my self-destructive and aggressive issues. We discussed my nieces over and over—whether I wanted to be or felt capable of becoming their father. I kept looking for guidance from others too. I kept yearning for my father to tell me what to do. Why did I always return to that age-old script? Again, the repetition compulsion. I began to think that maybe I felt guilty over his death, that unconsciously I felt responsible. The psychoanalyst Hans Loewald wrote that instead of repressing Oedipal guilt you should examine and try to accept it. Then you can move ahead by your own agency. After years of cogitation I realized that *I* was the father now. By accepting this role I gained the power to help myself and the girls, and I could mitigate my feelings about my father.

Now I was determined to finish my book. Self-doubt still crept in, as it always does—the absurdity of sitting alone in a room for hours writing, while the rest of the world whirled outside, as if I were a sloth in a tree surveying all the hubbub down below—but it was easier now to shout down that negative voice. To paraphrase Frank Conroy and a Nike ad: You have to put your ass in the chair and *just do it*. I did, and I finally finished the damn book. It felt like a huge maturation, a willful act, and a separation from some parental attachment. The book was *Bloodnight*, and like most first novels, it's a coming-of-age tale, this one based on my childhood and adolescence in Atlantic City, where growing up meant hustling and learning to be tough.

It took me two years and a zillion rejections before I found a publisher, a tiny independent in Virginia. They said they'd do a little marketing, but had no budget for advertising. If I wanted to sell the book, I'd have to do it myself. So I highlighted it on my website, set up readings and book signings, arranged talks with book groups, found reporters to write articles. I got a radio interview with the local NPR station, which went well and helped move a lot of copies. I joined Facebook and other social media. I considered going door-to-door in my apartment building or pulling up to Rittenhouse Square in my Honda and selling stacks of books out of the trunk. Selling books wasn't easy. But I was excited about doing it, and the book was finally out there.

Everybody in the workshop was happy for me and probably relieved that I had a book published (and a decent one). They and other friends threw book-signing parties, with the obligatory wine, beer, cheese cubes, crudites, chips and dips, small chocolatey confections—nothing too salon-y, just nice. I read from *Bloodnight* or from new stories I'd written. It felt great standing behind an improvised lectern and looking out at all the people I'd become close to over the years. Of course Adrienne and the nieces were there too. The nieces seemed so poised—the way they introduced themselves and talked to everyone. So well behaved, so mannerly. I was proud of them; maybe they were proud of me. Maybe Adrienne and I had done something right.

Even the Psychoanalytic Center held a book-signing and reading. My analyst showed up, smiling—another proud papa. Many of my instructors and mentors showed up. Fifteen people sat around a polished seminar table; others perched on chairs behind them. The room was packed, almost SRO. A woman sitting near me wore a coconut musk body spray, the scent so rich it made me dizzy. I was nervous but not nearly as much as I'd been for my first workshop twenty-five years before. I still wanted to do a good job, wanted people to accept me. Sweat still prickled my forehead and neck, but it wasn't the waterfall it had been back then. I didn't read an introduction, just talked about my background and presented a new story, and they liked it and applauded when I finished. Afterward I enjoyed the Q&A. One member of the audience said that my book should be standard reading for the Child Psychotherapy program about boys and gangs and absent parents. One of my mentors whispered, "You're all growed up." At the end the group thanked and congratulated me.

27

As I write this, Rittenhouse Writers' Group is almost twenty-eight years old, still meeting in the Ethical Society building. It may be the longest-running independent fiction workshop in America. No attachments to a university. No state or federal grants. Paid for by folks who want to write good fiction in a safe, serious, honest environment. The writing keeps getting better, and, I think, in number of publications you can put our publishing record against any top MFA program. So many great writers have come through the group.

Recently Gwen's son joined. (Gwen appeared in Chapter 12, tamping down my hypothesizing.) Her son is a sturdy, goateed young man who already writes at a high level. He's talented, self-aware, and willing to make that tough journey to where shadowy images reside. And like his mom he works hard. Like Romnesh, Dan, Diane, and so many other RWGers.

Gwen was first published while she attended the workshop. A few months later she moved away from Philly, wrote a story collection, found an agent, fired him for not working hard enough, wrote two novels, revised them through several drafts, and finally found a better agent—who sold Gwen's third novel, *Montana*. Now she's got a four-book deal. Talk about commitment and determination. Most of us would've have given up long before. It tickles me to say that her son also had his first publication while he was in the group. Genes are inherited, and so, it appears, is the inclination to repeat what your parents have done, hopefully by utilizing what's best in them.

So Rittenhouse Writers' Group has become a multi-generational enterprise. We continue to do what we're supposed to do, which is foster better fiction writing through hard work, self-awareness, and possibly greater self-acceptance. With a few laughs along the way.

Both of my nieces like to write. Maybe one of them will lead a workshop one day.

Epilogue

THIRTY YEARS AGO, while I was writing *Gettin' Dumb*, the first draft of the book that became *Bloodnight*, I discovered halfway through that the narrative was predicated on my yearning for a father. Father figures haunted the pages—a boxer, a psychotic carpenter who paid attention to and challenged me, and a new best friend who was older than I and a mentor.

The revelation sickened me. Suddenly I saw how much I missed my father and how much my personhood had been shaped by his death. Then I was upset that I hadn't conceptualized my yearning for him from the outset. I felt dumb, again. Back then I didn't understand that a first draft is exploratory, a journey where the story and characters are discovered along the way, and that you should expect these revelations, value them, honor them. That's where the magic resides for the writer, the surprise or the shift in expectations that makes the narrative richer. Often when the writer is surprised, the reader is too.

What did I do three decades ago with my newfound knowledge? I came up with the idea that I should craft the novel around a teen-age boy who'd lost his father. Every chance I got, every scene where it seemed pertinent, I couldn't wait to scream: His father died! His father died! He's looking for a father! I made explicit what should have remained implicit. If I hadn't over-emphasized it, it might have worked, but instead I blew the book. I stopped writing it. That draft and another are tucked away, buried, in a plastic container with a bunch of other failed compositions. (Buried? Container? Who am I thinking of?)

With this book, to my amazement, a similar moment occurred. This time I made it almost to the end. I thought I was writing about my desire to have a family, that all through the workshop, my marriage, the arrival of my nieces, and my involvement with the analytic community, belonging to a family had been my motivation. Then it hit me. That wasn't really true. What I really wanted, at a deeper level, was my mother, or at least a symbolic one, who loved me unconditionally and wanted to take care of me. And this felt like an age-old desire.

Then I wondered if yearning for my father had been a notional scrim, and family had been a scrim as well, for my deepest desire. Once again a revelation had unmoored me, through writing. Again I felt stupid. (I thought I knew myself so well. *Please.*) In one of his final papers, Freud wrote, "I find myself for a moment in the interesting position of not knowing whether what I have to say should be regarded as something long familiar and obvious or as something entirely new and puzzling. But I am inclined to think the latter." Ha. I didn't know if I were so inclined.

I wanted my mother. Adrienne was certainly a loving, nurturing force, but she couldn't be a mother figure to me. Did everyone want their mothers? Or, at least, their primary caregivers? Didn't men and women *in extremis* cry out for their mothers?

I was filled with a great emptiness and sadness. I yearned for my mother the way I had for my father. I thought maybe I'd blown another book. But I was older and more attuned to the process. I scrutinized the book and looked for places to sprinkle the idea. I used a salt shaker this time instead of a front-end loader.

Then I had another thought. Maybe my reaction to my mother neglecting me in my early years (though she became my ally after my father died) had been to become a mother myself—a nurturing, loving force with my students, friends, nieces, wife. Perhaps I wasn't quite the father figure I fancied myself as. Now I was upset again. I felt emasculated—I wasn't the big man after all.

I talked these ideas over with my mentor. (Yes, I still look for guidance.) He said we all want to be taken care of, all our lives, and we're all both fathers and mothers. At the same time we seek to be ourselves—separate from our parents, autonomous, independent. Of course. It took me a while to accept the idea that I had been expressing a maternal side all along. It was time to leave the book alone; these themes were already there.

So I wrote this epilogue. I feel more forcefully, now, that we're all haunted by the good and bad we receive from our parents. Maybe "motivated" is a better word. Consciously and unconsciously we recall them by replicating their actions, emotions, and ideas. All of us carry their representations forever.

Some of us strive to untangle our authentic selves from our parents. Some of us strive to turn our parental ghosts into ancestors or at least find better ways to accommodate them.

All of us eventually end up as orphans, alone. There's a terror and a comfort in this.

TEN STORIES

This book wouldn't be complete without an RWG sampler. I've picked ten stories, a fraction of the ones I could have included. Eight were workshopped in the group. "The Conference Rat" was written after Samantha Gillison left RWG (and Philly). Alice Schell wrote "Kingdom of the Sun," before she joined. We work on novels, too, but I didn't feel excerpts could adequately represent the books.

All of the stories affect me emotionally, which you probably know by now is a crucial factor. Some move me by the voice, the depth of the characters, or the convincing depictions of setting and situation. Most convey a beautiful pain—a feeling that I'm partial to. Some are funny, with nuggets of incandescent humor.

Most anthologies present their stories alphabetically. I opted for an order that's more in line with a "collection," as if representing a single writer. I wanted a variety of subject matter, and a narrative with an emotional cadence.

So many elements go into creating a good story. RWG addresses them all, from locating the heart of a story, to intent, point of view and distance, and how characters evolve (or not). We discuss issues of craft such as structure and dramatic action. Toward the end we may narrow our focus and talk about word choice and grammar. We do most everything to improve a writer's work, employing a disciplined subjectivity as best we can. But it's hard to know what a writer will hear that will translate into significant changes. That process is still a mystery to me.

Writing workshops are complex enterprises, like people, like characters on a page. What makes them successful is another mystery, no matter what methods or rules are used. The instructor's attitude and intellect generate the group dynamic, along with the intangibles that connect participants. It may sound coy, but it's unclear to me what makes the Rittenhouse Writers' Group thrive. I do know there's magic in that room above the Square.

—J. R.

GWEN FLORIO

On Fire

Even without the radio, or the calls to the Forest Service for updates, Jack would have known. He could smell it, taste it, an acrid tang on the tongue. The air got heavy, took on a yellow tinge. Outlines blurred.

But he wanted to see for himself. So he took the road that climbed the rimrock north of Billings, leaving the pickup with its rusted Swiss-cheese side panels in the airport lot and hiking to the cliff edge. He looked west sixty miles, to the smoke cloaking the peaks of the Beartooths. Behind him, the afternoon 757 from Denver came screaming in. He leaned back against the noise, imagining himself already at the fire, deafened by its roar. Then he went home and packed.

The crew chief came by when he was only half done. He stood in the doorway of Jack's rented room, leaning heavily against the jamb, working a wad of bubblegum in his cheek. Kayla had made him give up chew. Jack looked at him, belly straining against belt, and thought, You're almost done, buddy. Arlie was thirty-two, nearly a decade older than Jack, beefy. The only way he'd hung around so long was by sticking with the hand crews, working brush fires, a few controlled burns.

Arlie nodded toward the bed, the backpack lying open on it. "You should of done that last night," he said. He kicked at the floor, where Jack had laid a trail of plastic sandwich bags stuffed with socks and underwear and energy bars and wet wipes and cornstarch powder and glove liners. It was September, days still hitting the eighties, but mornings in the fire camp would bring hard frost.

Jack ignored him. The pack had sat ready since the last fire and
Arlie knew it. But Jack liked to go through everything one last time
before he left. He methodically began stuffing everything back into it,
underwear at the bottom, salve handy near the top, only half-listening
to Arlie jabbering about how if things went right—if the fire went
wrong—they could each pull down about a thousand bucks, allowing
for sixteen-hour days and hazard pay.

"A thousand," Jack repeated. Hand crews like theirs, the ones that
worked the edges of the fires, only got paid by the job. Not like the
smokejumpers and the hotshot crews, the ones who fought the fire at
its heart, and for that got guaranteed salaries all season.

"Kayla's got her eye on a new sofa," Arlie said. "She told me on the
way out the door: 'Get your butt up there and don't come back till it's
paid for.'"

Jack thought of the tires on his outfit, silvery steel threads glinting
beneath a membrane of tread; of the new boots he'd been paying on,
the kind the hotshots wore. He hefted the forty-pound pack.

"Come on," Arlie urged. "They're waiting on us." The rest of the
crew would meet them over at the Forest Service office, where they'd
pick up their tools. Arlie would drive the bus from there up to the fire
camp outside Red Lodge.

Jack shook his head. "You go on," he said. "I'm going to drive up
myself. Got some business in Red Lodge I want to take care of after
we're done." He thought of her voice, low and clear through the telephone, the last time he had worked out an excuse to call her. "No,"
she'd said. "Not now."

Arlie turned to go. Jack took a breath, risked the question he'd been
living with since he saw the smoke corkscrew up from the mountains. "Hotshots coming in, I guess," he said.

Arlie paused in the hall. "You bet. This thing really took off this
morning. They called in Flagstaff, Bitterroot, Chief Mountain," he
said, ticking off the names of the hotshot crews. He shifted the gum
to his other cheek. "Lolo's coming, too." That was the hotshot crew
from the Lolo National Forest, over on the other side of the state,
where the tourists went.

Jack let his breath out. He forced himself to wait until Arlie's outfit had turned the corner before jumping into his own. He gunned it all the way out to I-90, picking up speed on the on-ramp, letting the new housing developments named for old ranches blur past. He could see the mountains from the road now. The plumes from the peaks were dark, roiling, streaming across the sky. Soon, Jack told himself. Soon.

He'd met her at the start of the summer, over where Montana flattens out and slides on into North Dakota. The blaze began as a regular range fire, wandering with the wind through grazing land, eating up a few dozen acres of sagebrush here and there, forcing ranchers to waste a lot of time shifting sheep and cattle around, but otherwise causing little damage. Arlie's crew and a couple of other hand crews came up, but mostly they just dug a few fire lines to turn it back from the occasional ranch house, finishing up in plenty of time each day to make last call at one of the nearby town's two bars. But a few days into it, the wind had tacked hard to the north and the fire charged up into the Missouri Breaks. There it had a field day feeding on the thick stands of willows and alders that clogged the narrow canyons pleating the Breaks. The wind kept coming, picking up speed as it swooped through the draws, shoving the fire up higher, into the tinderbox of Ponderosa pine, its roar drowning out the rattle of the hastily summoned smokejumper planes as they circled once, then again, looking for level spots in that jagged, tilting landscape to drop the crews.

It was five nights before the crew saw town again, and Arlie had to punch Jack awake when the bus that hauled them jolted into the gravel parking lot of the bar. Inside, the air was thicker with smoke than it had been in the Breaks, but after Arlie stood him a schnapps and a beer, and then another, Jack felt life burning back into his wooden, deadweight limbs. He started feeling his face again, too, blisters rising along his cheeks from where he'd sunk his Pulaski into a tussock that hid a hot spot, sending sparks spraying upward.

He looked around for Arlie, but he'd shifted down the bar, talking to a girl. Jack got a look at dark, watchful eyes in a strong-jawed face with long, wavy hair pulled back away from it. Just like always, he thought, putting the moves to the locals. Well, who could blame him? Fires left everybody pumped up and restless, wanting to go off with somebody afterward. Jack worked out on the weight machines in the basement of the high school, and ran the rimrock road on his days off, staying in shape for the day there'd be a slot on a hotshot crew. When it came to the after-fire frolicking, he did all right.

The place was packed with ranchers ending up their day in town, crowding three deep at the bar with the fire crews, eager for some-body new to talk to. A group of Indians, still in their heavy yellow Nomex pants, sat at a table that they'd pulled a little ways away from the others. Jack knew them to be one of the reservation hotshot crews, Blackfeet from up by the Canadian border. They were big men, taller and broader than the Mescalero Apache Hotshots who'd come up from Arizona and were even now headed for Billings and the airport, hoping to catch the late plane back to Phoenix.

One of the Blackfeet—six feet or more, with broad scars furrowing one side of his neck and face—rose, brushed roughly past, reached for the girl Arlie was talking to, wrapping both arms around her, hold-ing her tight, swaying a moment, nearly pulling her from the barstool. Jack felt things slow down, everybody pulling back a little, setting down their beers and getting ready. He reached for the man, intend-ing to get him off the girl, but Arlie stepped between them.

"It's okay," he said, and then, looking at the men around them, said louder, "that's Leonard Old Horse and this here is Annie Brach. She's with Lolo, out a Missoula. They were at Los Verdes," and Jack saw it register on the other men's faces just as it did on his.

The Los Verdes fire had been in New Mexico, he knew, in the redrock mesas in the north. Three Hotshot crews and a hand crew had come in to fight it, forty-two firefighters in all, and nobody had pulled them out of a box canyon when the winds started. The fire blew up, flames climbing two hundred feet tall, and took ten firefight-ers with it. Two were women. Until Los Verdes, it hadn't occurred to him that women could be hotshots.

Jack looked at Annie, at her arms, fire-tanned and corded, wrapped around Leonard's back, her boots doing a tap dance against the legs of the bar stool. The boots should have told him: three-hundred-dollar handmade Nick's like the ones he'd been saving for, with the extra-deep lugs on the bottom that would dig into baked earth and save your life if you found yourself running uphill, fire hot behind you.

Leonard finally released Annie, and she smiled and caught her breath, holding out her hand to Arlie, then Jack, forming them into a tiny circle. Her handshake was quick and powerful, and Jack looked at the outlines of her shoulders and arms beneath the tight tee-shirt she wore. From the back, he figured, she'd have looked like a man, hard and compact, but in the front, her shirt tented in a way that made him turn his attention to his beer so as not to be caught looking.

Luckily, Arlie was talking, distracting everybody. "You know how we talk about being on fire when we're out on the line," he said to the ranchers who crowded close, wafting a mix of cowshit and Saturday night cologne. "Well, Leonard, here, he was really on fire at Los Verdes. He must of still been half-froze from one a those Hi-Line winters because he walked right up to that fire, they say, trying to thaw out, and the fire obliged him, ran right over him. They brought him back into camp smelling like so much barbecue, and he was smiling. Smiling!"

"You got that exactly right," Leonard said. "It was the first time I'd been warm all year. You know what they say about the weather up on the Hi-Line. Just one month of summer, and that month comes one day at a time." Only the right side of his mouth moved when he talked. The left trailed up into the sheet of scar tissue that shone pink and oddly tender against his brown, pockmarked skin.

"You were smiling because your nerve endings were burnt." Annie's voice was still hoarse with smoke, but it cut through the laughter, and the men stopped and listened to her. "It only happens with third-degree burns. That's why there's no pain. At first. You felt plenty later, if I remember."

"Ignore her," said Leonard. "She's a fire geek. If she's not on fire, she's on her computer, trying to figure out where the next one will be, e-mailing those poor people at the Fire Center in Boise three times a day, driving them crazy."

Annie smiled, unperturbed. She had undone her hair, which from a distance had looked nearly black, but turned out to be dark blond, hanging down past her shoulders, frizzing in the heat and closeness of the bar. "Called this one right, didn't I?" Leonard lifted a longneck in acknowledgement. Jack hung back, wondering how to get in on the conversation. A fire geek, Leonard had said. Jack touched her arm.

"What was Los Verdes like?" he asked, and signaled the bartender for more beer and schnapps when she smiled and swiveled to face him, her gaze scanning the blisters along his cheekbones. He thought maybe there'd be some tears trembling at the memory—with a girl, you didn't know—but she spoke of perimeters and sequencing and wind speed, while he kept waving his arm, calling for more shots as her eyes grew glittery and her cheeks flamed red, and he bent his head close to catch her analysis of downslope spreads and fireline overruns.

She stopped for breath, licked dry lips. Jack fished around in a fuzzed brain for another fire question to keep her going. She put her hand on his arm and her mouth against his ear. "I'll dance with you if you quit staring at my tits."

She didn't flinch when he pressed up against her on the dance floor. He bent his head to kiss the side of her neck, just below the earlobe, but she turned her face until her mouth met his. She tugged him toward the door. "Let's get out of here."

Outside, they fell up against the rough log wall, his hands under her shirt, her breasts a soft surprise after the hardness of her arms and back, her tongue inside his mouth, her hair falling around his face, its silkiness smelling of cinders and ash. "Does this hurt?" she said, her fingers tracing the stinging blisters. It was cold and her breath wreathed around them, her words so low he could barely hear them. He was used to girls with high, sharp voices, who talked and talked, demanding reassurances, promises of Saturday night dates and Sunday dinners with the family before locked knees parted. Annie was silent as she tugged at his belt buckle, pulling him close, kissing him hard as he worked his leg between her thighs.

"Not here," she said, and he took her to the bus and wrenched open the door, the two of them falling across a seat, him on his back, her tugging his pants down, the vinyl slick and icy beneath his bare legs. She sat up to strip the tee-shirt over her head. In the dark, her nipples were sooty smudges. When he kissed them, he tasted smoke.

"Wait." She bent and untied her heavy boots and kicked free of them, then peeled off her socks and pants and underwear. "You, too."

"It's cold.

"Let's do this right."

Jack scrambled out of his clothes. He reached for her but she held him at arm's length, then nodded and he lay back and for a few moments forgot about the cold and the bar and anything but the woman moving on top of him. Then a light flashed across her face as the door of the bar opened, letting out a blast of noise and a knot of ranchers fumbling for their keys, their heads turning curiously toward the bus. Jack pulled Annie close, as the ranchers hooted and whistled.

"You see that?" someone said.

"Indeed I did. One a them fire boys. They like it hot, you know."

"Local girl?"

"Naw."

"Hell. I thought maybe your wife got lucky."

They guffawed their way into their respective outfits, hitting the gas when they drove past the bus, spraying it with grit. Jack pulled Annie closer, but she stiffened. "That'll be last call," she said. "They'll all be out soon." She sat up and felt around for her bra and shirt, pulling them on slowly, calmly.

"We could go to a motel," he said, hating the pleading in his voice.

"Can't. Smokejumpers took all the rooms. Besides, your bus is heading back to Billings when this place closes tonight. Arlie told me."

He reached for her again and she let him kiss her this time, though he sensed her eyes open, watching the door to make sure nobody else was coming out. He asked for her phone number. "The crew gets over to Missoula sometimes," he said. "I could call you."

She shook her head. "Not a good idea. You'd come up and I'd be on fire someplace else."

He held out his hand to her as she climbed down from the bus. She took it. "I got to see you again," he said.

She leaned against him a moment, then backed away. At the door of the bar she called to him, "Maybe I'll see you at the next fire." She pushed open the door and stepped into the blaze of light.

When he pulled in to Red Lodge the bus was waiting for him, Arlie hanging out the door, waving him over, calling, "Move your ass." The bus bounced along a logging road, following the fire's tracks through a no-color landscape still smoldering in spots. It climbed higher, past the burn, and stopped with a wheeze alongside a high meadow.

"If we can stop it here, turn it back on itself, it'll die out," Arlie said. "At least, this piece of it." Jack and the others spread out along the edge of the meadow, hefting their Pulaskis, letting them arc down through the dry, matted grasses into soil so dry it flew up like powder, settling in the creases of their clothing and skin. Jack wet his bandana and tied it across his face. The hills west of them glowed orange.

"It's real bad over there," Arlie said. "Flared up sometime this afternoon. Lolo and Chief Mountain are there, trying to get a handle on it. Planes been dumping retardant on it all day, trying to quiet things down, but I don't see as they're having any luck."

So she was there. Jack swung his Pulaski, sidestepped, swung, sidestepped, moving down the line, trying to get into the rhythm of it. He thought how things could go after the fire, how if he could just get her alone for a minute in camp, he could talk her into coming down to Red Lodge with him, maybe having dinner at one of the tablecloth restaurants that the ski people liked. He worked slow and steady for two hours, trying to keep his mind blank, but he finally let himself think what it might be like, her sprawled beneath him, sweat slicking her skin, her hair plastered damp across her forehead. He swung the Pulaski wide, almost taking the toe off Arlie's boot.

"What's wrong with you?" Arlie said, grabbing his arm.

Jack thrust the Pulaski deep into the dirt, and bent over it. He felt Arlie's hand on his back. "You okay?"

He nodded.

"Just take it easy a minute. They're going be taking us back to camp soon, anyway. They've got things pretty much under control down the line."

The Chief Mountain Hotshots were already back in camp when the hand crews came in. Jack went right to the radio tent and saw Leonard Old Horse there ahead of him, pestering the girl with the headphones, the pink swath of his scar smeared dark with smoke and sweat. While the operator twirled the dials and spoke a lot of numbers into the radio, Leonard told Jack what he knew, which wasn't much.

"This time they paid attention to the wind," he said, and was quiet for a moment, both of them thinking of Los Verdes. "They sent a couple of helicopters up for us. We were over by a flat place, and they got us out. But Lolo was up higher on the hill. All twenty of them are still up there, spread out all over creation. The crew chief is talking to all of them on their radios, then he's calling in to us."

The radio girl spoke up then, in a nasal singsong Jack recognized from past fires. "Not anymore he's not," she said. "We lost them about ten minutes ago. He said the wind was up and the fire was moving again. Look up there. You can see."

Jack looked through the tent flap, up at the mountain, watching the fire burn a band across it. Along the rows of tents, crews were stepping outside, looking.

"Hell," said Arlie, coming up behind Jack, "it's crowned." The fire was up in the treetops, racing, feeding on the wind flowing above it, sucking oxygen from the air below. Jack knew anyone beneath it stood as good a chance of suffocating as burning.

Jack turned, shoving past Arlie, stepping out onto the trail. He would go up there. He would find her. He would bring her back. But Arlie grabbed him. Others did too. "What the hell you think you're doing?" Arlie yelled.

That night Jack lay in his sleeping bag, trying not to think. Fire camps were usually noisy places where crews who only saw each other a few times a year got reacquainted, but this was the quietest camp he had ever been in. He feared for Annie, and all her crew, and sensed dozens of others just like him, awake, straining toward the mountain. One of the ranchers from Red Lodge had been on his way up with a mule train, and Jack had seen the pack saddles, body bags folded onto them, and he knew what they expected to bring back.

He lay there in the dark, his mind pulling him up the mountain. It would be like daytime there, everything lit up, with hard, sharp edges like noon in December, except it would be hot, so hot. He pictured Annie, probably sweating in her Nomex, but cold, focused, her mind racing, eyes flicking back and forth across the flames moving along the hill below. The crew would be spread out above her. She'd stoop and yank up a handful of grass, that old test, hold it high, let it fall. But the grass would swirl and eddy in the wind currents the fire created. There was no way of telling which way the fire could go, and the crew was deep in tindery stuff. She waved her arm, pointing up. There were rocks up there, and the brush looked thinner; if they got caught down here they'd cook, no chance of smoke inhalation, nice and drowsy, just the flames wrapping them tight.

Then they were all quick-stepping, racing along ahead of her. They'd get to the top of the ridge and hunker down on the other side—then it was on the back of her neck like a hot breath, roaring behind her, the flames towering up into the pine canopy and beyond, carving their way high into the black sky, and now the wind bent the fire toward her, and she let her pack slide to the ground and sprinted to catch up to the others, the rocks still too far.

She pulled even with one of the crew and whacked him to speed him along, but he shook his head. He was tugging at the fire shelter on his belt, and she screamed, No, there's too much stuff here, the fire will stay too long, you won't make it, you'll fry, but he was already on the ground, pulling the shiny sheet over him, and she turned away, toward the rocks. Things slowed down. The fire was louder, the sound dropping and deepening. If she turned, it would be an orange wall shimmering fierce behind her, but then she was at the rocks, hitting the bare patch of dirt behind them headlong, shaking out the shelter, hooking hands and feet into the loops in the corners, spread-eagling face-down, sucking in dirt.

The fire came licking under the shake-and-bake bag, braceleting her wrists where they stuck out from the Nomex sleeves, then it was on top of her, too, moving across the shelter in waves, lifting her up, letting her down. Her breath was leaving her, her lungs filling up with heat, nothing but noise all around now, and she floated up one more time, and things were quieter. She was on fire.

Jack came to, sweating. Light seeped into the tent, with the sound of feet rushing past. Somehow he must have slept. He'd left his clothes on, even his boots, and the laces flapped around his ankles as he ran to join the crews. They lined the trail, a gauntlet of yellow-clad men, a few women, the Indian crews standing together. The rancher came down first, leading a mule gone lame, and as it stutter-stepped behind him, the rancher stared down at the ground and shook his head in response to the unspoken questions. The first mule's cargo was draped over its back, the bag swaying slightly as the mule lurched down the steep slope into camp. Behind it were three more, and Jack tried not to see how the contents of the bags were oddly abbreviated. A man sat on the fifth mule, slumping low in his saddle, his bandaged hands and arms crossed before his chest, his face filthy and black with smoke except for the wet smears beneath his eyes. He stared down, like the rancher, studying the mule's neck, and the men lining the trail reached out to touch his calf, his knee, to caress the mule's flanks.

"They left some up there," somebody said, the whisper floating down the line like the wisps of fog burning off in the early-morning light. Jack's stomach twisted. He choked back a sour taste in his throat.

But there was one more still coming down the trail, this one on foot, and it was her, Annie, moving slow and stiff, but walking just the same. The tips of her boots were black and peeling, and her hands were bandaged up past the wrists, and she held them like oversize mittens away from her sides. She had cleaned her face, and the skin there was red and angry and shiny with salve, but her eyes were dry. He stepped forward as she approached and her gaze flicked toward him. A muscle jumped in her cheek and he started to bring his arms up to wrap them around her, let her know she would be all right now, but she hitched her shoulder and edged past him, heading for the Chief Mountain crew.

She stopped where they'd assembled and the rest of the crew read her face, seeing the fire that each of them knew, and then they turned and walked together, not touching, cutting across the field to the medical tent, while Jack stood on the hillside watching, the others heading for their buses in slow, silent groups.

Mother—6/7 Months

I HAD A dream once. There is a woman I know, but she is in a kind of shadow, or else it is dark and I cannot recognize her. We are in a boat on a lake and she is rowing. In the dimness of my dream the lake seems endless. I think I ask the woman if I can take the oars, row a little, isn't she tired? And this is where the problem starts. I've had a similar dream, many times. The end varies slightly but basically the same thing happens. The woman raises the oar as if to give it to me but then hits me with it. She hits me hard, and in my sleep I can always feel the pain, it is so familiar, the ache that starts in my head and courses through my body, pain like a deep sorrow, felt in my blood and in my bones.

John, my friend who is an artist, told me where my dream is from. It's a scene from a movie about reincarnation whose name I forget, but I swear I have never seen the film. We dream, he said, from a shared consciousness, what we've seen, done, been told. The thing is, I'm not sure what the explanation is, or what it all means. I think the answer lies in the identity of the woman. Sometimes I think it's my mother, the way the woman crosses her ankles only her toes touching the boat's floor. But other times I'm certain it's my wife, who doesn't know about this dream. John told me the woman in the boat is "Woman"—all women and all the women I have known—but I can't believe him. I love women, woman, mother, wife. My wife is expecting our first child, and I believe it will be a girl.

Serena, my wife, is a photographer. These days she's a bit introverted, quiet. She stays home a lot and appears to have lost interest in her freelance work; she says she is taking a break from photography.

I know it must be her pregnancy, but I am worried about her being alone all day, having nothing to do, even though she is quite capable of looking after herself. I call her often during the day and sometimes the phone rings and rings, and I imagine her asleep on her back, her long brown hair spread over the pillow, dreaming perhaps another version of someone else's dream.

One day Serena is visiting her gynecologist, and I am late for work and need a large envelope in which to put the bills. I search through the drawers in the small front room she uses as her darkroom, knowing I will find a modest stock of the stationery I supply her with from my office. In the top drawer I see Bics, erasers, White-out, Scotch-tape, four Exacto knives, but no envelopes. Then a drawer full of yellow and black Kodak and Fuji rolls, some in little black canisters. I shut the drawer quickly, afraid I will expose film or unused paper. The third drawer is full of manila envelopes, none of which appears to be empty.

As I sift through the pile in search of my now elusive quarry, I see an envelope with "Mother—6/7 Months" written neatly in Serena's handwriting below my company's logo. The envelope is thick with what feels like 8 × 10s, and I am suddenly curious. Pulling the black and white photographs out of the envelope, I do not know what to expect, and all at once I feel that pain, the very same one from my dream, only now it murmurs uneasily in my stomach as though nervous of the reality of daylight. I walk over to the work table and begin to spread the two dozen or so prints across it.

Serena is the subject of the photographs and in every picture she is naked, her pouting belly always the centerpiece. Some photos frame only her round stomach, her navel gawking at the camera like a blind eye. In others she is lying on the bed. Her eyes are shut, her face is without makeup and looks fuller, less beautiful, than it usually does. The way her hands rest atop her stomach in these pictures makes her look like a distorted Madonna.

And then there are the ones that have a strange effect on me. These are taken in the bathroom, Serena sitting on the pot, the camera aimed at her vagina from below. I wonder for a moment how she placed the camera to achieve that angle. She must have used a special lens; her vagina, being closest to the camera, appears huge and detailed, behind it looms her seemingly enormous belly. Her face is only in one of these three prints, and in another she has begun to urinate, her pee frozen in its rush towards the camera.

The photographs shock me. Serena rarely does self-portraits and, being a commercial photographer, has never done any nudes before. These pictures have a shamelessness that scares me. I feel as though the subject is a stranger, not a woman I see every day, often in the same positions as Serena has assumed for the camera. The photographs do not arouse me, though the ones in the bathroom stir me in a way I don't like and cannot define. I think suddenly that we have not made love for two months. Serena had begun to find it uncomfortable, and now I am inexplicably jealous.

The ache in my stomach begins to tire me, and I sit awkwardly on the tall stool. I continue staring at the prints on the table until they begin to blur and look alike. I don't know this Serena, and for the first time in her pregnancy, her body, as displayed in the photos, repulses me. Why did she take these pictures? And, asking myself that, I am quickly open to conjecture. I look again at the table and realize there is a question I have been attempting to push into the back of my mind, but cannot ignore any longer.

Was Serena in fact the photographer here or simply the model? Some of the photographs taken on the bed have about them a tranquility that belies the usual rushed look of self-timer photographs. And others seem to be shot from impossible viewpoints, if the camera had been unattended. I convince myself these photographs are not self-portraits and yet I cannot be sure of anything. My wife is a shy woman, ill at ease around nudity, and it has taken many years for her to be comfortably naked in my presence. She would not bare herself to another photographer with the apparent ease these pictures portray.

Unless they were taken not by a photographer but by someone else? While a minute ago I didn't question technique or style, the photographs before me now appear amateurish and oddly intimate. Once again I am jealous of someone or something, a caressing camera or unknown voyeur, and I distastefully gather the prints back into a pile, unconcerned about recreating their original order. All thought of envelopes forgotten, I replace the packet in the drawer and leave for work, only now looking at my watch to see I have lost all sense of time and have been here for three-quarters of an hour.

At work I can think of nothing but the photographs, and I want to talk to Serena about them, but not over the phone. Yet part of me wishes I had never come across the envelope, or had left it unopened. I think of the word "Mother" on the envelope and wonder what it implies. Surely it suggests the pictures are self-portraits, an experiment prompted by some desire alien to me, a symptom of late-stage pregnancy? And why wasn't the packet hidden away? All day I run through the permutations and am irritable when my train of thought is interrupted by my secretary or one of my coworkers.

When I get home at six, Serena is out again and has left a note to say she will be having dinner with Lisa, her friend who works in an advertising agency. I am tempted to go at once to the photographs, but at the same time I don't want to see them again. Instead I open a beer from the fridge and turn on the news in the living room. A man speaks into a microphone in front of a large warehouse, and I press the mute button on the remote so I don't have to listen.

Then I hear the lock turn in the front door and the door slam shut, and it can only mean Serena is home. I wonder if I fell asleep, but I see the same newsman on TV, still in front of the warehouse. Serena walks into the room and shrugs her shoulders.

"She couldn't get out of work and didn't have time to call, so I'm waiting at the bar and decide to call her and of course she apologized like crazy and I said it's okay, I can spend time with David, and here I am, so let's spend time."

She smiles and lowers herself slowly onto the leather chair across from me. She is wearing one of those loose and shapeless smock-like dresses that I find so unflattering, and it is hard for me to picture her naked body underneath, which is what I am trying to do. She reaches over for the remote and turns the sound back on.

"What should we do for dinner?" is all I can think to say. I still haven't decided what I'm going to do about the pictures, but they are now vivid in my mind, and I am flicking through the imaginary sheaf of prints, trying to reconcile them with the woman in front of me. When I recall the bathroom pictures, I feel my penis begin to grow erect.

"I left last night's pasta for you, but I don't know if it's enough for two," she says. "Or three," she adds after a pause, looking down into her lap. "We could go to Julia's, it's that new restaurant I was telling you I read about, Lisa and I were going to go there, they don't take reservations, so, you know."

Today of all days she is annoyingly cheery, and I have trouble responding to her chatter.

"Why don't we stay in," I say. "I'll cook something, or make some salad."

Serena nods as if to say she doesn't care what we do tonight. I stare at her watching the news intently, something I can never do with much patience, and am confused between a feeling of detached arousal and one of disgust. I am repelled by the very images that now stir me and am reminded of the way some weird pornography once affected me. But this is my wife, moreover, the slight body in front of me with its hidden round burden appears no more than homely. Yet those photographs, coarse and disembodied, will not stop dancing before me. Serena must notice a strange expression on my face, because she looks at me and says, "What's the matter?"

"Nothing," I answer and rise to go to the kitchen. "I'll start dinner."

Before Serena got pregnant, when we talked about having a baby, we always started our discussions seriously. Did we want the commitment, the changes in our lives? We had seen the effects on couples we knew. But we never reached a conclusion. There was always the next day to talk about it, and our conversations were often cut short by a certain feeling of excitement that invariably led to lovemaking. We made sure Serena had her diaphragm in, because we didn't want to have the baby until we were ready. And then, somehow, we stopped talking about it, and Serena left the diaphragm on the bathroom shelf, and we both knew what we were trying to do. But we couldn't communicate these thoughts through words anymore. It was as though we thought talking about it would be unlucky and spoil our chances of success.

And so even as Serena's body changed its shape and this thing, this event whose occurrence we knew would alter so much, took on an inevitability that drew closer every day, we never again discussed the momentousness of what was happening. Like other prospective parents, we talked about clothes and toys and reminisced about our own childhoods. But our earlier conversations, which were so typical of our relationship, were never resurrected, and now, as the photographs have begun to obsess me and I think about so many things, I wonder about that change in our relationship and when exactly it happened. It was as if we had decided to give up forever a certain level of intimacy in order to admit another person to our marriage.

As the days go on, I think increasingly of this distance between us that began to grow long before I found the pictures. In my mind the photographs have taken on a greater meaning; they must be symbolic of larger events in our lives. I find myself staying later at work and, when at home, avoiding Serena whenever I can. Serena notices this change in my behavior, I think, but does not comment. We spend evenings of polite formality together, and I wonder if she knows that I know and is afraid to talk about it.

But I am still unsure of what it is that I do know. Did Serena take the pictures or did someone else? If it was another person, is it someone I know? Is it a man or a woman? Does this person mean anything to Serena? And yet I am sure there is no one else. I keep track of her movements and can account for most of her time. Now, as if guarding the pictures against my perverse curiosity, she rarely leaves the apartment. Since that first time I haven't been able to see the pictures again, and I don't know if I even want to.

Yet they continue to torment me, and the longer I wait, the less inclined I am to confront Serena. If I am in the room to see her undress for bed, I stare with a fascination I try to disguise, comparing her body to the photographs, as if they, not the aerobically fit and slim woman I married, are the frame of reference against which her pregnancy should be measured. I have begun to masturbate every day in the men's room at the office, guilty behind the seemingly flimsy booth dividers, pausing every time someone walks in. Sometimes I imagine the photographs as I remember them, particularly the explicit ones, and often I think of Serena's pregnant body being made love to. She has a man in her mouth or is lying on her side, and he is trying to enter her. The man is obscure; it could be me or anyone else. It is Serena's image I picture in detail.

Afterwards, I find it all sickening, but the next day I cannot stop myself from doing it again. It is harder and harder for me to put anything in perspective. We are having a baby together and are creating life, and I am proud of that, yet I have let some stupid photographs warp my view of how special this time could be for us, is what I think half the time. And then again I'm amazed that I am having a baby with a woman I feel I don't know, who has a secret she wants to hide from me. I think maybe I should talk to someone about what is happening to me, to us, but in order to do that I feel I have to show them the photographs, and I cannot do that.

Then one day I decide to destroy the photographs, to find the negatives and burn them, together with the prints, and when Serena realizes what I have done, it will all go away, we will never mention it to each other, and everything will be as before. This course of action seems so simple and appropriate, I am surprised I haven't thought of it before. I wait for the next time Serena will be out and begin planning my day so that I can sneak in while she is gone.

She has to shop for a present for her mother's birthday, and I call twice at lunch to make sure she isn't home. I drive home, flushed with the import of my mission, hoping I have estimated the timing correctly. At home, in Serena's darkroom, the packet of pictures lies in the same drawer, and I am apprehensive as I hold the envelope close to my face, as if to inhale its scent. I stare at the words written on the front, and they now appear strangely private and forbidding.

And then I hear a sound and I almost drop the envelope because the noise is from inside the apartment, and it sounds like it is coming from the bedroom. I stand still and silent, waiting to hear more. I am sure there is someone in the bedroom, and I quietly put the envelope back in the drawer and slide it shut. I am drawn to the passage lead-

ing into the bedroom, and I see the door is shut, but now I can hear
Serena's muffled voice. I wait again, closer to the door, but it is quiet
again. I don't know whether to open the door, to knock, or leave the
apartment and enter again, banging the door shut loudly behind me,
to let Serena know I am home.

I wait indecisively; I don't know what lies behind the door and I
am afraid to find out that it may be nothing, or it may be something
else altogether. And then I hear more movement and it is coming towards the door and before I can move the door is opening and Serena is standing, naked, looking at me as though she has just entered a
room she knows well, but the furniture has been rearranged and now
she cannot recognize it.

In the same instant, I look at her and notice her breasts seem larger,
yet disproportionately small compared to her stomach, and I look
past her into the room and see the naked back of a man sitting on the
bed. The man has our piano-shaped phone in his hand and has just
begun to speak into the receiver, but I cannot seem to hear what he
is saying. I glance again at Serena, who has not moved, and I see in
her look neither surprise nor the confusion I saw a moment ago, only
a blankness that suddenly reminds me of her expression in the photographs. Standing there, I wonder about the photographs, why they
upset me so. They depicted nothing other than what I see before me
in the frame of the bedroom door: my wife, Serena, naked and with
a big stomach carrying a baby, a daughter perhaps, who could have
been mine.

And then I turn and walk out of the apartment without looking
back and feel this is something I have done before, or dreamt, or seen
or been told, but that it is not happening to me, now, here.

DIANE McKINNEY-WHETSTONE

Moon Penitent

THE MOON was a dot in the sky as Cartha watched her husband, Raymond, come home. He was a capable accountant but fairly impotent when it came to her needs. The deep needs nestled in her softness like that spot the size of a dime that the doctors had assured would be easy to shrink. She thought about the spot, and the dot of the moon against the navy glazed sky as Raymond laughed his way onto the porch.

A stranger with him. Always bringing someone home to fix things. The dishwasher hose, the motion sensor on the upstairs deck, the timer on the gas grill. This one was tall and thin and dark as the space surrounding the moon. His shirt was a baby blanket blue and made of cotton gauze: a red twisted licorice protruded from the pocket of the blue gauze like an up-turned drill bit.

"Babe, meet Cole," Raymond said as he leaned into the porch swing and mashed his lips against Cartha's cheek. "Never believe it, babe, I'm at the gym, stopped at the gym after work that's why I'm late, anyhow, I'm doing the life cycle, complaining to the guys about the damned closet door being off the track, how I got that crap all over my hands, axle grease or whatever the hell it was when I'd tried to fix it earlier—"

"And let me guess," Cartha interrupted in a voice that sounded like it wanted to fall asleep, "Cole here is an expert on sliding glass doors."

"No expert." That's all Cole said, then he extended his hand to Cartha and smiled.

Cartha thought that his hand was too large for his slender build, and his smile too slow, at least that his mouth took time to catch up to the rest of his face when he smiled. She ignored his hand and stared instead at the moon.

"She doesn't mean to be rude," Raymond whispered as he motioned Cole in through the front door. "Hasn't been feeling well, otherwise lovely wife, couldn't ask for a better wife."

His voice drifted and Cartha didn't strain to hear. She was angry that he'd brought another stranger home. Not the crackling anger that used to leap like a brushfire when the wind was right, but a muffled one like a low groan covered with wool and pressed deep inside where the dark spot was growing.

She pushed her bare feet against the wooden planks of the porch floor to get the to and fro motion of the swing. The air had been still and thick with moisture but now it moved with the swing and even lifted her hair weighted down in locked tussles. She at least hoped this stranger would stay until she fell asleep. She couldn't tolerate Raymond's cheeriness, his monologue about how uncanny that he should run into this guy at the time they needed him most.

She did fall asleep until she felt Raymond lift her tiny sagging body from the swing. She kept her eyes closed while he carried her up the stairs and pressed her gently into bed and covered her feet with the white down comforter. The ceiling fan clicked predictably as she listened again to Raymond cry.

The moon was a small crescent and reminded Cartha of the jewelry the Fifty Second Street vendors sold on green felt-covered tables in front of Hakim's bookstore. She could smell the incense and oils, almost taste the lemon pound cake she'd buy from the Cookie Jar when she still had her appetite and could swallow well. She stared at the moon and thought about the city—how long it had been since she'd barreled through its caverns on the train. Raymond insisted she not drive in, even when she'd still had the strength to drive. "They'll stalk you," he'd threatened. "Car like ours they'll kill you for, stuff you in the trunk like a rag doll."

She pushed her bare feet against the porch to move the swing to the beat of Raymond's voice in her head. She wondered where he was anyhow. Wondered if maybe the carjackers had gotten him, stuffed him in the trunk every night this week, as late as he'd been. She stopped the swing when she heard footsteps. Thought that she would try to pull together enough strength to greet him standing for a change. But she was tired. And then it wasn't even Raymond making his way up the steps. Nothing like him. This figure was taller, darker. The one who'd fixed the sliding glass door.

"Raymond's not here," she said quickly, as if her weak voice had the power to stop a determined man in his tracks.

He did stop though. They all did. When they showed up a few days after they'd made right whatever Raymond had said leaked, or hung wrong, or was cracked or frayed or confused (one had even told him that wiring gets confused), they'd stop at the sound of her voice, in deference to her frailty, she thought. This one, Cole, leaned slightly in a bow, showed his palms as he did, said, "I don't mean to disturb you, Cartha, may I call you Cartha?" And not waiting for a reaction slipped into the chair across from the white wicker swing where Cartha sat straight and still. "I just left Raymond at the gym, said he's got to go back to the office, high-powered account he's on. So I just thought I'd come by and check on you, you know, sit with you for a while."

She scanned his shirt as he talked. This shirt was cotton gauze and naturally wrinkled. She moistened her lips when she saw the red twisted licorice peeking from his shirt pocket, her favorite little girl candy. She wanted to ask for it, wanted to stretch it and break it into bite-sized pieces she could chew on for a while, but it would take too much work. "Did he send you?" she asked instead.

"He didn't send me, he told me you're sick though, I hope you don't mind."

"That he told you, or that you just popped over here unannounced?"

"I like your hair." Cole ignored her question as he sat forward in the chair and leaned his arms against his knees. "It's very political. First thing I noticed about you the other night."

"No politics, just too tired to comb it. It's all I can do to wash it."
She watched his face. He didn't believe her; she could tell by the way
his eyebrows came together in a V. Raymond had believed her. After
she'd patiently twisted each wisp of her hair to nudge it into locks
he'd offered to get someone over there to fix it up for her. Now that
they'd left the city, he'd told her, she couldn't just let her hair grow
wild like those Jamaican Rastas. And when she'd insisted that she
didn't have the strength to keep it up, he'd relented, said it would be
okay only until she was able to start going out again.

She leaned slowly against the swing back and started a gentle
to and fro. "So you noticed my hair so I noticed your hands." She
watched his eyebrows curve up in a question.

"What about my hands?" he asked as he extended them into the
moonlight and almost touched her to-the-floor dress.

"Too large for the rest of you."

"They are, yes, I know they are."

"From shooting up?"

He nodded. "I should have known that you would know, your
husband told me that you're smart. Quite, quite smart."

"Not all that smart. I used to be close to some people who did that
when I lived in the city, raised in the city you know."

"Well this must be hard for you, living way out here. You miss it,
don't you?"

"What's to miss? Drive-bys, guard always up, half-dead men
soaking up the rank steam from sidewalk vents." She said it with determination. Kept her saucer eyes wide-open. Raymond used to tell
her that he knew when she was lying because her baby doll eyes
went to slits. She didn't want this Cole to think he understood her.
Next thing he'd think he knew her well enough to ask her how it felt
to die.

"And you like your hair, I noticed that about you too," he said as if
he'd read her mind.

"I noticed your eyes smile before your mouth."

"Meaning?"

"Meaning your reaction's sluggish. Meaning you're still shooting
up."

"Well I admit it," he laughed softly. "I did it before I came over here the other night. Only because I'd be working, helps me concentrate."

"And tonight?"

"I'm not working tonight. Like I said, I only came to sit with you awhile."

"Ritalin's cheaper."

"What?"

"If you really want to concentrate, Ritalin's cheaper than heroin. Thought shooting up went out with disco anyhow." She turned to stare at the crescent moon. The moon relaxed her. And so too did his presence on the porch. She thought that if she looked at him right now his face would be opened in a smile. She noticed that about him too, he had an expansive face that widened when he looked at her as if to give his face more room for drawing her presence in. The wicker creaked as she shifted on the swing and the fluffy white pillows exhaled softly. "So you came to sit. So you sitting."

The moon was half full and hanging low as Cartha stilled the swing and fought the sleep that was covering her like the dark cottony air. Raymond was late. Had been late every night that week. He'd be late again tonight, he told her. Big account. Very big. So big he might have to work all night long. Might as well pack a change of clothes just in case, would she be okay? he'd asked. Should he call the hospice and arrange for someone to stay the night? She insisted not. She liked the still quiet. But this quiet was irritating now as it pranced through her head and mocked her in this over-sized house on the private road. The house that Raymond had promised would be perfect for raising children far away from the decadence of city life. She imagined him at his late-night desk with his spreadsheets and Mont Blanc pens working with sterile, passionless intensity to maintain their lifestyle. It was easier for her to imagine him that way.

She fell asleep on that image until much later she felt herself being lifted from the swing. She kept her eyes pressed shut so that she didn't have to hear the litany of "Sorry I'm so late again, babe." She let her head roll away from his chest the way someone in a deep sleep would. Her locked hair dropped and swayed and pulled at her scalp as he moved up the steps. She hated this part. The way he'd just let her head dangle and bob like she was already dead. The cramp she'd get in her neck while her head bounced roughly as he took his time up the steps, punishing her with heavy, erratic foot stomps. By the time he reached the bedroom, it felt like he would just toss her down in disgust or even hurl her against the scalloped wooden moldings that framed the wall. But then he'd soften. Maybe from the vanilla-scented candles she'd burn, the ones that she'd bought on South Street when she'd had her palms read. His humanity would return and he'd place her gently down.

Except tonight these footsteps were lighter. These arms stronger. Tonight he cradled her head, protected it with his arms, moved his fingers through her scalp as he carried her up the steps. Tonight she felt his heart beat as she nestled her head against his chest and then the texture of his shirt against her cheek. The cracked softness of cotton gauze. Tonight he stopped midway up the stairs to press his mouth against hers. She kissed him back with lips that were fleshy and full, the only part of her that still had a fullness to it. She smelled the licorice on his breath, tasted it, opened her mouth wider to draw in more of the taste, to swallow it up.

She was wide awake by the time his slow, soft footsteps navigated the winding hallway into the master bedroom. He eased her delicately on the bed. She kept her eyes shut and almost held her breath as he walked into the bathroom and let the water gush into the porcelain sink. She pictured the lather of her soap melting into the blackness of his hands and then silence as the rush of the water went still.

That's when she heard it, the urgent smack of rubber against skin. She knew what he was doing then. Pictured him holding one end of the rubber tourniquet between his teeth and the other with his free hand as he tightened it around his arm until the erection in his vein pulsed. The swish of matches struck in succession—three, four, she counted them and wondered if they still used bottle caps and bent spoons. She heard him suck his breath, lightly. She knew he'd just plunged it in, probably for the thousandth time, and now the blood was bouncing around in the syringe like a bright red tide when the moon is full.

His footsteps dragged slightly as he walked back into the room the way that Cartha had noticed his smile dragging the week before. She wondered what he'd fix now, since he'd insisted that he only got high when he was working. She was about to challenge him, tell him to get his drug-using ass out of her house. But she wanted more to feign sleep, keep her eyes closed on what he was doing, the way she'd done with the people she'd been with before Raymond.

Her feet were cold and she wanted to push them under the white down comforter. At least Raymond knew to cover her feet. She rubbed her feet together. It sounded as if a burst of static had just whooshed through the speakers of the built in sound system. She could smell the soap mixed with Wintergreen alcohol as he neared the bed. Her feet were blocks of ice and she was about to sit up, about to snatch the comforter open to cover her feet. But right then he took her feet in his hands.

His hands were warm and he stroked the soles of her feet and covered them with his hands. At first it tickled and she almost giggled. She hadn't actually giggled out loud in weeks, since she'd smoked a joint to kill the effects of the chemo. Then he used his thumbs and pressed against her feet and she was far beyond giggling. The repeated press of his thumbs, the velvety feel of his fingers as he stroked her feet from her insteps to her heels, her toes to her ankles. It was every pleasure she'd ever felt, lassoed from the beginning of her life, roped in, and then centered right there in the soles of her feet that he touched. She wondered if death would feel this good.

He moved then from her feet and blanketed her body with his. She thought then that she would die if she didn't cry out. She made a sound from the back of her throat and then another until there was a continuous stream of sound and she imagined that he was touching that spot that had grown unrestrained all these months. The chemo, the radiation hadn't touched it but it felt as if his heaviness touched that spot right now.

His heaviness was familiar and reminded her of the people she'd been close with who'd shoot drugs and then couldn't do anything with their heaviness. Cole couldn't either. So he just rested still against the spot. She imagined that the spot was being consumed by his stillness, bursting into sparks like a fire cracker on Independence Day, and then fizzling into nothingness.

⌒

THE MOON exploded into the night with its fullness. It seemed to take up a whole side of the sky. Not even the stars could compete as Cartha bounced on the swing and hummed "Heat Wave" the way she thought Martha and the Vandellas would. She crossed her legs and smoothed at her shorts splashed with bold purples and reds and felt good about the dinner she'd prepared for Raymond tonight. Her locks were piled high on the top of her head and she felt like a queen as she pushed her sandaled feet against the porch floor and got the swing going to the beat of the song. Tonight she would tell Raymond she was ready to return to work. Just a couple of hours once or twice a week for now. No she'd insist, her hair wouldn't be a problem. They were so glad to hear her doctor's report, that the spot was finally showing signs of shrinking, they'd take her back however she'd choose to come. They were good that way.

She jumped to her feet when she heard Raymond's footsteps on the porch. She ran to him and hugged him and kissed his neck. Her chin mashed the knot of his hand-made silk tie. His cologne was strong and stung her nose and made her sneeze. "Thought you switched, you know that cologne messes with me."

"Sorry, babe," he said as he stretched his arms and gently pushed her from him. "I thought now that you're better you could handle it, but if it still bothers you I won't use it anymore. Promise, babe."

She could feel his thumbs pushing against her bare arms as he held her. She shrugged her shoulders to make him move his hands and then adjusted the straps on her deep purple tank top. "Well loosen your tie," she said. "You can have wine out here. I'll throw the veggies in the steamer. Salmon's on the grill. Made your favorite herb sauce too."

"It's so good to have you back, babe," he said as he undid his tie and slipped off his shoes and propped his feet in the white wicker swing. "I was just telling the guys how much better you've been the past week. That lab report did miracles for you." He rocked the swing and the chair squeaked. "Chain sounds too tight," he said as he leaned his head against the chair back and closed his eyes. "Need to get someone over here to take a look at it."

"What about that guy who fixed the sliding glass door?" Cartha asked it with restraint as she turned to go in the house to get the wine. She could hear the wicker breathe and the swing creak as Raymond readjusted his propped feet and nestled himself deeper in the chair. "You ever hear from him?" She fought to keep an even tone.

"Heard he overdosed yesterday or the day before." Raymond's voice drifted like he was falling asleep. "Not sure when. Wasn't like he was a friend or anything. Just somebody with a habit who maintained equipment at the gym."

Cartha had stepped inside the front door. She leaned against the wall in the marble foyer to steady herself. The wall was cold and smooth and unyielding. No! she shouted inside her head.

She groped her way into the kitchen. Tried to focus her eyes through tears that were hot and thick. She thought that she should cut the red and yellow peppers to throw on the grill. The smoke from the salmon was dark. Now she thought she should rescue the fish from the grill. She remembered then that she'd come into the kitchen for the wine. She managed to get back out on the porch with a modicum of composure. Raymond had fallen asleep with his feet in the swing. She banged the wine bottle against the wicker-bound glass table. Pushed at his feet trying to knock them off the swing. He stirred and shifted and smiled in his sleep.

The porch was too small suddenly with Raymond asleep with his feet in her swing. She looked at the moon in its climax. Wished this light would perforate the porch air and outline Cole's frame. Wished Cole would step through the darkness like a cut-out doll coming to life from the page. Wished he'd lean toward her holding a licorice stick red and sweet and strong. But the air was flat and still. No forms moving through it.

"He wasn't just someone with a habit," she said through her teeth. Raymond shifted and snored. "And fix the swing your own damned self." She spit the words as she walked off the porch and took the long way around to save the salmon from the heat of the grill.

TOM TETI

The Last Confession

THE DAY before Christmas vacation was to begin, at precisely ten minutes to three in the afternoon, the nuns of the Immaculate Heart of Mary ordered their seventh and eighth grade boys and girls into line. The students made a procession through the halls of Saint Pascal's School, maroon blazers and uniforms filing out the grey metal doors, down the concrete steps, along a path lined by woody yews. The smells changed as they went, from the austere cleanliness of the school's scrubbed wooden floors and the sisters' ironed habits to the crisp December air with its transient whiff of fallen leaves. Inside the big oak doors at the side of the church the smells changed again to the sweet aroma of burning beeswax candles and the piney resin of the freshly cut balsam that decorated the Advent manger at the altar rail.

Sister Ludmilla was directing the pupils into three queues: one straight down the side aisle to the back of the church; one down the center aisle; and one down the aisle on the far side. At the end of each aisle was a confessional booth, where the young students would cleanse their souls so that they could receive Holy Communion at Mass on Christmas Day. The white wafer they would take onto the tongue represented the Body of Christ, and to accept it while harboring sins not forgiven was, the youngsters had been told, a big sin, a bad sin, an excommunicable sin—but the students didn't believe every word the sisters said. A red light above the middle door of each of the three booths meant a priest waited inside, sitting, listening, praying, rosary in hand, stole draped around his neck, in a posture of gravitas and only dimly seen by the confessee through a special window that blurred vision but allowed voices to be heard through its network of holes.

Nick had a favorite confessor: Father Conroy, a sincere kindly man, with white hair and horn-rimmed glasses. He was deliberate with his few words, gentle of voice and gentle with his penance. Father Conroy was always in the booth at the end of the nearest aisle, and his light was on. Sister Ludmilla was deciding the lineup, however, and she was waving the kids in front of Nick down the center. What priest occupied the center aisle confessional Nick had no idea. The students had always been told they could select their own confessor, since that's what the priests and nuns themselves did. Nick was considering asking to go into Father Conroy's line when, just in front of him, Bugsy Malatesta asked first.

"Sister, I'd like to go to Fa—"

"Shhh!" Sister Ludmilla widened her eyes; it was the universal nuns' warning that a child was about to be in trouble.

"But S'ter, I—"

"You stay in THIS line!" she spat in a ferocious whisper, thrusting a forefinger toward the center aisle. "Brazen as brass!"

Emile "Bugsy" Malatesta was a perennial ne'er-do-well, conspicuous all over town, a boy who could not, no matter what he did, avoid the full-throttle consequences of discipline. Now he had spoken during the somber process of preparing for confession, he had asked for something counter to the Sister's plan, had done it too loudly, too boldly, too oblivious to the deference necessary—too Bugsy—which had provoked her, which in turn made it his fault that she was upset, which meant he would pay. He, and every stupidly timed thing he did, signified something bad in the world of Saint Pascal's in 1962. He was Bugsy Malatesta, big, bad, dumb, hairy Bugsy Malatesta, and his presence was too much for the sisters at least once a day.

Bugsy followed the Sister's finger. As Nick watched him go to the center aisle, he again contemplated asking Sister for himself: Could he go to his trusted confessor Father Conroy? After all, he wasn't a problem boy, he did his work well, he came to school clean, he put covers on his books—he wasn't Bugsy Malatesta, or anything like him. Couldn't he get that one favor? But Sister Ludmilla already had

the glare trained on him. He was frozen in front of her; he had de-
layed too long.

"Move!" she hissed, and shot the same forefinger in Bugsy's wake.
Nick went to the center aisle line and brought his hands to his chest
in prayer pose.

As he stood in the waning light that seeped through the long
stained-glass windows, he began a silent argument with himself: I
could've asked for Father Conroy's line. No, it's good I didn't. Trust
and adjust. But I wished I'd asked first.

The column progressed. Each confession took about five minutes.
It would be over soon. The pastor, Father Hagan, crimson-nosed
and quavering, would be in the confessional on the far side. Father
Hagan was careless, often disinterested. He was known to leave his
confessional door open. He often asked confessees to start over because he hadn't been listening, even fell asleep during confessions.
Behind thick spectacles, Father Hagan's eyes roamed as if he was
seeing everything for the first time. Sometimes he would say: "What
was that?" in too loud a voice. No, Father Hagan was a bad option.

Bugsy spoke again. "Who's in there?" he asked George Shonegger
in a hoarse whisper as George approached, on his way to the altar.
George casually surveyed the pews as he slowed to cruising speed
and pushed the words out of a tiny opening at the side of his mouth.

"New one, Bonselle! He's a bastard! Don't tell him anything!"

Nick had seen Bonselle before. He was a square man with a stiff
voice, who had already gained notoriety for screaming at a girl who
took a piece of straw from the manger on her way back from communion, right in the middle of Mass. None of the students had yet made
a confession to him.

Nick watched Bugsy go in. If Bugsy really confessed all his sins,
the whole truth and nothing but, he would be in there until Easter.
But the boys of the eighth grade had a system, based on the examina-
tion of conscience the sisters conducted in class every week, modified
so as to not say too much, to admit a plausible amount of wrongdoing,
yet always include some genuine sin so the penance would not go to
waste. Father Conroy was consistent, with five Hail Marys, five Our
Fathers, and "a good Act of Contrition." He would sweetly give his

blessing and then Nick would exit the booth, go up to the altar rail, kneel, say the penance, and go back to sit with the class. At any given time five or six boys and girls would be at the altar, kneeling and saying their penance.

Father Bonselle's voice bassooned from his booth in a forceful mumble. Bugsy, who never had a good idea of how to behave, could be heard as well. When he emerged he looked relieved. Passing close to Nick on his way to the altar, he shook his head. "Keep it short," he whispered. Nick nodded. He stepped forward into the confessee's side, and closed the door.

There was always a darkness in the booth before the priest slid his shutter aside and began saying those mysterious Latin incantations that sealed a pact in ritual. To Nick it was an inviting, seductive darkness, a deep shadow that lured one into a feeling of warmth and safety. It was God, Nick knew he was supposed to believe, the Almighty, who threw His arms around you in this sheltered quarter where you knelt to free yourself of yourself, where your bad deeds were erased from the record, all violations rendered forgettable, where the hurt of exposing yourself to a stranger was exchanged for the mercy of the Lord on High. It was God bringing relief to the grateful and contrite, deciding not to condemn you to hell—for another week, at least.

The window slid open. Father Bonselle began: "In nomine Patris, et Filii, et Spiritus Sancti . . ." a rumbling invocation, stentorian and utterly unapologetic, for neither the self-important fervor of it, nor for its disregard for the privacy of the lamb waiting on the other side of the window. Father Conroy's voice was a respectful whisper, understanding, humble, that closed the circle of confessor and sinner, in which there was an almost audible pain from the burden of hearing someone's, especially a child's, private admissions. Hearing Father Bonselle, Nick felt immediate longing for Father Conroy. For him Nick always said his penance, and both together, confessor and priest, sought forgiveness for the ways in which a boy in eighth grade could wound the Lord.

Nick did not feel any peace in Bonselle's presence.

"Begin," came the order.

"Please b-bless me Father, for I have sinned, it has been one week since my last confession."

". . . Go ahead."

"I have cursed, I have lied to my mother and father, I have been disobedient in school—" There was a form to the confession, things that he always said so as not to feel ridiculous. The students had to go every week and it was sometimes hard for Nick to do anything confessable in that time. He went to school, played sports, ate dinner, did homework, watched television, slept, then started over on the next day. No one had ever said it was fine to go in and say, "I've had a pretty good week, Father." He was instructed to be a sinner, and a sinner he would be.

Nick's formulaic confession, like many of the other boys', started with lying, which was, ironically, always believable; then moved to disobedience, also believable; then to misbehavior like talking or laughing during Mass, also easily believable. At the end came an obligatory salute to the more prurient offenses, bundled together in a trinity of its own: impure thoughts, words and deeds. This packet had been part of Nick's confession for about a year and had been accepted by priests like Father Conroy as the usual signs of weakness for a boy becoming a teenager, as a topic about which a pubescent youngster should have only the sketchiest knowledge. Perhaps some kids had real, juicy firsthand sins to confess, perhaps Bugsy Malatesta and all the others who had been left behind so many times that they were sixteen and just finishing eighth grade had authentic experiences of the flesh to trade in for mercy. Nick had no such exploits. He and his friends padded their resumés in the confessional because they were always convinced of their guilt; they didn't need to have done the sin to be sorry for what they would be doing if they could. It was smoothed over by the Father Conroys, the good shepherds tending their flocks, so that the boys could exit, not feeling perfect, but able to look at the face of Jesus in the mural above the sacristy and feel right with Him.

Nick's hopes for tolerant understanding were dispatched with the disregard of a brute wrestler for the boos of the crowd when he hurls the nice-guy favorite to the mat. In Father Bonselle's booth, the quality of mercy was indeed strained. There was neither patience, nor compassion, nor anything like love wafting through the bubbled screen. The round, bespectacled head issued, instead, pious wrath and the power of God. Nick did not want to call him "Father."

"COME ON." The priest's voice exploded like a bomb in a subway station.

"I have engaged in impure thoughts, words and deeds," Nick recited in a soft voice, hoping a priest's preoccupation would send the tedious child out of the booth with a good Act of Contrition and maybe ten Hail Marys and ten Our Fathers.

"WHAT?"

Nick didn't know what to say. Father Conroy had never asked him for more. He recalled Bugsy's telling him to keep it short.

"COME ON."

"Pardon me, Father?" Nick felt his voice getting smaller.

"I CAN'T HEAR YOU. COME ON."

"Father—"

"IF I CAN'T HEAR YOU THE LORD CAN'T HEAR YOU!"

"Sorry, Father, I . . ."

"WHAT HAVE YOU DONE? TELL ME!"

And then Nick blurted out: "I have impure thoughts when I look at Eleanor Donlon, and Maureen Pfeiffer, and Alicia Randazzo, but that's all I ever did, and you can't expect that not to happen. And . . . maybe . . . I don't mean to, but . . . boners . . . uh, erections . . . during Mass. I'll try to stop, I will. But I don't do it, the jerk thing . . . Not yet! I haven't! I mean I touch myself in the bathtub, it feels good but I don't do it for too long! Really. And I've never even touched a girl, let alone kissed one!"

In the silent space Nick offered him, Father Bonselle released his thunderous voice again, impersonating the outrage of the Almighty. "HOW OLD?"

The words emerged from underground. There was no real question. There was a foregone conclusion that he, Nick, the little sinner, was disgracefully young to carry such blights on his soul, which would be damned, damned, damned, unless Father Bonselle could drive out the evil that had taken hold of him. "What?" Nick said.

"How OLD are you?"

"Umm, thirteen."

"Thirteen—MY GOD! OH MY GOD!"

Nick began to shake. He was sure that the entire church had heard. He felt as if the whole world was shaking.

He tried not to look directly at the priest through the window, but he couldn't help himself. The figure of Bonselle held the top of his head in a cradle formed of his index finger and thumb. The rest of his fingers were splayed out in the air as if he dare not sully any more of himself by touching the head that had been made unclean by all he'd been hearing. Bonselle's next words descended like a moaning meteor from a distant galaxy. "YOU PLAY WITH YOURSELF. YOU SEEK IMPURE GRATIFICATION FROM YOUR BODY. YOU MUST STOP. NOW!"

"Y-Yes, Father." Nick's mind left the booth for a moment wondering what his classmates and the nuns had heard.

"WHAT DID YOU SAY?"

"I said, yes."

"YES, WHAT?"

"Yes, Father."

"WHAT?"

"Yes, FATHER."

"STOP, DO YOU HEAR?"

"I do."

"IT IS IMPURE, DO YOU HEAR ME?"

"Yes, Father."

"YOU WILL STOP! YOU HEAR ME?"

"I hear you, Father."

The priest took three deep breaths in the silence, and to Nick they sounded as bombastic as his words. "Say two rosaries and an Act of Contrition!" Father Bonselle shut the window on him as Nick began the prayer that initiates a release from the wages of sin: "Oh my God, I am heartily sorry for having offended thee, and I detest all my sins . . ." Nick couldn't tell if Father Bonselle heard his apology to

God and his plea for forgiveness. He couldn't even be sure he was absolved. All he knew was that it was time to leave.

He made his way to the altar slowly, stunned. How was he going to say two rosaries at the altar without drawing attention to himself—because his penance would take forty-five minutes, minimum, even if he sped through it? Everyone would think he'd murdered his beloved parents, or worse.

Halfway to the altar rail, he saw Sister Ludmilla nodding off in the middle pew, a small singular stroke of good fortune. The faces of his classmates, however, waiting in line to make their own confessions, seemed to show that they knew the awful things he'd done. Good girls, future nuns, like Kathleen McQuigan and Mary Peluso, looked away, eyes filled with horror and disdain; bad girls, especially Noreen Dehart, thin and pigeon-toed, in her sloppily ironed, grey-tinted blouse and drooping knee socks, gave him a lingering glance and smirked. Noreen was famous for inviting inexperienced boys over for comics and lemonade, and other stuff, after school because her mother worked and no one would be home. She raised a fuzzy eyebrow as Nick passed her that just about sealed the offer right there in the nave. Bugsy Malatesta, his paltry penance completed and on his way back to his pew, passed Nick, shook his head and sniggered, pretending to look at his prayer hands.

There were probably twenty paces left between Nick and his own personal D-Day, decision time. He considered a change in lifestyle: walking home with Bugsy, enjoying the freedom to be a bad boy, raiding trash cans or hunting rats in Cobb's Creek with sharpened sticks. Saying goodbye to Noreen, asking her with a knowing smile whether she had her Christmas tree yet. She would invite him to come over and see it, the kingdom would be his, and his next confession would be different, easy; he'd just have to remember not to ask Noreen if she was going to get her tooth fixed.

Nick fell onto the kneeler at the altar rail. Each movement he made was watched very closely, he was sure of it. But the painted face of God the Father, with his white beard and flowing mane of white hair, being ministered to by cherubim, did not look down from the dome above the sacristy. The statue of Mary, the Blessed Mother, which usually permitted the fantasy that her eyes returned the supplicant's gaze, today was frozen stiff. The large crucifix of Jesus, straight before him, though depicting an expired Lord, looking to the side, hands bleeding, body slumping, feet held impossibly to the beam by a single nail, as always, had the most life in it.

It spoke to him.

It did.

"It's all right, Nick." The voice was clear and slow, and gentle, but strong. It resounded in Nick's head and he could have sworn it spread throughout the hallowed air of the church, where silence was more resonant than a gong. The subtle smells of white candles and wood polish, the soft light, beginning to darken with the close of the afternoon, the prevailing itch of his wool trousers, all were present in the quiet and made a backdrop for the voice. "Forgive them, for they know not what they do."

"Oh, Jesus!" Nick whispered. "Oh . . . sorry."

Jesus's eyes were closed, but his head was tilted toward Nick, like a blind man able to see more without his sight than what a hundred people would tell him he was missing. Jesus's voice had a tenderness in it, though his body strained and twisted against the nails that held him to the infamous gibbet.

"I don't need those rosaries, Nick."

Nick wondered if he actually heard the Christ call him by name, but it didn't matter. He felt the glow of His presence, felt it shining on him above all, which couldn't be truly fair-minded, if Jesus were really Jesus—but he did feel it. Maybe that's what made Jesus Jesus, that anybody could know him if they just talked to him.

Nick mouthed the words "Thank you" and went back to his pew. His head was spinning. They were supposed to believe the Lord saw them—each boy and girl, man and woman—and heard their prayers. But he, Nick, heard Him.

Nick was lost in thought, staring at the altar and the sacristy. "Are you planning to spend the night?" Sister Ludmilla was standing over him. "You're talking to yourself."

"Sorry, sister."

She shook her head. "Get in line. Since you're last, you can close the doors."

Outside, at the foot of the church steps, Nick saw Bugsy across the street.

"Hey!" Bugsy shouted. "What'd you do?"

"What?" said Nick. He tried to be loud without shouting.

"You were in there a long time. Bonselle was screaming."

"Did you hear anything?" Nick swallowed; he felt weak at the knees.

"I heard him. What did you tell him?"

"Too much I guess." He thought of Jesus. Maybe not enough.

Bugsy shook his head. "Stupid."

Nick nodded.

"Confession blows." Bugsy laughed.

"Yeah." Depends on who you confess to, Nick thought.

Bugsy pulled out a pack of cigarettes from inside his jacket pocket. "Got matches?" he hollered.

"Nah."

"See you tomorrow."

Nick watched him ramble off toward the center of town.

Nick walked home alone, by Fairmount Park, along Cobb's Creek. It was the darkest day of the year, and at four o'clock, night was coming on, and would close the light down within the hour. There didn't seem to be any dusk in December; the day went to night like a door blown shut by a gust from out of nowhere. Most days, Nick would take another route, just to walk with others, but today he was overwrought, still shaky, from his confession. He was far from putting the confession behind him. It was a day to travel alone.

Down the hill, the dull gleam of a streetlight reflected off the creek, which was beginning to look black. He turned away from the park and crossed the street, where the first headlights of the evening pinned him in their beams. While trudging uphill toward the traffic light on the main drag, he halted. He felt sick, and as if he would cry if he could, but it wouldn't come.

When he got to the light it was red. Nick leaned against a telephone pole, watching the traffic, feeling chill air about his face, the moment held; winter's stillness became his own, apart from the noise and movement around him. Calm had come back to him. He fancied a challenge to himself—how long could he keep perfectly still? and in the small space of time where he didn't move, he felt totally powerful, as if he might never move again if he didn't say so.

The light changed, the cars slowed and stopped, and he looked at the green an extra second longer than he normally would, then hustled to the far side of the street.

His olive drab book bag was heavy, but a good kind of heavy, a friend. Other friends awaited him: his sneakers, his sweatshirt, steaming dishes of dinner, parents, sister, brother, Granddad, his shows on TV, the clank of the radiators. In the basement, where the encyclopedia was kept, he would say the rosaries while pretending he went down there to look something up for homework. It would be a parting gesture, complying with the order he'd been given, if not with the one who gave it. Then it would be done, and he would be done with confessing sins, forever, not even to Father Conroy. If he needed to unburden himself, he would try Jesus.

As he climbed the back steps to the kitchen, the smell of tomato gravy cut through the sharp chill his nose had felt for the last twenty minutes. He hoped they were having the short macaroni with the curly shape. He would offer to grate the cheese for his mother.

CAREN LITVIN

Ivory Is Wrong About Me

IVORY AND I were outside on one of our cigarette breaks last summer when she told me, "Cathy, I think my son killed someone," and I said, "Ivory, quit foolin'," and then she said, with her face all serious, "No, Cath, listen. LeVan wasn't home Tuesday after school when I called so I called his cell and he was crying but couldn't say why so I told him, you get home, we'll talk after I get there, and then some girls on the bus were saying Mrs. Edgar's grandson got shot and they think it was boys from the neighborhood. I didn't say nothing, but I was wondering, and LeVan wasn't home when I got there, and now it's been three days and he still ain't home."

"Oh, Ivory, LeVan's a good boy, don't think the worst," I said, but afterward I checked the newspapers in the break room and there was a story about Anthony Edgar, 16, shot outside a pizza shop and then I didn't know what to do. I wanted to tell Clive about LeVan, but I didn't cause I knew he'd say something ugly, and I didn't tell my mother cause she's got high blood pressure.

I was still friends with Ivory back then. We were the only two cashiers who smoked and we'd take our cigarette breaks together, even when it was 20 degrees outside, and we'd talk about the Store Manager Bill and the squishy sound his shoes made when he walked around the supermarket which he'd do for about 10 minutes every morning, then go to his office and spy on us with the security monitors and wait for the pretty housewives and then he'd be back in the aisles in those squishy shoes saying, "Good morning, Mrs. Franklin, are you finding everything you need today?" That Mrs. Franklin comes in to buy her groceries after she works out next door at the gym and she always wears a tight tee shirt showing off her big titties and she never seems sweaty like I do when I run up and down the stairs at home, trying to get some exercise—only I can't do that when Clive is in the house because he'll yell, "Cut out that stomping, the TV's gonna fall off the wall."

I got promoted to Assistant Front End Manager a few weeks after Ivory said what she did about LeVan, and it was still bothering me, so I asked Edith, the Front End Manager, "Can I talk to you in confidence?" and she said, "Of course, you can always talk to me." I told Edith what Ivory had told me, although I never said it was Ivory, I just said that *somebody* said that she thought her son killed someone and the police didn't know, and what should I do, cause I want to be a good friend, but maybe I should tell them. Edith's eyebrows scrunched together and her lips puckered up and she didn't say anything for a minute, and then she said, "Cathy, I think you need to tell the police," and I hesitated, and then said, "I think so too." When my shift ended, Edith drove me to the police station and I went in and told a detective what I knew, but I said he should say that he got an "anonymous tip" cause I know about that from CSI.

A few days after, Ivory told me that the police had come to her house to talk to LeVan, and that she told them about her phone call with LeVan and the police found him and arrested him. Then right before Labor Day, the police gave LeVan's lawyer their files which showed it was me who went in there and talked to the detective, and Ivory called me at home, screaming at the top of her lungs, "You fucking told the police about my boy. You fucking told the police. How could you? I'm gonna kick your boney ass," and I told her, "I didn't mean to, I didn't mean to." Then she hung up. I was scared of her, not cause she's black but because she outweighs me by 50 pounds and she could kick my ass if she wanted to. That's when I stopped smoking cause I didn't want to have to go outside with Ivory. I was scared of LeVan too, that he'd come after me, but the newspaper said he was in jail until his trial.

I stopped asking Edith's advice after that and realized how wrong I was to go to the police. I missed talking to Ivory and I felt bad that her life wasn't real good to begin with and then I made it worse. She used to tell me about all her problems, how LeVan got held back two times and how her mother broke her hip. With her I didn't need to pretend that my life was perfect. I told her that I thought Clive was cheating on me cause he worked a lot of nights but his paycheck didn't always have overtime, and when my daddy was real sick I admitted to her that sometimes I wished he would just die since he wasn't getting better and I was afraid my mother might lose her job if she missed any more time. Ivory and I talked about the other cashiers and the Managers and we joked about how we were going to smear peanut butter on the lens of the security camera so squishy shoe Bill couldn't spy on us.

But I was nervous whenever I saw Ivory around the store, though she wouldn't speak to me or even look at me. Then last week she went to the new Store Manager who took over from Bill and told him that she heard me use the N-word and then I was put out of work on investigative suspension because the Company has a zero-tolerance policy about racial stuff.

But Ivory is wrong about me. No, it's true that I used the N-word to Johnny the Assistant Deli Manager but I was just joking, cause Johnny calls me the N-word all the time even though I am 100 percent Irish Catholic. Johnny is as dark as pumpernickel but he told me he was mostly Cherokee and he gets mad when people call him "African American." Nobody knows that Johnny and I are special friends, being that I'm married and Johnny is, too. I didn't expect that I'd ever be friends with a black man but after I became Assistant Front End Manager it seemed like none of the cashiers wanted to be friends with me anymore. It's like all the non-Managers are friends and all the Managers are friends cause Rita, the Dairy Manager, and I never talked when I was just a cashier, but after I became Assistant Manager we had lunch together in the break room and she told me about her daughter in Afghanistan and her son who works HVAC. Rita is married to the Meat Manager and we're all friends with Dottie, the Bakery Manager, although she's kind of a bitch.

Johnny started working at the store slicing cold cuts just before the business with LeVan last summer, when I was still a cashier. I told Ivory that I thought Johnny looked like Mr. Clean with his big bald head and an earring in one ear but I never really talked to him other than to say "Hi." Ivory said she thought Johnny was "fine."

Johnny and I became Assistant Managers at the same time and we had to go to Corporate for management training classes and they said, "Johnny doesn't have a car. Would you mind driving him? We'll pay you for mileage." "No, I don't mind," I said cause I wanted that two-dollar an hour raise, and then I thought, What would I say to Johnny for an hour each way?

That first day driving him, he told me he was a Mets fan, which surprised me cause I thought that black people don't like baseball, that's what Clive said, and then we talked about the Mets, even though I know next to nothing about baseball except what Clive tells me. It sure was different talking to Johnny about the Mets cause he just chuckles when they're doing bad like that's what he was expecting, but Clive never laughs about them.

Boy, Clive gets so mad watching that team. Every year I think it'll be better, then he starts saying, "Two weeks to pitchers and catchers," and then counts down to Opening Day, and he's so excited during that first game you'd think they actually won the World Series. But in no time he's back to being miserable old Clive, shouting "the Mets suck," like it's my fault. But even though they make him mad, he watches every single night game unless he has to work, cause that's time and a half which is really good money when you're making $17.39 an hour, though Clive says it kills his back. I used to work overtime at the supermarket when CJ was little cause we had so many bills to pay, but I've been working at that store for over half my life and even if they were paying me $30 an hour, I couldn't stay one minute past 4:30 p.m. when my shift ends and I think, Hallelujah! Get me out of here.

Johnny and I had to do that drive to Corporate five days in a row and we ran out of things to say about the Mets pretty quick. So, we talked about Bill and his squishy shoes and Johnny told me that Bill had a stack of porno magazines in his office and that the guys from Meat and Dairy went up there on their breaks and talked nasty. Then we made fun of the people at Corporate who were supposed to be teaching us to be Assistant Managers cause it seemed like none of them had ever been to a supermarket in their whole lives and they only wanted to talk about "diversity" and "functionalities." Johnny and I knew that being Assistant Manager meant we had to wear white jackets with name tags, but it was worth it to get that extra two bucks. When we were talking during those drives, I stopped thinking about Johnny being black cause I was looking at the road and not at his dark skin. I thought that he smelled like chocolate and bleach mixed together whereas Clive smells like Brut and potato chips.

That last day we went to Corporate I picked up Johnny and he was upset. He told me that he wanted to divorce his wife but didn't want to leave his little girl and I asked why he wanted a divorce and Johnny said that his wife weighed 250 pounds. I thought that was mean, but then he said she watched TV all day and never cooked supper for him and I thought, That's not right. I always fix Clive's dinner, even when I'm tired and would rather just relax on the sofa eating popcorn cause I know Clive looks forward to eating a home-cooked meal when he's driving his truck and lifting those boxes and feeling sorry that he didn't get his GED like I told him to so he could have been a Supervisor.

I told Johnny that if Clive died I would never get married again, although I didn't even know I was thinking it until it came out of my mouth. I was so crazy about Clive when we were in high school together, but now he comes home from work and doesn't hardly talk to me, other than saying, "Those brussels sprouts smell up the whole house." or "Don't tell me we're having meatloaf." I'm still skinny like I was when we met, not like some of my friends who got fat after they had kids, and I look pretty good now that my skin's cleared up, except when my roots come in dark and you can tell I'm not a real blond. Clive was handsome back in high school, even though he's short for a man, but I'm only five feet one so it never really bothered me. Clive's got one of those big bellies now, just like his brothers, but when I brought home light beer once instead of regular he stared at me like I told him to go put on a dress. I feel bad that life didn't turn out the way he wanted cause I got pregnant with CJ and Clive had to drive a truck when he really wanted to be a mechanic. My daddy used to say, "Clive's done right by you, don't forget it," and it's true. And even though he never changed a diaper, Clive was a good father, showing CJ how to pee standing up and how to pitch lefty. CJ lives with his girlfriend now and they're going to have a baby in a few months. I was hoping CJ would go back to school for HVAC like Rita's son, but CJ has to work nights with the baby coming so he's just a warehouse worker.

Johnny is a foot taller than Clive and wide as an oak. A few months after Johnny and I became Assistant Managers we were both working in the store when a huge blizzard hit. Nobody on the late shift could get to work cause the buses stopped running and Bill said, please, he'd pay us double time but could we stay at the store that night, cause food was flying off the shelves and he desperately needed us to unload inventory from the back.

Johnny and I stayed and Bill worked the cash register. Johnny filled the dollies with boxes from the loading dock and wheeled them out to the aisles and I raced to put the food away before he could get back, like it was a game. I'd know where the regular canned corn goes and where the creamy corn goes even if I was blindfolded, so I usually won. Johnny and I were so tired from working a double, but it was fun being in the store at night with everyone gone, like a sleepover party. Around nine o'clock I had to get more cereal boxes down from the top shelf for the customers, and I didn't feel like getting the ladder from the store room so Johnny lifted me up by my waist and I felt like a ballerina. Johnny was so strong, holding me in the air like I was a feather and I said after that, "Let me feel your muscles," and he got a big grin on his face cause he's so proud of them. I felt his arm and it was as thick as Clive's head and solid as a frozen turkey and it had a tattoo on it that said "Montel 7/15/96" and I asked, "Who's Montel?" and he said it was his brother who got killed. Johnny chewed his bottom lip for a minute, then said real soft, "Cathy, I will tell you about Montel someday but not now because I don't want to spoil tonight."

I knew right then that Johnny had a thing for me and I lifted my hand and touched the side of his face and we just looked at each other. Then we carried another load of windshield wiper fluid and road salt up to the front of the store. There were a bunch of people in line and I asked Bill whether I should open up a register but he said no, just keep bringing out inventory so Johnny and I went back to the store room and had sex right there on the boxes of Chicken-Noodle-O's.

That night it was like he and I were in our own little circle of happiness and everything outside the circle was blurry. I didn't think about how would I ever get my car home through all that snow or even about the fact that what I was doing was a sin. My mother goes to Mass every morning before work and I think her veins would pop out of her neck if she ever knew that I was running with Johnny, even if she didn't know he was black. I was glad my daddy was dead, too, even though I miss him, cause he'd have died all over again if he'd seen me and Johnny together. And Clive, well I never think about him when I'm with Johnny. I try not to think about Johnny when I'm at home but I wind up missing him because Clive never wants to talk. I used to tell Clive everything that happened at the store, but he would call me "Chatty Cathy," even though I told him that that hurts my feelings, so I don't tell him much of anything unless it's about CJ's baby coming or when the toilet gets clogged.

Clive never did those things to me in bed to make me feel good that Johnny did, even though we were just in the Butchers' changing room after they left for the day. Johnny once told me, "I love the way you taste" and I said, "You're so bad." Sometimes I think I love him but that doesn't mean I don't still love Clive, cause I do. Me and Clive have been married 21 years and we're gonna be grandparents together. I'd get real sad sometimes thinking it was wrong for me to be with Johnny, but then I thought about how I love the way my pale hand looks on his dark arm, like the moon against the sky.

I started driving Johnny home from work and one beautiful spring afternoon we stopped at a bar, even though I hardly ever drink, but we were celebrating that Bill got fired after Mrs. Franklin complained that he followed her around the store every time she did her grocery shopping. Johnny wanted to go to a bar right near his house and I said, "Aren't you worried your wife might see you?" but he said, "No, she's lying in bed watching Oprah." So we went in and I was the only white person there and at first I was scared, but then no one stared at me or acted funny so we ordered beers, and a song came on that Johnny sang when we were in the car, *They say you can't turn a bad girl good, but once a good girl's gone bad, she's gone forever,* and everyone in the bar began singing, including me, and I felt about the happiest I ever felt, other than the day that CJ was born and I saw he turned out just fine—all ten fingers and ten toes.

One afternoon, I was worried that Ivory knew what was going on between me and Johnny, cause when we came out of the Butchers' room, there she was, long after she should have left, and she stared at us but didn't say a word. I told Johnny we'd better cool things off a while and we did, but he wasn't happy. I stopped driving him home and we stayed out of the Butchers' room and we didn't talk much, except when I went back to Deli to get Clive's ham and cheese sliced real thin and Johnny waited on me with that sparkle in his eyes, and he sliced the meat real slow with his back to me, and I'd watch his elbow move back and forth, back and forth, and I wanted to put my arms around his waist from behind and rest my head between his shoulder blades.

The day of the N-word incident, I was in the break room eating lunch with Rita and Johnny came in and sat with us and then Rita got a call and left me and Johnny by ourselves. Johnny said, "Tell me something bad about yourself Cathy so I won't want you so much," and I thought about it and said, "I never learned to ride a bike," which is something even Clive doesn't know about me. I'd tell Johnny lots of stuff I would never tell anyone else, like how at night sometimes when I can't fall asleep, I pretend I'm having a conversation with my daddy up in heaven and I tell him all the things that happened since he passed.

Johnny said, "That's not bad not knowing how to ride a bike, do you know how to swim?" and I said, "Of course I know how to swim." Then he said, "Well it's more important to know how to swim in case someone throws you in the water," and then he grinned and said "Mmm, mmm, niggah, I'd like to see you in a bikini," and then I said, "Shut up, niggah," just as Ivory opened the door to come in.

I thought I'd die a thousand deaths. Ivory sat down at the next table and started eating her egg salad sandwich, and at first I wondered whether she'd heard me. I started talking to Johnny about the Mets and I heard Ivory mumble something about "white folks." Going to the police about LeVan was the biggest mistake I ever made and I wished that I could go back in time and be a good friend to Ivory and keep her secret. She doesn't have a husband, and her boy was locked up in jail and it wasn't fair that I had two men plus CJ who stops by every Sunday and helps me fix stuff around the house cause Clive's back is always hurting.

That very day after she finished her egg salad sandwich, she called HR and told them that I was creating a hostile work environment against black people. I worked at the store for 20 years. I worked with black people, Filipinos, Puerto Ricans, Haitians and two female Produce Managers who were "roommates," and I'd know what that meant even if they didn't have short hair. I'm not like Clive when it comes to these things. Besides, I try not be hostile to anyone, not even Clive when he deserves it. Ivory and I were such good friends for so many years, she knows I'm not hostile to black people.

When the new Store Manager told me that Ivory complained, he said I shouldn't talk to Johnny or Ivory until the investigation was over. I burst out crying and sat in his office sobbing for almost a half hour till he asked if I wanted to make a statement. I said no, and just kept crying some more. That's when he put me out on investigative suspension.

I didn't tell Clive or CJ or my mother or anyone else what had happened. Every morning I got up at the usual time and made Clive his oatmeal and coffee and left the house right at 7:35, like I always did, but then I drove to the mall and waited until it opened and walked around inside, not buying anything, just looking at the shops pretending I had the money to buy whatever I wanted.

This morning I went into one of those fancy women's clothing stores and tried on low cut blouses even though I've got nothing up top to show off and I looked in the mirror and pretended I was getting ready for a date with Johnny and that we were going to Applebee's and then home to sleep in an actual bed and then I got sad cause I knew that was never gonna happen.

I was missing Johnny so much this afternoon. He doesn't know my home phone number, being that we never needed to talk on the phone. I don't have a cell phone cause Clive says they're too expensive. I decided I would drive by the store and wait in the parking lot to catch a glimpse of Johnny when he came out of work. So I went and sat in my car and waited and waited but he didn't come out at 4:30 and I wondered if he left early or maybe wasn't working that day or maybe I didn't see him come out, but he's so big how could I miss him? All of a sudden, I heard knuckles rapping hard on my window and I almost jumped out of my skin and there's Ivory signaling me to roll it down.

If there wasn't a minivan parked right in front of my car I'd have stamped my foot on the gas pedal, but there I was trapped with Ivory looking right into my eyeballs. I hesitated then cautiously rolled down the glass. "Hey, Ivory," I said.

"Hey." She shifted most of the flesh in her face to the left side like she does some times when she's thinking and said, "I ain't mad at you about LeVan no more."

"Then why'd you file that complaint on me?"

"Because you never said you was sorry."

"W-What? Oh Ivory." You never know about people. I looked up at her and said, "I'm so sorry I made things worse for you and LeVan."

Then her face got all soft and she said, "Well, they're gonna call you to come back to work tomorrow."

"Really? That's great. Thanks for letting me know."

"And I just found out I'm gonna be Assistant Deli Manager. After I filed my complaint, Corporate decided I should get a promotion, seeing how all the white cashiers got promoted but the black cashiers never did."

"Well, hey, that's terrific. Are there two Assistant Deli Managers now?"

"Nope," she said. "Johnny don't work here no more."

"What are you talking about?"

"Johnny got transferred to another store," she said, smiling. Then she turned and walked away from my car towards the bus stop.

I jumped up so fast to get out of the car that I forgot I still had my seat belt on and it nearly choked me. By the time I got it unsnapped she was already at the bus stop and I ran up to her and shouted, "Why'd you file that complaint against me? Why'd you do that?" My face felt hot and my heart was hammering. There were about four other women waiting for the bus, and they were all black and they looked at me real nasty and formed a circle around Ivory, who stared at me, with a satisfied look on her face.

"You were my friend," I shouted at her.

"Was," said Ivory.

I just stood there in shock, and tears filled my eyes. Then I realized I'd left my keys and purse in the car and ran back and got in and slammed the door so hard my whole body shook.

Tears flowed down my cheeks and I tilted my head back so my makeup wouldn't look bad. I sat in my car for a while, thinking how I never got to say goodbye to my daddy before he died cause the Good Lord took him before I could get to the hospital and now he's taken Johnny from me, too. I messed up real bad about LeVan and now I'm paying the price. How could I ever go back inside that store? 20 years, Assistant Front End Manager, but I was sick over Johnny, and now Ivory hated me.

I sat in the car until it got dark, then I drove home to make Clive his Shepherd's Pie.

SAMANTHA GILLISON

The Conference Rat

THEY FIRST slept together at an American Anthropological Association conference in Denver. It was six months after her baby was born and Fleur Radkowicz had flown out West with the child. Jon had had a ferocious crush on Fleur in graduate school and he flirted with her at one of the panel discussions. The next night, after dinner, Fleur went to Jon's hotel room with her daughter in a Baby Bjørn and they got drunk on Jim Beam and warm Coke. She and Jon avoided the subject of Paul and then had sex while the baby slept on the couch. The second time had been five months later at a New School symposium. Fleur couldn't come to a week-long conference without her baby, Patsy. She was still breastfeeding. She hired a graduate student to baby-sit almost around the clock but Jon still freaked out after they made love in his room.

"I can't," he said. "I just can't when your daughter is so close. She makes me think of Paul."

It wasn't until a seminar at Oberlin on the Ethnography of Identity that Fleur committed adultery again. She ignored Jon and sat next to Vance Rutland at a dinner in honor of the presenters. Rutland pursued Fleur with the ardor of a man falling in love. Jon watched from the other end of the table in despair.

Vance didn't last past the Oberlin seminar. And, anyway, after that Fleur and Jon started sleeping together again. Eventually, their affair became normalized, almost like a marriage: they were always together, Patsy with a babysitter. And since they could only meet at the conferences neither one of them missed a professional gathering of American ethnographers for four years.

Not long into their romance Patsy got nicknamed, "The Conference Rat." There was quite a bit of pathos about the situation with Fleur Radkowicz's daughter and nobody really liked the topic that much. However, a significant portion of the American Anthropological Association had unwittingly watched the child grow up; she was omnipresent at these things. Toddling around institutional dining rooms, complaining of boredom at the back of lecture halls during panels, being chased by varieties of babysitters across the well-groomed lawns of academe year after year. It was inevitable that Patsy would become a kind of totem to the meeting clans of social and cultural anthropologists.

Jonathan Thomsen was tall with the white-blond hair of his Norwegian grandfather and his mother's distracted, pale blue eyes. He was 32 and his relationship with Fleur was the first significant emotional connection of his adult life. Before Fleur there were only passing flirtations and the occasional stunted affair with the women who crossed his path. But since college through graduate school and into the first couple years of his tenure as an assistant professor at Swarthmore, Thomsen was mostly either in a classroom, writing, or getting high and riding his bike for hours.

He only allowed a little bit of how much he understood about Patsy and her mother into his awareness. It wasn't clear whether he was in love with Fleur; he would be if she weren't married with a child, he thought. He wanted her to leave her husband—but not for him. And the wish that she could wind back time and undo her daughter resided, uncomfortably, in a remote corner of his mind. It was a mystery to him how Fleur, independent to the point of hermit-like standoffishness in graduate school, had morphed into a frightened hausfrau who spent all her free time in yoga class and couldn't finish her dissertation. If Thomsen wondered about it too much the prospect of a real life with her started to seem gray and confused.

"Why can't you leave him and see what's really going on?" he would ask. "Why do you need a guarantee from me if you're unhappy with him? We can't move in together so fast, you know? It's not healthy."

Thomsen also avoided, with the intensity of a Motuan aversion taboo, Paul's name. He had been friendly with Paul Bruce once upon a time. They had gotten drunk together, talked about books, sports, ideas; a lot about Don DeLillo and Pynchon, some about Elkin and Gaddis and Gass. Paul, heavyset, a joke-cracker, bald before he was 25 but preternaturally socially at ease and attractive to women, had wanted to write novels. At the time, Thomsen had envied him his life-to-be—publishing books, married to the brilliant, beautiful Fleur Radkowicz, throwing dinner parties and traveling. Paul and Fleur had seemed like birds about to take wing and fly off.

Right then, though, it was mid-July and Jon Thomsen was with Paul Bruce's wife and daughter in Middlebury, Vermont (at the conference, Pockets of Change: Cultural Adaptations and Transitions), while Bruce taught summer school in Baltimore. Jon's panel had just broken for lunch and Fleur left him and Patsy together sitting on Adirondack chairs while she went to buy sandwiches.

Thomsen could feel the child looking at him. Patsy wasn't pretty but there was something about her, something in addition to her childish softness, some ineffable quality of Fleur's which had rubbed off on the child, that made people want to touch her. She was promiscuous, too, always trying to escape her babysitters and rush over to the aging, female academics who tended to be soft touches and would cuddle her and read Ping and Olivia which she kept tucked in her pink Dora the Explorer backpack.

Jon didn't know what to think when he saw the girl at work on these women, holding their hands, her soft little fingers in theirs, regarding them with deep-brown eyes that were sad and expressive and made her seem as defenseless and unconscious as a calf.

Thomsen leaned back into the wide slats of his Adirondack chair, looking out across an immense lawn at the mountains in the distance rising up in gentle, deep-green colored slopes. The air was full of the New England summer; Queen Anne's lace and mowed grass and blooming lilacs.

"Do you know my daddy's taking me to Florida when I get home? We're going to see dolphins," the girl said, breaking the silence.

"Oh," Thomsen said, smiling out at the day, avoiding the child's face. "How cool."

"Um, and," Patsy said, "we're going to swim in the ocean." She had a doll that was always with her, a stuffed unicorn, which she was gently twisting.

"That sounds like lots of fun," Thomsen said.

He felt the girl looking at him again, and he willed himself to turn and meet her gaze and the charm of her enormous, soft, dark-brown eyes. It occurred to him how much she looked like her father; she was big-boned like him—even her full mouth was his.

Fleur emerged from the cafeteria, holding a tray piled high with plastic-wrapped sandwiches and cans of Pellegrino.

"Oh, wow, look at your mom," Thomsen said. "She has lots of food. Yummy."

Patsy stared at him contemplatively.

"I got egg salad sandwiches," Fleur said.

"Mommy, I told Jon about Daddy," the girl said looking up. "About that we're going to Florida."

The unicorn was being pet vigorously now, Patsy's little fingers fondling and tugging the doll's matted white fur. Her mother looked quickly over at Thomsen, then blithely unwrapped a sandwich and said, "Well of course we're going to Florida, Miss Lovey. Maybe we can send Jon a postcard if you want."

The girl shrugged her shoulders. "Oh," she said, quietly. "Okay."

The egg salad was salty and chalky and tasted delicious to Thomsen. They ate in silence. The girl took a few bites of her sandwich and then wandered off with her unicorn. Thomsen decided that Fleur had moved the chairs to the perfect spot to absorb this landscape. The sky was inscrutably blue-and-white. A bright yellow butterfly lazily floated across the grass. And all the while the mountains were there in the distance, green, full of life, breathing quietly, as though they were waiting for something. Fleur was eating the potato chips that Patsy had left untouched; she looked unreasonably sexy to Thomsen, placing one chip at a time on her tongue, licking her fingers, sighing, her large breasts nudging at her t-shirt.

"You have a dirty mind," she said, and turned to smile at him.

"How do you know what I'm thinking?"

"I just do."

In the sunlight he could see the fine lines around her eyes crinkle as she smiled. She looked tired and was breaking out—a rash of angry, red pimples had erupted on her chin. Thomsen was always surprised by how attracted to Fleur he was; she could be wearing anything, look tired and rumpled and unshowered, it didn't matter. He always wanted her, and the deeply sexual intensity of his feelings was usually mingled with a chest-tightening anxiety. Sometimes, if he wasn't watching himself, he would get angry if she left his side to go to the bathroom or to talk to someone else at a cocktail party. But at the same time the thought of her wouldn't cross his mind for weeks when they were apart. And there was always the specter of Paul looming in the background since he had first known her in graduate school.

"Are you ever going to leave your husband?" he asked, not really meaning to say the thought out loud.

Fleur glanced at him, her green eyes flickering across his face. She attributed the color of her eyes, which could turn from a green-flecked-gold to aqua to violet, to the Cossacks who, she said, raped her great-great grandmothers in the Ukrainian shtetls.

"Do you want me to leave my husband?"

"What kind of question is that?"

"Do you want me to leave him? I mean, you probably won't be attracted to me if I'm not married," she said, wiping the salt off her fingertips onto the grass. "You're like a fly stuck in ambivalence-flavored Jell-O."

"I don't know why this subject always turns into a conversation about me. Either you are happily married or you're not."

Fleur looked out at Patsy who was lit up, the sun in her hair. "We don't have to talk about this now, right?" Thomsen could feel her floating out into the afternoon, eluding him.

"She looks like an angel, doesn't she?" Fleur said. "I wish I had my camera."

"It's not at all good for her, for Patsy, either, I don't think."

"What's not good for her?"

"I don't know," Thomsen said, gesturing towards the mountains, at her and then himself. "This whole thing. You. Us. Your out-sourcing of the intimacy from your marriage."

"I'm not sure that you're qualified to make judgments about Patsy." Fleur was frowning. They almost never talked about the girl. Thomsen didn't like to. But he was angrier than he realized at Fleur's withdrawal and casual dismissal of him.

"Well, am I qualified to make judgments about you? You know what they call her, right? Everyone calls Patsy the Conference Rat. The. Conference. Rat. I think there's a consensus that what you're doing is not bring-your-daughter-to-work day, but pretty much just some super unhealthy mothering."

"That is disgusting." Fleur was staring at him, her face suffused with color. "Never, ever bring this up again, ever. If you don't want to be with me just say it but don't bring my daughter into it." And then she burst into tears. Patsy looked up and came running over, the limp, dirty white unicorn at her side.

"What's wrong, mommy? Don't cry!"

Fleur wept uncontrollably. Thomsen stared, surprised at what he had just said. He watched mother and daughter, roles reversed, the girl stroking her mother's long, dirty blond hair, kissing her part, whispering, "I love you, mommy, don't cry. It'll be alright," over and over. Unbidden the image of Paul appeared in his awareness; masculine and big, deep-voiced, reassuring. Thomsen closed his eyes until the vision left.

It started to rain after lunch. The whole world became the smell of the wet earth and grass, the leaves and flowers dripping, wood smoke seeping out of chimneys. Thomsen walked outside and breathed in the fragrant air. He wanted to feel the rain and he left the dorm without a jacket or shoes, plunging his bare feet into soft, cold, muddy grass. He walked along the road for a while, uphill, sheltered a little by the trees. A lawn-covered clearing emerged on his right.

A farmhouse stood in the distance and the rich smell of cow manure filled the rain-wet air. A group of birch trees across the property beckoned. Soaked, his bare feet sore from the roots and rocks and prickly grass, Thomsen realized it was the first time in months he felt free of Fleur. He started to laugh. It occurred to him that he might be having a nervous breakdown.

Thomsen followed a narrow, packed-earth path through the dripping birches that led to a pond which was surrounded by ferns and flowering Queen Anne's lace. A small wooden dock bobbed in the middle of the water and three rusted folding chairs leaned against an old, thick pine tree. Thomsen took off his clothes and waded into the water. The bottom was muddy, cold clay on his feet and as he began to swim he could feel plants and small fish brush up against him. He rolled over and floated on his back and opened his mouth and tasted the rain and the muddy pond water. He wished he had some weed.

I don't love her, Thomsen thought as he floated, the rain pounding down on him. The realization drifted across his mind slowly, easily. He saw himself, the girl, Paul and Fleur as though they were all together, swimming in the chilly, murky pond water. He saw, too, that the whole world knew what he was doing—his colleagues and graduate students, people he didn't know—that he was sleeping with another man's wife. And all Thomsen's theoretical training and understanding of cultural mores and codes, the strictures of religious belief and their dissemination into human social constructs; all of the psychoanalytic and Marxist theory he had read—none of it relieved the heavy judgment he felt.

Thomsen took a shower and started the reading for his panel. The book bored him. He fell into a light sleep and heard Fleur when she knocked at his door. The tentative, soft knocks and her whispered, "Jon, please, come on," penetrated his unconscious state but he didn't want to wake up. Later, he went to the vending machine in the basement and bought a bag of Fritos, peanut M&Ms and two cans of 7 UP so he didn't have to go to the dining hall and see her at supper. As he sat at his desk working, Fleur's distress seeped into his room like acrid smoke. But knowing that she was looking up, expectantly, every time someone walked into the dining hall soothed him.

Eventually, Thomsen wandered down to the dining hall. Dinner was over and only the cleaning staff were still there, mopping and wiping the tables. The smell of the bleach and soap stirred up an odd, old memory of having kitchen duty at summer camp. He was beset by the image of his pubescent self cleaning out the empty cavernous dining hall after the vibrating noise of 300 children shouting over their lunch had abruptly stopped. And then, lost in memory and thought, Thomsen found himself staring at the stacked dirty trays wondering which one had been Fleur's.

In the morning Thomsen went for a run along the college hill road. Everything was mist and dew and filtered green light and the smell of wet grass. He went to the dining hall for breakfast but didn't see Fleur. She didn't come to his panel and at lunch, sitting alone, reading, he decided that they needed to have it out. He tried on the idea of doing whatever she wanted—renting a house in Swarthmore big enough for her and Patsy, supporting them. He imagined her going to yoga class, knitting, baking cupcakes, distracting herself from her dissertation. All the things she said that made Paul furious. For the first time Thomsen fathomed a domestic life. He smiled to himself. It was as though he had been initiated by his little swim in the dirty pond the day before; taught the allure of being a man in his own culture with all its responsibilities and privileges. He even thought he might like it.

Thomsen heard Patsy before he saw them. The girl was singing Frère Jacques in a loud, off-key, happy voice. The girl stopped singing abruptly when she saw him. Her parents were walking a few paces behind her, holding hands.

"My daddy came!" she announced to Thomsen, triumphantly. "He surprised us!"

And then before Thomsen could escape he was face-to-face with Fleur and her husband.

"Oh, hi, Jon," Fleur said, smiling, removed.

"Hey, man," Paul said and put out a warm, engulfing hand. "How you doing?"

Thomsen stood there in agony, talking to Paul, feeling Patsy's wary eyes on him. Fleur was far away; he could barely see her. Paul was telling him about the route they were driving home, to Baltimore.

"Are you leaving right now?" Thomsen asked, all of a sudden realizing what Paul was saying. He felt panicked. Fleur was leaving. He wanted to shout at her. Stay.

"Yeah, we're going down to Fort Lauderdale to stay with my folks so I came to get the girls early."

"Wow, yeah that sounds so great."

"Fort Lauderdale with my parents sounds so great?" Paul laughed. "Dude, man, you need to take a holiday."

"I guess I do," he said. Fleur was neither avoiding him nor engaging him. He needed to hear her voice.

"So, are you going to the Micklejon conference in September, Fleur?" he asked.

"I don't know," she said. "I hadn't really thought about it yet."

Thomsen glanced down and saw that she was still holding Paul's hand. Was that for him? How could she do this? Didn't she understand that he loved her? That he had changed? That he was ready for anything she could throw at him?

"Well, I guess I'll see you there, then."

"Yeah," she said. "Maybe."

And then they were gone, the three of them, mother, father and child, safe and cocooned in each other, walking to the lower parking lot.

Only Patsy looked back to see Thomsen standing there, bereft. He waved but she ignored him.

SARAL WALDORF

Dropping a Line
into the Murky Chop

His DAD always pontificated that eels were the ones to put up the best fight, so, in hopes he didn't hook one, Fred wetted his line, and started to cast in a big arc, but the line never even hit the water, getting all tangled in the thick-branched, willow-like tree above him. This is what usually happened when he used to fish with his dad. And Fred saw again his eight-year-old self, his ten-year-old self, his twelve-year-old self on banks of other rivers, the Sacramento, the Truckee, sometimes the Pacific itself, his dad yelling *For God's sakes, cast higher, idiot! Jesus Christ, can't you even bait the hook?*

In those days Fred would have resignedly climbed the tree or picked through the bush to get his line unsnarled to show he was a good boy, a good sport. Now he just got out his knife and, after wiggling and twisting to set it free, he cut the line, reeled in what was left, and began packing up. It had been a bad idea to begin with. He'd just get back on the borrowed motorcycle and go home to his *case de passage* in the small northern town of Mbe in Cameroon where he was working as a nurse practitioner in the Lutheran private clinic there.

However, as he turned away from the main river of the north they called the Bay-new although it was spelt Benoue, a water-sodden mass of what looked like clothes began to surface and move slowly and heavily by. At first it looked like some kind of village rubbish washed away from a muddy bank upstream, but then he saw the drifting half-submerged stuff take form, take flesh. Long strands of hair floated ahead as if pulling along what he could now see was a girl. Her body for a moment swirled around as if caught in some underwater eddy, then, picking up steam, it went right past him.

Fred, frozen by surprise, at first did nothing, the sight so amazing, so beautiful in a way, just this girl—she looked young—her blondish-looking hair strung out before her, floating past him in this kind of surreal calm. Then, coming in diagonally, again on the surface, were some bubbles and what could be two nostrils pushing out of the water; Fred, still rooted to the spot, said to himself fucking shit, this was just his kind of luck, a dead girl in the water, and now a croc after her! Or if not a croc, a big snake or something, but whatever it was, it couldn't be good, so yelling and using his rod to hit at where the bubbles had appeared, he jumped in and grabbed one of the drifting arms. At first it seemed that something caught at the other end, at one of the girl's legs, and he yanked frantically at his end, the croc or whatever at first holding fast at the other, until he and the dead girl finally popped out of the water and onto the sandy bank.

Fred knew crocs and hippos could travel on land at very fast speeds, so he dragged himself and the girl further behind the river bank and, after catching his breath, hoisted the now heavy water-sodden body over his shoulder in the way he'd been taught in training, then staggered as fast as he could to where his bike was. There was going to be no way to get the body upright on it. She was already amazingly floppy—he couldn't think of any other word—rigor mortis either not yet started or long gone, but he had to get her away from there, to safety.

He was sure he could hear some thrashing through the bushes right off the river. His instinct was to flee, just get the hell out, leave the body, let someone else find her. But, even in his fright, he'd registered this was not just a dead girl, but a dead young woman about his age, and a dead white woman, maybe one of the Peace Corps volunteers up country at Garoua or further north.

If he did leave her, there could be a big stink; he might lose his job and lose his bonus for not finishing his two-year contract, get sent home, maybe even get arrested, have everything turn into an international incident. For who was going to believe that he just happened to find a dead white girl in this mostly flat dusty arrondissement of Mbe? Most of the other whites were in the bigger towns and cities north and south of him, and the only Peace Corps volunteer he'd so far met was Tim teaching English in N'Goundere, the big town south of his town.

His dad said categorically that if Fred got himself into some kind of mess in Africa, don't look to him or his mother to save him, *Isn't that right*, his father yelled to Fred's mother in the kitchen. His father had been against everything from the beginning, and when Fred finally got his nurse practitioner's license, his father said, *Well, I guess you won't kill anyone as a nurse, will you?* He'd been amazed, then scornful, that his son didn't want to be a doctor, only a nurse—a woman's job. And when Fred came home to tell his parents he was going to work at a private medical clinic in Cameroon for two years, his dad sighed ostentatiously. *Those poor slobs*, he said, shaking his head.

Before leaving, Fred asked if his parents wanted to come out and maybe visit him for their holiday, see Cameroon, take a safari at one of the parks in the north or west, even go fishing because some of Cameroon's rivers, he had read, carried the legendary Nile perch that could weigh up to over a hundred pounds. It was his mom who came out fast from the kitchen on hearing all that, saying what could he be thinking, she and his dad always went to Las Vegas every year. And his dad added, *Are you crazy? Catch something like a hundred-pound fish? You could hardly catch a goldfish in the old days, boy! You should give away that fishing pole of yours I gave you to the Salvation Army!*

Fred didn't, he took it and his other fishing gear with him to Mbe because he had to put on his application some hobby, and fishing was the only one he could think of that sounded wholesome. And now this was the first day he decided to try it because the one thing he hadn't counted on was how boring the town was, and N'Goundere on the *falaise*—"cliff," it meant—where he went by bus once a month for supplies, wasn't much better. In Mbe, there was generator electricity four hours a day if he was lucky, but no TV, no movies, and no books outside of school ones, and things weren't all that much better in the bigger town.

So Jean, his houseworker, said why didn't Fred try fishing since he brought his gear. People usually needed a fishing permit or had to go with someone who had one, for the permits weren't cheap and only available further up the highway where the southern gates to the Benoue Park stood. But the locals didn't bother. No one would stop him if he just took the wide dirt path west of the town, went past the cemetery, past the hamlet of Tcoleree, where he would then see the green banks of the river with lots of trees and bushes because that's where there were always trees and bushes, near the rivers. Jean warned of possible crocs and hippos, but only when the river ran wide and fast, so he should stick to this smaller channel with its eels, a local delicacy, and fish, including at times the famed *Le Grand Capitaine*.

Still, Fred had been fishing illegally. He couldn't get away from that, and now he was also claiming to find a dead female body he'd never seen before. The embassy had warned that if he or other Americans chose to work in Cameroon, they would come under the country's laws, and if they got into trouble, with drugs or other illegals, there wasn't a thing the embassy could do. Remember *Midnight Express*, he had been told.

Fred suddenly thought maybe he could put her back into the river further upstream so some local might find her. But if he did this, what else might find her? She'd become like bait, like a meal, fed on by crocs and eels and fish, and who could identify her after that? And even if nothing fed on her, the sunken body just rotting away, it would eventually come apart, *disarticulate*, it was called, the head usually coming off first, they had been told in class. She didn't deserve that.

Even while asking himself all this, he was taking off from the motorcycle's back metal rack the strapped-on thermal cooler box he

used for village vaccine visits and where he had intended to put any
fish he caught.

Leaving the cooler under the tree against which the girl was sitting, he then dragged her carefully to the bike and, hoisting her up,
sat her on the back metal rack. Holding on to her, he edged himself
onto the seat in front, letting her fall against his now own wet back
and then strapped her to himself with the cooler straps. He revved
up the bike, feeling her clammy, cold body against his, and moved
away slowly, really afraid she might fall off. When he got to the main
paved road to town, he came to a slow stop, pausing not only to see if
there was any traffic, but also to worry again what he should do.

Should he go back? Put her in the river? Go get his cooler and fishing gear he'd left behind and pretend to fish again? He recalled the
story of some fishermen who'd found the body of a woman in the
river and tied her up, so they could keep fishing before calling the
police, and all the trouble they got into afterwards.

No, he had to bring her in. He had to do that. Her parents would
thank him. She had to have parents. He saw his dad coming out to
Cameroon to identify his body, shaking his head, saying that boy
never could do anything right and now look at him, dead! Fred tried
to imagine his father then falling into racking sobs, but he couldn't
see it.

As he and the girl leaning tightly against him began to approach
the outskirts of town with its wooden food shacks, first kids, then
some adults began to follow behind the bike, someone exclaiming,
C'est la femme d'Americain, sa femme! By the time he got to the small
district hospital where his own clinic took patients they couldn't
help, more people had come to watch the procession. At the hospital,
he went to the new annex where he asked for Madame Eugenie, the
only female nurse at the hospital and married to the town's mayor.
The district was mostly Muslim as was most of the north and so only
used male nurses except for her. She carried a lot of clout as the may-
or's wife and spoke pretty good English. Fred knew he wasn't going
to be able to explain everything in French.

The dead woman was carried into the hospital, put on the metal
table in the surgery room, and after being examined—and that was

all, just stared at and touched minimally—she was turned over on her stomach and pressed on so water ran out of her mouth. Then, laid back on her back, she was wrapped in two thin hospital blankets and carried off to the small one-room brick hut behind the hospital that served as the morgue. All this speedy efficiency somewhat silenced Fred and he did as Madame Eugenie told him to, helping to push the dead girl now on a gurney to the morgue.

Two of the morgue's eight shelves were already taken, males from the size of them, also wrapped in thin hospital blankets. They were bodies waiting to be autopsied, legally demanded in the country if the cause of death was unknown. But no one at the hospital would do autopsies unless forced to because it was considered disrespectful to their families. However, until some settlement could be reached, the bodies finally declared to have died of "pneumonia," or some other respectable disease, the bodies could not be buried, and, if not buried, the bodies stayed in the tiny morgue, decomposing slowly but powerfully in the dry climate.

The woman was put on one of the lower shelves. The stench was already strong, and Fred put an arm to his nose as he backed out of the room. Madame Eugenie then told him to go home and change his clothes; he was to meet her at the police station when he had cleaned up.

Later there, he was left alone. Although the town chief and other local bigwigs owned some of the European cell phones now sold in Cameroon, here at the police station someone went to the back room to get the old rotary kept in a box. Fred explained again that he had been fishing in the river above Mbe when the woman had floated by and, on thinking he saw a crocodile making its way towards her, went in and pulled her out.

Even to Fred's ears, his recitation, however awkward in French, sounded good, even brave, maybe medal-deserving. After all, hadn't he jumped in and saved a dead woman from a crocodile! He could have been attacked himself! *Un crocodile?* The police officer's pen lifted off the page a moment so Fred had to repeat the word. He gave it both its English and French pronunciation for it was the same word in both languages, and then the police officer, looking skeptical, began to write again.

He was impassive, showing no further emotion as he continued taking down Fred's account, the only hesitation that initial one over the word "crocodile." Had Jean been wrong and there weren't crocodiles in the Benoue? When the policeman asked if Fred had *un permis de pêche*, Fred said he didn't know of a *besoin de permis*; there hadn't been any signs and the policeman locked up again staring at Fred before continuing. When he finished writing, he pushed the papers towards him and indicated he was to sign each page. The account had been written in French, of course, and Fred tried to see if it agreed with what he had said in his mixture of languages. On one page, it said the woman brought in was a *jeune fille blanche*, and when Fred tried to correct this to say *jeune femme*, the police officer said "*ça va, ça va*," which Fred knew meant generally, Okay, okay, who cares? So the police officer didn't correct it. The woman hadn't been at all a *jeune fille* once he had been forced to see her clearly on the examining table; she was probably older than him, maybe in her mid-thirties. She still had on a T-shirt and shorts, now wet and flat against her body, her small breasts and nipples prominent under the thin cotton.

He was then told to *attendez* again, and so he sat in the small office, waiting. He wished he'd brought a paperback. He had learned it was imperative to have something to read as waiting times could be legendary, people promising to come and never coming until after lunch or dinner or the next day, buses breaking down before they even left the depot, or breaking down halfway to somewhere, or just stopping because it was prayer time.

He was sleeping sitting up when Madame Eugenie came in and said the hospital's one ambulance was going to take him and *la mademoiselle morte* up to N'Goundere to the big private hospital there. He recalled that it had once been part of the Norwegian Lutheran mission network in the country, but now had been taken over by missionaries from the States. The doctors there all spoke English. People from various embassies would meet him there as well because it was

believed the girl may have been a European or American volunteer,
like him, or tourist. Fred started to say he wasn't a volunteer *or* tourist, but Madame Eugenie bustled on, telling him there were many
volunteers and tourists in Cameroon and it would take time to see
who was missing. Meanwhile he and the dead girl would stay at the
hospital in N'Goundere. Madame Eugenie seemed to say it in a way
that suggested he and the girl were sweethearts, and Madame Eugenie was booking a hotel for them.

Fred repeated, more vehemently this time, that he didn't know
who the woman was; he'd just found her floating down the river. He
didn't know if she was a volunteer or whatever, but he did know she
might have been eaten by a crocodile or hippo if he hadn't pulled her
out! Although he acted very upset, he actually was feeling great relief
that no one had suggested so far, or at least wasn't voicing it directly,
that he had known the girl or had anything to do with her death. And
he had done his duty. He had saved the woman! Then he heard his
father saying, *You saved a dead girl? How is that saving her?* Fuck,
fuck, fuck, why had he decided to go fishing? Fred asked himself.

When the ambulance arrived it was already jammed with people. The dead woman's body took up most of the space on the long
seat on one side and across from four riders who sat on the other.
The driver and a police officer sat in the front, and two of the male
nurses from the hospital were in the seat behind them, one with his
wife, who held a nursing baby. Fred saw that he would have to ride
in the empty space beside the dead woman, who was now emitting
a peculiar odor, which wasn't entirely unpleasant. Madame Eugenie
had said lime powder was sprinkled on the body to help preserve it.
She also told him that the other passengers were just hitching a ride
as they had business in N'Goundere. No one but him seemed nonplussed to be riding with a dead body. For a moment, Fred felt a kind
of hysteria rising up in him as he climbed up through the back of the
ambulance to take his seat. He didn't like strong smells. It was the
one thing about his profession he didn't like, having to deal with people who smelled bad or had died. The blanket, now damp from the
body, sagged, taking on the shape of the dead woman under it.

"I'm sorry," he said, edging gingerly next to her. "Look, I'm really sorry. But it wasn't my fault!"

The ride to N'Goundere took about two hours up the *falaise* to the plateau above where the town sat. It was a paved two-laner, a steep, winding road that passed small groups of baboons congregated on the sides of the road, looking as if they were begging. When the driver honked his horn they didn't flee, but opened their mouths, grimacing and chattering. Coming down on the bus that first time from N'Goundere, Fred had seen a baboon actually leap on the hood of the bus and ride about a mile before jumping off. His seatmate had explained that baboons never strayed beyond their territory. He also told Fred that if he were in a bus or car accident to stay aboard because baboons ate flesh, any flesh. And there were a lot of accidents on this road. That's why the baboons came out when cars went by.

Fred asked the two male passengers across from him if it was true that baboons would eat people if they could. The brothers—at least they looked like brothers—regarded him blankly, then nodded and smiled.

Fred felt a mixture of hysteria and anger arise again. Would everyone throw the dead woman to the baboons if the ambulance crashed on the way up? Or would they throw *him*, believing that baboons only ate live flesh? And why wouldn't they? Who was he anyway? Just a stranger making a nuisance of himself, taking away a job that any local could do and, as no doubt some Mbeians would soon be claiming, fishing for dead bodies in the rivers so he could eat their flesh.

Adventures were overrated. His mother was right. He should have gotten a job at home, no, not at home, but in another state. Fred concentrated on thinking of home, his mother in the kitchen when he used to return from school. Then one day, she wasn't there anymore because she had gone and gotten a job. He felt betrayed. Now when he came in from being bullied or something at school, there was no one to comfort him. She just left notes, saying to heat this or that for dinner for him and his dad for she worked a three p.m. to eleven p.m. shift at the 7-Eleven, and continued to do so until she retired at the mandatory age. She hadn't retired when his father did. She stayed on. Fred didn't blame her. It had been all so unfair, those fucking evenings with his sarcastic Dad! No wonder he had decided to get far away when he grew up.

The hospital was big and on a hill, and, by the time they got there, all the other riders had been dropped off except for Fred and the policeman. The policeman told him to *attendez* again while he went in, and after a wait, came out again with several people, two of them more male nurses who started to take the body out of the ambulance with the help of another policeman, and a tall, white-haired man in a dark suit and tie who identified himself as Dr. Anderson in a definite American accent. He was in charge of the hospital.

"That was a brave thing you did," he said immediately to Fred. "Her family will be very grateful. Do you have any idea who she is?"

"No," Fred replied firmly. "I was just taking a day off to fish. My father and I used to fish together. He taught me. He liked to fish for eels," he heard himself adding gratuitously.

But the doctor by then was giving out commands in French about where to take the body. Fred didn't see him again until later that night, while he was waiting in a lounge area, not knowing what else to do, to see if he were still needed, or should go back to Mbe. The officer had told him to stay, but Fred didn't know why; he'd told them everything he knew. When Dr. Anderson passed through around 8 p.m. and saw him still there he seemed surprised but told him to come along and got Fred a room to sleep in and money to buy food from one of the food vendors outside.

"You saved her, after all," the doctor said when Fred protested about being given money. "Someone may want to talk to you later. Stick around." Then the doctor rushed off.

Two days later, Fred was still at the hospital, still being told to *attendez, attendez*. An autopsy had been done, Dr. Anderson explained at one point, and the woman had drowned so Fred need not worry.

Fred protested that he knew she had drowned; had people really thought he'd hurt her? Was this why he was being kept at the hospital? "No, no," soothed the doctor. In unusual deaths the staff had to do autopsies just like in the States. Besides, Fred was like kin because he had rescued her body. She had been identified and her parents were on their way from the States; they would want to talk to him to thank him.

And the parents did come, arriving wild-eyed, red-eyed, wearing clothes as if they had been interrupted in the midst of a vacation, the blonde-streaked white-haired wife in jeans and heels and looking as she was about to collapse, the father short like his wife and wearing a flowered shirt, his gray hair tied in a ponytail. When he met Fred, the father grabbed him and held on.

"You saved her," he kept saying, "you saved her, or tried to, we're in your debt forever." Much later, when things calmed down, Fred tried to reassure the couple that their daughter—Heather her name turned out to be—had not suffered, had been very happy from what he had heard while she was in Cameroon as a Peace Corps volunteer in Garoua, for that's where her post had been the doctor told him once the hospital found out who she was. Fred hadn't really known her very well, he told the parents, just seen her now and then, and he felt guilty claiming even that much kinship, but the parents seemed so desperate to know about her life in Garoua and his life in Mbe, and to tell him everything about their beloved daughter.

By the time Fred got back to Mbe, he did feel as if he had indeed known her, although he had to say over and over again that no, he never dated her. No, he never really knew her in *that* way, and it was crazy gossip to think he'd gone down to the Benoue to fish as an excuse to meet her. Just ask his houseworker, Jean, but now and then he thought Jean was giving him the wink as if he and Jean shared a secret.

He told his father the whole story when he went home on his annual leave. It was really challenging fishing in countries like Cameroon, he said, where one had to look out for dead people in the water, like the girl he had rescued. People were always finding dead bodies in the rivers, sometimes just body parts because of some ritual killing where a witch doctor had cut up someone to make magic out of their body parts and, now, sometimes even sold the parts to medical suppliers looking for organs. Fred wasn't kidding. Then, too, most of the rivers in Cameroon had hippos and crocs and snakes as well as eels and fish like the Nile perch. His dad would have really enjoyed it.

"Not like our days on the Sacramento!" Fred said. "Pretty lame stuff compared to the Benoue!" He laughed, but for once his dad didn't say anything, just looked smaller and older than he had remembered. For a moment he felt a sudden longing for the odd security of his childhood where he could count on his dad's sarcasm and his mom's steadfastness to keep him safe.

But the longing quickly passed, and Fred, searching for something to say to keep his dad interested and maybe even jealous, started his baboon story.

They were everywhere, he said, each tribe having its own territory. One had to keep riding right past them when they collected along the road because they were just waiting for someone or some animal to come along and do something stupid. Like walk past them, or stop their motorcycle or Land Rover to get out and take their photographs, like some tourists had done.

"Did they pay for *that*, people told me! And baboons eat everything, even the bones."

Fred looked expectantly at his father, but his father said nothing, his head having fallen down onto his chest, and he suddenly heard his father begin to snore. At first Fred felt great resentment. He wanted to yell at his father, shake him, Let's see you rescue a dead girl from a croc-infested river! He sat there furious, staring at his father. His father continued snoring. Finally Fred got up and, like the nurse he was, got a small pillow and put it under his father's chin. Then he went to find his mother.

LISA PAPARONE

What She Missed

I<small>T SUDDENLY</small> occurs to me that I am sitting on the piano bench in the living room with my back to the piano, which is an odd choice because I've been here for possibly an hour replaying the horrendous events of the day. I haven't moved from this spot since I returned home, and I might have gone on like this even longer had I not leaned back and hit my right elbow on the keys, which jerked me out of my stupor. That's a good word, stupor. Sounds like stupid, which might be how I feel, but I'm not sure yet. I will have to rerun more reels, events of the last couple of years since I have been with my husband.

When I woke up this morning, I was the wife of a good man, a successful real estate developer, a loving man. Now, I don't know. I don't know what to think about him. Now my head is filled with words like "fraud," as in "conspiracy to commit" and "justice," as in "obstruction of." The images are even more distressing and peculiar than the words. When he was taken away this morning, I noticed that the suit jacket he was wearing was the very one I had just picked up from the tailor. Among other alterations, the sleeves had been let out, but not enough to hide the metal cuffs they placed around his wrists before leading him out the door. None of it makes sense to me, except maybe this wretched piano bench, possibly the most uncomfortable piece of furniture in this big beautiful house. There is no cushion, only wood and sharp angles, and because of that it feels just right, as if it is exactly where I am supposed to be.

I grew up in a house where everything was soft. Our feet were cushioned by wall-to-wall carpet (not as pretty as this marble, but back then I thought marble was only for palaces and princesses). In my parents' house there were, and still are, quilts my mother made that were washed regularly enough to make them feel like velvet. We'd wrap ourselves up in them and eat the soft foods she prepared, like creamy soups, smooth applesauce, orange juice without pulp and white bread that was spongy and ever-present. Even my mother and father were soft, with rolls of flesh that I've inherited and do battle with on my own body. On theirs it was different—comfortable, inviting, even nourishing like the bread.

Now everything seems so hard, even breathing. I feel hollow but filled with pain at the same time, to the point where it is actually physical. A trembling has started in my stomach, has worked its way down my limbs, and I am wringing my hands and rocking my feet. I want to stop but it seems as if I would have an easier time playing a concerto with my elbows right now. I have a million things to think about, that I am thinking about, practical legal things like the matter of our frozen accounts, and how do I get my husband back home, and what will I do without him here.

For a short while, I could delude myself by going about my day as if he's just on a business trip. I skid to a halt with that thought. Deluding myself feels natural, comfortable, like one of Momma's quilts wrapped around me, so much so that I think maybe I have been deluding myself all along. Certainly for the last several weeks, as I read in the paper about investigations into people who had business dealings with my husband. We knew them all. Some of them we entertained right here in our home, feeding them a beautiful tenderloin and filling their glasses with an aged Bordeaux.

I try to remember what we, what they talked about those nights. Certainly the Oswego tract, which he considered the brass ring for most of his career. We celebrated his success, although the zoning hurdles were not officially cleared. His work dominated many of our conversations. His devotion to it is one of the things I love most about him—and his brilliance, his tenacity and dedication. I see that I've allowed myself to consider only his admirable qualities. Should I have seen more?

My mind is off, racing again. Only now I am focused on my emotions, trying to put labels on them, using words I never use. Bewildered? Hoodwinked? Nonplussed? Or not surprised at all? I want myself to be innocent as much as I want him to be.

I run out of words and thoughts until all I can do is feel, or not feel, as my legs have grown numb from sitting on this hard bench. I should get up and move and allow more blood to flow through my veins. As I stand I realize the room is dark except for a hint of light coming through the blinds from the ornamental trees outside lit by our timed system. I'm still trembling and weak and not sure whether I'm trembling from the weakness or the other way around. Logic tells me eating would help, so I move toward the kitchen. My heels clicking across the marble floor are absurdly loud in the stillness of the house.

The light I flick on is blinding and I immediately turn it off, preferring to find my way in the dark. The thought of eating is not appealing, which is odd and unfamiliar, because I've always had a bit of a love affair with food, though for the most part I've been able to keep the upper hand, as my husband would say—taking into account that I am naturally big-boned and the degree of extra weight common in my family. I am always careful to hide my indulgences, so that even I forget about them, except for the special times I allow myself to enjoy the foods that remind me of home.

Toast with a little bit of butter seems like a good choice, but when I reach into the back of the breadbox and pull out a fresh loaf, the bread alone seems sufficient, the toasting hardly worth the trouble. I sit in the head chair at the kitchen table—excuse me, the farm table, as I am told to call it, as if we are the Waltons. Actually it's just the two of us, unless you count my cleaning woman. Carefully I unwind the twist tie and pull one piece of bread from the bag. WONDER, it reads, and so I do. That easily I am pulled back into mulling over the last two years and the last two days, and how much or how little I knew about my husband's work. I can't help but WONDER if there is any possibility of truth in the charges, and if so I wonder who was hurt by these actions and who else was involved.

The slice of bread is still in my hands, intact except for my thumb prints. I squeeze my fingers together and work my way around until I have completely flattened the middle. Laying it directly on the table I am able to pull away the crust and flatten it even more using the heel of my hand, until it is as thin as a patch of cloth. I peel it off the table and flip it over, revealing a lovely pattern made by the natural distress marks in the wood.

I remember how I used to like squishing soft bread between my fingers, then rolling it into balls, and it makes me think of Momma and what she would say to me now. That makes it sound like she's passed, but she hasn't—she's still here, just a few hours' drive or a phone call away. But I don't want to call and talk about all of this, not yet. Right now it's easier for me to just imagine our conversation, so I can control both sides of it. In this conversation she's loving and doesn't judge me or my husband and has no words of advice, no words of encouragement, offering only the good gift of listening. I'm pretty sure that's how it would actually go. Slice after slice I pull from the bag, feeling the soft bread between my palms, working different parts of the table for different patterns, until I have an empty plastic bag and blocks of the flattened bread arranged across nearly the entire table top.

The darkness suddenly deepens as the outside light-timer clicks off, and a weak glow comes from a half-moon. I am so tired and can't focus enough to wonder about anything any longer. My trembling returns and I feel cold as I sit and look over the array, with nothing left to work between my fingers. My own arms wrapped around me are useless to stop the tremors so I unfold them and find something to do with my hands. I change the position of some of the squares, rearranging for balance in the patterns, and I move them closer together to pinch seams between the pieces. Now up out of the chair, I make larger blocks from smaller ones, sliding pieces into place and pinching the soft bread together into ridges that run throughout. Only the bread isn't bread anymore, it feels like dough, as if I have reversed the baking process and returned it to its former state. The last section comes together nicely as I have perfected the method. I lean back in the chair and behold my creation.

What I do next seems so natural and obvious that I can't imagine others haven't done it before me. Maybe they have, I don't know. But I am done thinking and all I can do is feel, my nerves quivering, my insides roiling. I am very careful as I slide the Wonder-quilt toward me, stopping a couple of times to secure the seams that threaten to separate as I pull it from the table. It is no larger than a crib blanket, but there is enough to cover my arms, and the bottom edge rests on my lap. It holds together perfectly and I am not at all surprised how it warms and settles me.

I tug it gently up around my shoulders and the smell of the bread is soothing, its softness like home, like Momma and Daddy too. Leaning my head back on the chair, I close my eyes and imagine the first calm waves of sleep.

ALICE SCHELL

Kingdom of the Sun

My father came home, cured of his enchantment with the dusty little towns where he'd lost himself barnstorming, sometimes playing as many as three games a day with one inchmeal team after another. Always hoping to make it with one of the big ones, the Crawfords, the Grays. Never making it at all except for a game in Pittsburgh once, where he'd managed to sit close to the bench, a spectator only, coming home with autographed snapshots of Satchel Paige and Josh Gibson and a clouded half smile. This time he was back for good, he said.

There was no steady work in those years, not in New Sharon or any place else, but he pieced together odd jobs, filthy work more suited to a younger man, someone whose armor of pride was less brittle. He cleaned toilets at the fairgrounds, hauled junk for Ottendorfer Salvage, unpacked maggot-riddled hides at the tannery. My grandmother, wordless and grateful, fixed his lunch bucket as before with baloney sandwiches and thermoses of hot tea, sometimes a chunk of gingerbread. As if nothing had changed, as if he'd never left. I was the one who sat close-mouthed and sullen when he appeared out of nowhere, who teetered dangerously on the edge of my chair.

Did he break his promises to Dory and Grammum, or just me? He was always leaving, saying he would stay but leaving even as he said it. My earliest picture of him, a winter picture, too far back to see clearly except for the colors: as he was going out the door, a quick flash of scarlet, the back of his hunting jacket pinned with a bright square of heavy flannel. He came home that day with a gunshot wound, an accident, he told us, runnels of blood streaking his face.

When he was taken away to see Dr. Holt, he promised to come right back. I stood at the window where I could see all the way to the end of the street. My mother, still alive but coughing up blood, already sleepwalking toward the last week of her life, whispered to me from her chair: *Elizabeth. Littlebits.* She tried to coax me to sit on what was left of her thighs, to take comfort in the bony cradle of her arms. But I refused to come away from the window, fighting to stay awake, at last being put to bed to the sound of her dry gasps for air, the certainty that both she and my father would disappear for good.

He did come home after the hunting accident, but he left the summer after my mother died to travel with a baseball team on the other side of Harrisburg. I was to begin elementary school that fall and he'd promised to wait for me when the first day of school was over; he said he'd take me with him to batting practice; we'd go to the picture show with Dory and Gram on Saturday afternoon. He was gone, of course, weeks before I entered school.

I tried to pretend it was a game like hide-and-seek: he had not disappeared like my mother, he'd hidden himself somewhere. I looked for him among the bushes and weeds in the yard; at the post office when I went with Gram to pick up the money he sent in thin dirty envelopes; in the colored cemetery where they'd sunk into the earth a blunt little stone with my mother's name on it. I ran up the alley, across Lafayette Street to the ball field behind the school, searching for him. Grammum came after me, telling me I should be ashamed of myself, a big girl like me, six years old, crying for her daddy.

I learned to sheer away from myself, to separate from my body and its incessant threats to blow apart: the vomiting spells, night terrors, dizziness, sieges of holding my breath. I often woke Dory up with my nightmares, my stomach aches, punching at her until she stumbled out of the bed we shared and groped her way to Gram's bed across the room—"Grammum, Lizabeth's sick, wake up, Grammum!"—all the while my heart dithering under my ribs, alert for her voice—*go back to sleep, Elizabeth.* But she never failed to appear at my bedside, if I asked, never failed to stay with me until morning, the three of us squeezed together tight, the way I liked best, with Gram and Dory on the outside, me safely in the middle.

When my father came home at last, limping up on the porch as if he'd just gone to the store for a poke of Silver Cup, I stood on the other side of the screen door, my mouth walled shut, while Dory leapt into his arms with happy shrieks of *Daddy*, and Gram stood smiling at him, her last living son, her hands lightly touching the banister for support. When Dory snatched at his yellow baseball cap, knocking it to the floor, he lifted one hand quickly to smooth his hair, still dense and woolly but stippled with flecks of gray.

He set my sister down and reached for the screen door, peering through the mesh with that two-sided look of his—bashful, even reserved, but agitated too, like water with unseen creatures abruptly disturbed by light. "And how's Littlebits? How's my girl?" I fled through the kitchen into the back yard, glancing quickly behind to see if he'd followed me. He had not.

That evening when we sat down to supper I saw a change in the grudging light that usually filtered in through the kitchen window. A tense, glittering brightness touched the room, as he told us the stories I'd waited for with such longing, such resentment. The places he'd been without us, the teams where he'd picked up jobs, playing every position from shortstop to second base to left field. Once, even the catcher's spot for a team called the Hill Hawks, a team too poor to own a catcher's mask or uniforms, he said, but who sported bright yellow caps with a brown hawk design on the front.

He told us about Brockridge where a shallow creek lay on the far side of the outfield, about the balls that wound up in the creek and the right fielder with water in his shoes, sopping wet up past his ankles. About the coon games he'd refused to play up there; clowning, Tomming; foot shuffling and boot licking just to fill up the maw of the white crowd, making them forget what it was that made them hungry.

He said he was batting close to four hundred. He'd hit twenty-three home runs, five of them grand slams. He told us about the stolen bases, the double plays, about being gouged by cleats more times than he could count.

Sitting next to my father, I felt his heat, his sun-charged dreaming. I wanted to ease myself onto his lap but I kept my head down, pushing chicken pot pie around on my plate. After supper I waited for him to fold me against his chest, say he'd never go away again. But he only tugged mischievously on my plaits as he got up from the table. He said, "Seems like the onliest time I play real good is when I'm out there on the road."

My father started going to the ball field behind the school every chance he got. He would stay out there alone, batting balls into the wire mesh behind home plate. From the window of Miss Zieger's classroom I could see him, wearing his yellow cap. He would throw the ball just high enough to ready himself for the swing, sometimes missing, sometimes cracking it into the mesh. He would run to retrieve the ball, loping forward with his fast awkward gait. Every once in a while he would bend over and massage both legs as if he had cramps, kneading and stroking the slightly shorter leg he'd been born with. I imagined him looking over toward the school, waving his cap at me.

When we met after school, Dory stopped to watch him from the Lafayette side of the field. She called out, "Daddy!" but he didn't hear her. I jerked her arm and told her to shush. She screwed up her face. "Ow, that hurts!"

She hopped neatly off the curb, where she planted one foot on the sidewalk, the other in the gutter. "Why're you always mad at Daddy?"

I answered with a careless swing of my chin, tilting it up and away from her. "Who says I'm mad at him?"

"You're not mad at him?" Her voice was hesitant, hopeful.

"No, I'm *not*. Now come on, Dory, quit fooling around. You said you'd walk me home and you're not gonna break your promise."

She scuffed her feet and slowed down, but she kept walking; as always, afraid to displease me. Dory—my shadow, Gram called her because I insisted that she go everywhere I went—was a year younger, but most people took her to be the older one; she was sturdy, taller by at least two inches, with an almost adult air of self-confidence and a knockabout kind of fearlessness. Next to her I looked frail, someone who had yet to grow into her own face. I was left back in first grade because I missed so much school; all I had to show for that year was a paperweight I'd fashioned from a chunk of rock painted with bold swirls of color. I'd made it for my father. Dory joined me the following year when I repeated first grade, sitting directly behind me. My sicknesses scared her. If anyone bothered me with so much as a word or look, Dory would be there bristling, ready for a fight. "You leave my sister alone!"

My father went back to playing shortstop for the Corinthians, his old position. Grammum took us to his first game at home in over a year. I told her I didn't want to go, I had a stomach ache, but she cajoled me: "Elizabeth, that ache will fly away on its own wings soon's you get yourself out of this house." She propelled me through the front door with brisk pats on the backside. "Do you know, honey, sometimes you cut off your nose to spite your face?"

Dory hung on to Gram's fingers all the way to the ball field. I straggled behind them, rehearsing under my breath how I would say *I told you* when we found that he was gone again. But he was there, showing his autographed pictures to the rest of the team, spinning tales about night games he'd seen, with lights that were hauled around on flatbed trucks. I gave him a sidewise glance as I trailed Gram and Dory to the bleachers. Using her worn-out bandanna, Grammum dusted off her favorite seat just behind the first-base line. She placed herself between Dory and me, but I moved behind her to the next level, where she couldn't see me chewing at my lip. I settled on the edge of my seat, braced my toes against the warped board in front of me, and stared at my shoes.

Grammum turned to me. "How long are you fixing to carry that long face, child? Your daddy's home now. You should rejoice!"

He was standing at the water bucket, finishing off a drink from the gourd that was tied to the handle. Amos Fortune, the manager, looked him over and laughed. Well, ole man! Ain't you about forty by now? Ain't it time for you to quit them sorry-assed dreams?

The other players laughed along with Amos. My father let the gourd slip into the bucket and picked up two bats, swinging them together, smiling good-naturedly at the razzing. "Aw, you-uns don't know nothing! You ain't seen no ball like I seen. By George, I can tell you this much. I was batting just about four hundred all last season."

They groaned, rolled their eyes, laughing and shaking their heads. "Aw, tell us another one!"

Early Keyes, the second baseman, put in: "How 'bout batting four hundred for us?"

Amos, with a quick glance at Grammum, said, "OK, boys, get yourselves ready to play ball."

The Corinthians, a haunted ball club forever cramped by their fear of jinxes, were mired in another losing streak. During the first couple of innings, the spectators tried to talk it up as usual: *OK, OK, let's move it, move it, move it, look alive!* Before long, there were little firecrackers of discontent among the crowd: *Aw, come on. Aw shit, wake up, you boys.*

I kept my eyes down, covertly watching Grammum's back. Every time I caught the small shift in her posture, a barely visible quiver in her narrow shoulders, I knew my father was at bat, shaking out his muscles, shrugging and hunching himself into his stance as meticulously as a man trying on a custom-made coat. He had already popped out twice. The one time he got on base he was thrown out in a rundown between first and second.

Now Early Keyes was razzing him again. "Hey, here's the man that hits four hundred! Mr. Four Hundred, Mr. Four Hundred! Show us what you got!"

I looked at my father as he crowded the plate. He had just drawn three balls, but his stance was coiled tight, like someone staring into the face of a full count. The crowd grew quiet. Instead of taking the walk on the next pitch as everyone expected, he stepped into it sharp as an exclamation point. A lightning *thwack* splintered the silence as he connected with the ball, a bare, wooden clapper of a sound that jolted people from their seats. All along the bleachers startled faces turned up to the sun, eyes searching the sky. The sound of clattering shoes echoed on the boards as people scrambled to their feet.

Gram, rising halfway from her seat, then standing straight up with the rest of the crowd, turned to me and cried softly, "Look up, child! Look up!"

Something was prying me loose, catapulting me up, forcing my gaze to the sky, where the ball, swallowed by sunlight, soared over the centerfield fence. As I watched my father circle the bases in his strange, hurt-footed way I was suddenly on my feet, my small voice mingled with the others in one long jubilant roar.

Dory and Grammum hugged me, laughing, their eyes shining, and Grammum said, "You see, Elizabeth, you see!"

My father won the game for the Corinthians that day, but the victory was a lone shooting star, for him, for the team. They lost a string of games after that. One Sunday, when just about everyone on the street had made the trip to Blue Gap to see the Corinthians shut out by eight runs, Amos called the team together before they boarded the bus for home. He was afire with rage, disbelief. The Corinthians had flubbed balls and racked up enough errors, according to Amos, to fill half the almanac. And the times they'd swung at air! He nearly danced with the pain of it. My father, who'd been pulled from the game after five innings of strikeouts, stood outside the loose circle of players listening to Amos's tirade and looked down at the ground where he'd tossed his glove, digging the earth with his cleats.

I waited until the bus was nearly loaded before I said it. He was staring over my head, but I forced him to notice me, grabbing his glove and hiding it behind my back. I struggled to look up, squinting against the sun. "You're not gonna leave again, are you?"

His baseball cap shadowed his eyes. He said, "Leave? Course not, Littlebits." I stood looking up at him. He forced a smile. "Now gimme my glove."

My father kept his word. He stayed at home for the next eight years, finally able to get steady work when the Lester Ordnance Depot opened the year the war started, and played with the Corinthians on weekends. Night games had begun to put in an appearance here and there, but most of the ball fields around New Sharon were not equipped with lights, so he was home nearly every evening. Dory ceaselessly pivoted around him, chattering, giggling, asking questions, never shy about interrupting whatever he was doing, even able to make him laugh.

During those years I saw how greedily he studied the sun, the sweep of color striations above us, the massed cloud shapes. Not anyone I recognized. A sky watcher, chasing distance and light.

"Did I tell you about that game up in Brockridge, the time I hit that there ball right into the crick? Bases loaded, by George. And what about them other games? All over this damned state, and Maryland and West Virginia too. Yes sir, if I'da kept on like that, by George, I would've hit over four hundred . . ."

He often sat at the window, adrift in memory, watching yesterday's skies. When he sank into one of those reveries, bewitched and out of reach, I was silent. He talked on about the games as Dory and Grammum repeatedly asked the same questions. The more they asked, the more he worked and reworked his stories like fine pieces of stitchery. I did not ask him anything. But even as I tried to remain outside that bright nimbus of memory, I was lured into its radiance. I came to know every game he played, every town he traveled. I said, "Tell me about the time in Brockridge . . . Tell me about the time in Mount Eden . . . Tell me . . ."

By the time we entered high school, Dory had lost interest in my father's stories. She lost interest in the Corinthians too, unless it was an away game where she thought she could meet new boys. She was leaving me, by the smallest increments drifting away. She said she couldn't walk home from school with me on Tuesdays because she'd joined the Press Club; then she was on the committee to plan a trip to the battlefield at Gettysburg. She made the honor roll every term and frequently stayed after school for one special project or another. She joined the chorus. I taunted her about how they'd let colored students into their precious chorus but just try to get a part in one of their dumb operettas.

She said, "Lizabeth, I'm not just going to fold up and sit in the house all the time. What do you want me to do?"

Grammum intervened. "Elizabeth, you've got to stop this, all this grabbing . . . Dorothy has a life of her own, you know." She added: "Don't you want to get out of the house yourself? You're so smart, honey, don't you want to do things at school like your sister?" But I was barely passing most of my courses. The only subject I liked was English, where I wrote rambling essays, everything I could remember beginning with my father's blood-streaked face, the blood in my mother's handkerchiefs. I composed a jumble of verse, squandering page after page in my notebook.

By the time Dory's schedule filled up so much that she no longer had time to walk home with me even one day a week, I told her, "You lie, Dory, you don't keep your promises, you're just the way he is."

I heard a new sharpness in her voice. "He's home, Lizabeth. What's the matter with you? Do you want to hold a grudge forever?"

The years settled in my father's bones like squatters. There were stiff agonizing times when he would slump badly, times of shut doors and long naps. Times when he'd spend whole evenings looking over the photographs he cut out of the *Pittsburgh Courier*: the ball players, the big stadiums, especially the ones in New York he vowed he would see some day. His slump would start off with a steep drop in hitting, then his fielding would plunge, with one error after another and a fearful loss of power in his throwing arm. Finally, his legs, already a source of betrayal, would fail him, the muscles, ligaments, tendons undone, his base-running not just the usual hobbling accommodation but a series of jerks and stumbles. Amos, playing his younger men, kept him on the bench.

It was during one of his worst slumps that I wrote the poem for him. He wasn't batting two hundred then, not even close, and hadn't been for a long time. The poem, celebrating the dazzle of his barnstorming games, his sunlit home run for the Corinthians, was published in the School Corner section of the *New Sharon Bugle*. My father never tired of hearing me recite that poem. He clipped it out of the *Bugle* and mounted it on a piece of wood, shellacked its surface, and hung it on the wall in the parlor. He kept another clipping in his wallet and showed it to everyone. He could not read, so he would unfold the clipping with great care and ask who would like to read it out loud. He bought a half dozen copies of the *Bugle* and displayed them fanwise on the sideboard.

His slump worsened. Gram told him he should start to take it easy, maybe not play so much ball. She made gossamer-light jokes about his getting on in years. He shook his head. "Aw, there's plenty of other fellas out there . . . I seen them, in their forties, fifties. I seen plenty of them." He watched the sky, as if for a sign.

My father's shorter leg had always bothered him, sometimes causing a dull ache in his left hip, but that had never stopped him from playing ball. Now the pain was keeping him up at night. Sometimes I heard his uneven footfall as he made his way downstairs to wait out the night on the front porch. He took to packing ice around his hip in the evenings. Long after the season was over he continued his solo batting practice, regardless of the pain, regardless of the weather, even when there was snow. I followed him to the field one day, holding my breath as he ran hitching and stumbling after the ball, then massaging his leg, settling into his stance again, swinging at the wind. It was almost dark when he finally quit, muttering, "Them bats they make nowadays ain't worth a red cent."

One warm April morning during my sophomore year in high school, he left home again. Gram said he'd found a couple of fellows out of Philadelphia putting together an all-star team. They wanted to try their luck with the Mexican League, maybe Puerto Rico, Cuba. She talked too fast, too low, her back curved against me as she bent over the washboard.

I stood there, hating her, hating the smell of brown soap, the hot damp misery of the kitchen. I wanted to tear the words from my throat and fling them at her: Him, an all-star? Batting one seventy-five, if that, an all-star? *An all-star?* But she had gone out the door to hang sheets on the line, and I was left holding fast to the sink.

I said to Dory, "I'm going to find him. I'm going to make him come home. He can't just up and leave any old time he wants." I tried to talk her into helping me, but she shook her head, training her eyes on me like lamps. "Lizabeth, you're crazy."

I tracked him down that summer. My father wasn't on any all-star team. He'd been barnstorming with the Beacons, then jumped back to the Hill Hawks. They were due for a game on Saturday with the white team in Brockridge. A four-hour bus trip. Grammum didn't try to stop me. I kept telling her, every chance I got, that I was sixteen, old enough to take a bus ride by myself. She let out a wisp of a sigh. "If you're old enough to take a bus ride by yourself, Elizabeth, then it's high time you stopped acting like a child."

I winced at the way she delivered her reprimand, quiet, all pained forbearance. I'd rather she slapped me. But Gram had never lifted her hand against anyone; she'd never even raised her voice, and she didn't raise it now. "I will talk with you, Elizabeth, when you get back," she said.

The bus did not go directly to Brockridge. It went as far as Altboro, a much bigger town a couple of miles to the north. I got off there and walked. These were hard little towns, mostly white, on the edge of coal country, Brockridge itself an anemic huddle of two-story houses with slanting porches and air that weighed heavy and gray under a too-distant sun.

The game had started by the time I made it to the ball field, a scruffy space behind what looked like a defunct factory. I saw by the crude wooden squares on the scoreboard that it was only the second inning. There was no score. The bleachers were small, probably seating less than three hundred people. I took in the drabness of the place, the weedy outfield, the corrugated tin roof sheltering a small portion of bleachers. All this time, I had imagined my father playing before tier upon tier of enormous crowds in real stadiums with immaculate diamonds, banners flying. The sad squalor of the ball field made me uneasy, as if I'd pushed open a forbidden door.

Some of the spectators had come with folding chairs, three-legged stools, crates. The faces of the people who stood a short distance from me were a pale blur, except for a man who narrowed his eyes and looked at me as if he expected some kind of trouble. A couple of the others glanced at me and looked away. They'd left a dry little moat of space around me, but I still felt hemmed in. The Brockridge team moved slowly onto the field. Someone called to the pitcher in a loose, friendly baritone, "Let's git them coons today."

My shoulders tensed. Not because I was afraid of that kind of talk. I'd heard it before. My real fear was that my father would go hitless, the bat a fifty-pound weight in his hands; that his legs would trick him into a long stumbling fall.

I waited, looking for him when the Hawks took the field. Where was he? Maybe he wasn't barnstorming after all. Maybe he *had* gone to Mexico, an unimaginable distance. I began to sweat under the hazy sun. The game was still scoreless in the sixth inning when the Hawks snapped to life with a string of base hits, a solid line drive that turned into a double. They were up by three runs, then another three.

I felt the shift, the change in the air: restless movement among the spectators, a low rumble of voices arguing, something pulling loose. Someone threw a pop bottle that went skittering along the third-base line and into foul territory. The man with the narrow eyes looked at me again. The blur of whiteness around me sharpened into a frieze of faces, chiseled and grooved with frustration; yet soft, too, with anticipation, a blank soft yielding to the thing that had been tied up inside them.

There were still no outs when, for no reason that I could see, the Hawks sent in a pinch hitter. A black ragpicker of a man, painted with a minstrel-red mouth, who sidled up to the plate with an exaggerated limp. His mismatched uniform was a joke, a clown's outfit. Apple green trousers, like baggy pajama bottoms. Shirt with a garish black-and-white checkerboard pattern, at least three sizes too big. On the back of the shirt a huge zero in red paint superimposed on the checkerboard design.

He reeled in a slew-footed circle, swaying like a drunk. He did a little Stepin Fetchit footwork, repeating it several times, until the mutters in the crowd turned to cackles. He twirled his bat like a baton, dropped it, twirled it again, dropped it, pretended to lose his balance. He rolled his eyes, bending over to grin at the crowd, his head upside down, staring at them through the triangle formed by his legs. He adopted a wobbly stance, holding the bat high above his head. The crowd cackled, hooted, gleamed at one another: now that's more like it.

My father.

When he smacked a sharp grounder through the infield, almost clipping the pitcher, he made it to first, gimping and high-stepping all the way, then doffed his cap with an obsequious flourish, fanning his face, his feet, his buttocks. He rolled his eyes and flashed his teeth on and off, a macabre semaphore that sent the crowd into screams of laughter. He was fitting his cap back on his head when his eyes swept past those of us who stood behind the first-base line.

He saw me.

He fastened on me, so stricken the air between us seemed infected. He stepped forward, heedless of being tagged out when his foot left the base, crisscrossing his hands like windshield wipers, an odd frenzied signal: *No. Stop. Don't. Please.*

A small terrible sound was rising behind my teeth. I wanted to spit but my mouth was full of dust. A sheet of pain spread from my chest out to the margins of my skin. He was still trying to get my attention, but I looked right through him. I pushed blindly past the spectators and walked, then ran, toward the road that would take me back to Altboro.

At home in the parlor that evening, I pulled the poem on its plaque from the wall and took it with my father's copies of the *Bugle* to the kitchen, where Grammum and Dory were finishing supper. Earlier, in preparation for heating her irons, Gram had laid the stove with fresh kindling drizzled with kerosene. There I crammed my father's old copies of the *Bugle*, the plaque on top of them. Both Gram and Dory leapt up from the table when they saw what I meant to do. Grammum's voice reached me before she did with a stern *don't you do that, girl*, as she tried to grasp my arm. But I had already dropped the match. I did not step away from the heat as the flame etched its way to the center. Gram moved fast, pushing me aside, upending a teakettle of water on the fire, jerking her hand away from the rising cloud of steam as she slammed the stove lid back in place.

She touched my elbow. "Sit down here, Elizabeth."

I took the chair she thrust beneath me, turning my head to the wall. She moved back to the table, as if to cool the distance between us, and sat down. "Now look at *me*."

I turned my head stiffly and looked at her. Dory, eyes wide, stood behind the chair with her fingers on Gram's shoulders. My tongue felt thick, gritty. "If you could've seen him . . ."

Gram gave me a mild look, a warning. "I don't know what all happened up there in Brockridge and I don't want to know."

"But you should have *seen* him . . . Gram, you would have been so ashamed."

Dory's voice, fluttering. "What . . . what did you see? What did he do? What?"

Grammum reached up behind her to place a quiet hand on Dory's cheek. "Never mind, child. Don't fret yourself so."

When she turned back to me she shook her head, talking to herself, I thought, as much as to me. "There are times . . ."

I stared at her, heartsick. What was she talking about, there are times? What times? I hardly had the energy to speak. "He's a fake."

"Elizabeth, you do not know what you're talking about."

"A liar."

Grammum rose from her chair. "Not another word."

"A fake, a liar."

She supported herself on Dory's arm. "Do not speak ill of your father, Elizabeth."

Turning end over end in a flash flood of words, that's what my body remembers. "A fake, a coon, a dumb coon, a liar, liar, liar!" At the edge of the torrent, Dory shrinking against the wall; the sound of my father's broken step, his shadow in the doorway; Gram advancing on me like a monolith in a dream, a granite statue mysteriously in motion.

The light in her eyes was not steady. It flickered, enlarged by sorrow, the flame of her loyalty trembling in gale-force winds. I tried to push away from her, sliding my chair backward along the linoleum, but she was already there, leaning over me, close enough for a kiss. She did not raise her voice; in fact, she whispered. "Didn't I tell you not to speak ill of your father?"

And she struck me in the face with her fist.

The blow was fierce enough to snap my head sideways, but the pain floated free, distant, not my pain. I gazed up at her, stunned by the heartbreak I saw in her eyes. *Oh, Gram.* She had known about the game in Brockridge all along.

A time of ragged edges. I expected something to happen, some act of completion, but Grammum had closed the door on Brockridge. She expected us to go on as before, and we did. Nothing happened, except that my father became a fugitive. The depot no longer had a place for him, so he went back to doing odd jobs, including two nights a week as janitor at the high school. After dark I sometimes stood outside one of the narrow windows of the gymnasium, watching as he limped around that expanse of glossy floor with his cart full of buckets, bottles, brushes, mops. When we had classes in the gym I studied the varnish, searching for spots he'd missed.

He never returned to the Corinthians lineup or attended the games, though I saw him once in a while watching them from the edge of the ball field or from the other side of Lafayette Street. His hip was visibly worse now. It had begun to deteriorate into a crippling rheumatism. He looked worn, planed and sanded down like wood. Stripped, peeled away. His hair had turned completely white.

Sometimes I wondered how, in our small house, we managed to avoid one another, yet each of us found our own way: my father working at night, usually sleeping during the day; Dory filling herself up with school, looking away from me when I talked to her; Grammum, sitting in the rocker near the window, the way my mother used to sit, quiet, turned inward.

I found a place to anchor my rage, touch the roots of my grief. I retreated with one of my notebooks to the cemetery, where I sat on the ground near my mother's stone, writing the same word over and over in microscopic letters: *liar.* By the time I'd filled half the book, the pages were nearly indecipherable, dense with scratched-out words and interlinear notes. When I switched to ink, dark splotches leaked through to the opposite side of the paper, sometimes staining the next couple of sheets as well.

One afternoon, hunched over my notebook like someone trussed up in a straitjacket, I stopped writing and traced the numerals on my mother's stone with my finger: 1900–1935. When I was a child,

Grammum had tried to convince me that my mother had not really disappeared, she would be with me always. She had simply *gone to her resting place*. I never believed her. Still, I put my lips to the stone and whispered, "Mama?"

I didn't hear my father as he made his way up the gravel path and stood a few feet away from me, leaning off-center, favoring his bad hip. I jumped up and moved away from him. We had not spoken to each other for weeks. He looked at the notebook hanging open in my hand, his throat working. "Hey there!"

When I didn't answer, he coughed lightly and looked up at the sky, then back at the notebook in my hand. "You writing something about me in that there book?"

I heard a defensive tremor in my voice. "Why should I write about you?"

"I don't know. Maybe, I thought . . ." His words trailed away.

As we stood in silence, watching the western light, a surge of malice welled up in me, and I thrust the notebook at him. "Read it for yourself!"

He bit his lip and accepted the book, holding it away from him in both hands, peering at the muddled pages as if he might find a key to their meaning simply by staring hard, perhaps searching for his name. He shook his head and handed the book back to me.

"It's about what I done that one time. It's about me, ain't it?" I caught the tiny phrase: *that one time*. Was he trying to offer an excuse?

He repeated the question. "It's about me, ain't it?"

I held myself rigid, crumbling only a little when I saw how fiercely he struggled to stand upright, to correct his posture against the tug of pain in his hip. He waited for my answer. Still, I remained silent. His lips parted slightly, as he if he were about to speak, but he swallowed whatever it was he wanted to say. Instead, he lifted his hand in a half-wave, a small dignified salute, and limped away.

I sank to a sitting position next to my mother's stone. I opened the notebook, for a long time studying the pages crammed with my peevish script, tiny and sharp as tacks—a long list of grievances, a crabbed documentation of my father's every transgression from the time I was old enough to remember. Pitiless variations on the same sin: leaving me.

There was no sudden epiphany, no shaft of insight, only slow unfolding knowledge, the gradual opening of a swollen fist. I seemed to be walking out of a thicket, blinking in the light. I closed the notebook, wanting to call after him, but he was gone. "No, it's not about you, not at all. It was never about you. It's about . . . me."

I found him in the back yard, where Gram had set up a rickety old chaise for him. His legs were covered with a thin counterpane that had fallen to one side; the bottoms of his trousers were bunched up, exposing the twig-like shins, pocked with dark scars from the cleats that had gouged him years ago. I pulled the cover back over his legs.

He was dozing, his head nodding toward his chest, wearing his old cap turned backwards, like a catcher. His breath shuddered out in ragged little sighs; his feet twitched under the covers as if he were running the bases in a dream. Next to the chaise I found an upturned apple crate. His wallet lay there beside a glass of tea with ice chips thinned to a glimmering translucence. The edge of a newspaper clipping, held down by a yellow-and-green painted rock, stirred lightly in the breeze. My first-grade paperweight.

I picked up the clipping. Someone had printed in smudged pencil along the top margin: *New Sharon Bugle, September 10, 1944.* There was my poem, intact, the paper shredded to a fine lace where it had been folded and unfolded so many times. The breeze played with the paper as I read the poem, long ago buried in memory. The first part was an intricate chronicle about my father's barnstorming days, a stanza for each town. Mount Eden, Brockridge, Schillersburg, Blue Gap, Lester. The second and longer part of the poem described the game he'd won for the Corinthians.

I had sketched the picture with fine, detailed strokes, starting with a panoramic image of the sky, blue as glass rinsed clean of any cloud; the Corinthians lined up starch-stiff in front of the bench. The spectators buzzing and hustling bets; Grammum, Dory, and I in our accustomed place behind the first-base line. The game described inning by inning, an epic battle with heroic antagonists. My father's deliverance of the team with the home run. It was a school child's fable. The ball, struck by the lightning of the hero's bat, goes spinning into a mythic field, vanishing somewhere in the Kingdom of the Sun.

I knelt on the grass next to my father, adjusting his cap, turning the brim to the front. I saw that his eyes were open, but I could not tell whether he saw me, recognized me. He finally said, "Hey, Little-bits." He lay very still, his breath coming more easily. He closed his eyes. He was falling asleep.

I picked up the newspaper clipping again and re-read the poem. My father used to say he was partial to the last lines, the one stanza, I realized now, that I still knew by heart but had forgotten I ever wrote: where the ball leaps into the sun, for a jeweled instant pulling him along in its trajectory; where he is riding the stream of blue air yet miraculously touching the bases; hardly limping at all as his cleats come down with a soft *choof* on home plate, and we are there waiting, shining for him, all mirrors.

DANIEL R. BIDDLE

The Letters of
Hon. Crawford G. Boulton III

**CARTON C: PERSONAL CORRESPONDENCE
20 JUNE 1946–20 NOVEMBER 1946**

US ARMY CABLE TRAFFIC 21 JUNE 1946   1118 HRS
DESIGNATION CLASSIFIED

FROM >> HON CRAWFORD G BOULTON III JUDGE
INTERNATL MILITARY TRIBUNAL
PALACE OF JUSTICE   NUREMBERG GERMANY

TO >> MR UGO CARUZZI
ADMIN ASST DEPT OF JUSTICE
1200 CONSTITN AVE WASH 51 DC USA

WIRING $1000 YOUR ACCT RIGGS BANK DUPONT CIRCLE
NEED PERSONAL ERRAND   PLEASE AVAIL 29 JUNE 5 JULY
FURTHER INSTRUCT   LETTER SOONEST
    BOULTON

Palace of Justice
Nuremberg, Germany
June 22, 1946

Dear Ugo:

I trust you have received my cable and cash advance. Regrettably this matter will oblige you to postpone whatever other arrangements you have made for the Independence Day weekend. I would attend to this errand myself, except that as you know the Tribunal has not yet reached its verdicts, and although we are in recess we labor day and night at drafting the opinions. Thus I rely, as ever, on your loyalty and talent. Please accept my gratitude in advance and trust that I will reimburse you as usual for any additional costs.

I ask that you compile a report on the following persons: Mr. ISADORE KALISH; Mrs. ISADORE KALISH (nee Esther Greenglass); and their daughter, RUTH KALISH. I understand they reside in a "row house" on Federal Street in the Jewish section of Camden, New Jersey, and that Mr. Kalish is partner in a tailor shop known as Irv and Izzy's, situated in or near the family's home.

Please determine whether the Kalishes own property and/or automobiles, have been the subject of proceedings either criminal or civil, engage in political activity, practice their religion in any public fashion, speak fluent English, etc. Please also check whether Mr. and Mrs. Kalish are registered as aliens.

I understand the Kalishes will journey to the Catskills for the weekend of July 4. Please follow at a prudent distance, observe how they conduct themselves, and report to me soon afterwards.

My former client, the Pennsylvania Railroad, will provide you with travel and dining-car privileges as your needs arise. Please telephone the company's current counsel, Wallace M. Guttmann, who is my great friend and former classmate. His office number in Philadelphia is Hobart 3400. I will write to him separately. Note that the railroad's cafeteria in the 30th Street Station serves a fine, simple lunch of sandwiches and soup.

Also, be advised that you may observe my son, Geoffrey, in the company of Ruth Kalish. I trust you will conduct yourself, as always, with the utmost discretion.

Finally, Mrs. B joins me in voicing thanks for your acceptance of private employment at our Cape Cod house when my Nuremberg duties end. After so many years in Washington's damp corridors, it will do us all good to breathe clean salt air.

Yours truly,

Judge Boulton

Palace of Justice
Nuremberg, Germany
June 23, 1946

My dear Marguerite:

At your insistence I have directed Ugo to make inquiries about the Kalishes. Rest assured that he is a cunning old Italian who earned his spurs as a Philadelphia policeman and is quite good at rooting beneath the skin.

I would take up this matter face-to-face with Geoffrey if time allowed one last hiatus before we render our final determination. But now, in our recess for deliberations and writing of opinions, the Soviet judges quibble about semantics. What lies ahead are days and nights of toil, at least through mid-July, in this "palace" of bare light bulbs, broken fans and all-but-useless telephones. I so look forward to joining you on the Cape when this task is complete.

All my love,

Crawford

Wallace M. Guttmann, Esq.   Villa Conradti
Finchot, Shavers, Guttmann & Fisk   2 Hebelstrasse
12th Floor Quaker Trust Building   Nuremberg, Germany
Philadelphia 19, Penna. U.S.A.

June 24, 1946

Brother Guttmann:

Greetings, old confrere. For reasons that will become evident, this note is for your eyes only. Do not entrust it to Esmeralda for disposal. Set it on fire yourself.

I write, first off, to advise you that my old tipstaff, one Ugo Caruzzi, will contact you forthwith for railway tickets and dining-car privileges. You may remember Ugo from my Attorney-General days; he was the clever little wop who had the keys to every office. He has agreed to retire from the Department at summer's end and hire on with us at Wellfleet as gardener, handyman and chauffeur. In the meantime he will be my operative on a minor matter.

The problem, as ever, is with Geoffrey. Now 26, he has rejected my suggestion of following our path to Harvard Law. He remains content to teach in Philadelphia. (Marguerite believes his malaise goes back 15 years to the loss of his brother, but who understands such things? Not I.) Worse, he has taken up with a Jewish girl, the daughter of a tailor from Camden. Her parents are immigrants and probably not even citizens. This gives me no great qualm (you might even dub it fashionable up to a point) but it has driven Marguerite into a panic of codeine pills and trans-Atlantic cables. She has never fully shared my liberal sensibilities on questions of race.

To calm her, I have dispatched Caruzzi to discover what he can about the girl and her family. Geoffrey has told Marguerite that the clan will make a jaunt to the Catskills around Independence Day, and Ugo will pursue them under-cover. A symbolic mission, to be sure, but the better to convince my wife that these people bathe with soap and have no horns beneath their skullcaps.

As for your old, bald classmate, I officially work day and night at the Palace of Justice, drafting the Tribunal's final words about Goring, Streicher and the lesser-knowns. We have been in recess since June 3 for deliberations and writing, and at first we argued daily with the Soviet judges about such issues as whether the Tribunal's opinions are the proper place for discourse on the number of squares of epidermis clipped from backs, legs and chests, dipped in tannin, dried on Auschwitz clotheslines, and converted into saddles, riding breeches and ladies' bedroom slippers. (Speaking as the sole equestrian of this bench, I could have questioned how a tanner, whether Nuremberg Nazi or Colorado cattleman, could stitch saddles or breeches of any durability from such fragile hides. But I held my tongue.)

It went on like that for a fortnight. On June 17, having drawn up a reasonable draft, we agreed to break informally—and completely— until Bastille Day. In the hiatus I have forged an acquaintance with a bright and charming British writer. She is Judith Davies, 12 years my junior, tall and pretty and a quick intellect. She dubbed Goring "blub-bermensch" and now the MPs say it to his face. She writes 10,000-word articles on the trial for the *New Yorker*, and sends shorter pieces to the *London Telegraph*. Remember, though, my friend: If anyone asks, I am working like the dickens.

I have ridden benches and desk-chairs too long. I envy your remaining in the hurly-burly of advocacy, building your case up brick by brick, word by word, even if the client is our big-hearted old cow, the railroad. But I suppose I must be content to watch the young Turks from afar when I retire to the Cape. I look forward, nonetheless, to visiting the City of Brotherly Love and dismembering you at squash.

My best regards to Julie, and to both of your girls. I will recommend them once again to Geoffrey, but I cannot be optimistic.

Fraternally yours,

Crawford

Palace of Justice
Nuremberg, Germany
June 27, 1946

My dear son:

I regret to say I cannot avail myself to meet you in Paris, much as I would enjoy it. Though in recess, the Tribunal works on, night and day, to complete its monumental task of passing judgment on the Reich's surviving leaders. It is unfortunate that you could not interrupt your teaching when the testimony here was in full sway.

In belated honor of your 26th birthday, I enclose to you one of my five gavels, cut from India teakwood and donated to the Tribunal by the British governor.

I understand from Guttmann that his daughters are lovelier than ever, and miraculously unwedded. You should look them up.

Affectionately,

Father

P.S. After 21 hours of testimony and seven months of trial, Herr Goring has shed no avoirdupois. You may tell your students I have dubbed him Blubbermensch.

Palace of Justice
Nuremberg, Germany
July 14, 1946

My dear Marguerite:

I received Ugo's report in today's mail. In summary:

1. Isador Kalish, 54, is, as we feared, an alien, but legally registered upon immigrating to Philadelphia from Lithuania via Danzig in 1911. He works at least 12 hours each day except Saturday, the Jews' sabbath, at his tailor shop downstairs from the Kalish home. He has no known political affiliation, but the family's well-maintained maroon Hudson has a Roosevelt badge in its rear window. (This bodes well.) His English is poor but he otherwise seems, in Ugo's estimate, to be an agreeable and communicative Jew.

2. Esther Kalish also registered as an alien when she landed in Philadelphia from Kiev via Bremen in 1909. She, too, contributes a considerable number of hours to the family business, as do her three daughters.

3. Ruth, 23 years old, attends summer classes at the University of Pennsylvania, as Geoffrey told you, on a scholarship. Her work at the shop is limited to some evenings and Sundays. Her mother is publicly demonstrative in that she nearly strangles Ruth with an embrace on the steps each morning before the girl walks to the streetcar stop. (Ugo writes, "Judge, the old lady's just like my mama.")

4. In general: Other than marking the sabbath, the family shows little outward manifestation of their faith. The father does not wear a skullcap on the street. The Kalishes attended a public memorial service for Jewish victims of Nazi camps. (Apparently some Kalish cousins perished in the Ukraine.) At meals, the family tends toward boisterous conversation, in a tongue unknown to Ugo's ear but

which I assume is Yiddish. They all seem accustomed to Geoffrey's presence.

I find this information largely reassuring and hope you will concur. Our drafting sessions here drag onward but the end is now in sight: August 15 at the latest.

Love as always,

Crawford

Wallace M Guttmann, Esq.   Wellfleet, Mass.
Pinchot, Shavers, Guttmann & Fisk   September 16, 1946
12th Floor Quaker Trust Building
Philadelphia 19, Penna. U.S.A.

Dear Brother G:

In light of your gracious assistance, I would love to report that my man completed his reconnaissance without gaffe, and that a measure of domestic tranquility has accompanied my return from Nuremberg. This, however, strains the record.

The fault was not Caruzzi's. Crisscrossing Camden and environs, he developed quite a file on Geoffrey's paramour, Ruth Kalish, and her family. On the eve of the July 4th weekend, matching their every move, he boarded the Zephyr at 30th Street and stood, sweltering, all the way to the Catskills. His luck! He was packed sardine-like in a trainload of Jews.

At Grossinger's, Caruzzi dawdled at the restaurants and swimming pools as if on holiday. The Kalishes stayed at a cheaper boarding-house two miles down the highway, but ate and swam at Grossinger's for a daily fee. Caruzzi reported that at breakfast, lunch and dinner, the Kalish parents and three grown daughters shouted back and forth over steaming bowls of potato soup or plates heaped high with meats and scrambled eggs.

When Ugo arrived on the Cape last month, I asked if he had insinuated himself near enough to overhear the Kalishes' meal-time discussions. He had. And what was said? He did not know, because the group "talked in Jewish." By this he must have meant Yiddish. Had the family become loud or disruptive? "Well, excuse my language boss," Ugo answered, "but they might as well have passed out the fucking tambourines!"

All this was fresh in mind when Geoffrey came up from Philadelphia for the final week of August, and announced one morning over a poached egg that he had invited Ruth—and her parents—up to join us. He had it all planned: the Kalishes would stay in the clapboard bungalow across the yard from our old stone house. (To differentiate, we have nicknamed ours the Big House.)

He said they were driving up that day.

You can imagine Marguerite's reaction. She set down her teacup, looked at Geoffrey, said, "Really," and arranged her mouth into an inverted U. I said we must make them welcome. She said she supposed we must.

The Kalishes' maroon Hudson, Roosevelt badge and all, chugged down our driveway at half past six. Mr. Kalish, a stout and agreeable sort, wore a white dress shirt. Ruthie (as they call her) is a lovely dark-haired girl. Her mother's gray tresses were bundled tightly in a knitted yellow snood.

Over a roast of lamb, with carrots and corn from our garden, I pointed out the Boulton bell. This tarnished stalwart, "U.S.S. John Boulton" engraved along its lip, sits on the dining-room mantelpiece amid statuettes of Presidents from Washington to my beloved FDR. I recounted my ancestor's naval feats as humbly as I could. I noted lightly the fact that old John had served our first great leader, and I had served our last. (At this, six Kalish eyebrows went up. It seems that Geoffrey had told these people nothing about me at all!) I said I'd made Geoffrey, as a boy, memorize all of those little wooden Presidents, forwards and back. Perhaps he could recite them for us now.

My son answered me with a sidelong glance and said only, "Pa. Please."

From there the evening disintegrated.

As our kitchen-girl, Henriette, wheeled out a raspberry bombe and a dozen chocolate truffles, Ugo, wearing overalls, leaned in through the doorway. "Boss," he said, "excuse me, but their car is blocking mine."

Geoffrey trotted off with Ugo to move the cars. When he returned, Mrs. Kalish, silent as a mummy until now, turned to her husband, spoke Yiddish in his ear, and pointed at the doorway where Ugo had stood. I distinctly heard her say "Grossinger," amid a certain phrase repeated several times. (I tried to reconstruct it for Abe Weiss, Class of '10, our neighbor on the beach road. Weiss said the words were "gaknipt and gabinden," which he translates as "all tied in," or smacking of foul play.)

By now, the woman had the group's full attention. "Esther, shush!" Mr. Kalish said. He reached for her as Henriette was easing between them to serve the dessert. His elbow struck the ladle, which clanged to the floor and splattered raspberry ice on Henriette's yellow apron and Mr. Kalish's sleeve. His daughter laughed. Mr. Kalish said he was sorry.

We finished the meal in silence. Then Marguerite stood up and spoke, pausing at each phrase as if she were accommodating a translator. "We speak English at our dinners here," she said. "There will be no more meals at the Big House."

She plucked a truffle from the tray and walked out of the room.

What was I to say? I suggested coffee and liqueurs in the library. (It seemed important to preserve a semblance of decorum.) Mr. Kalish looked at his wife, then at me. He said, "I thank you, sir. We will go home now." I made no move to deter them.

For the next two days, Geoffrey, never a terribly talkative boy, said not one word to me. On the morning of his departure for Philadelphia, he said that he would write me a letter.

So it is that, having welcomed me back from Europe, my family has grown silent. Marguerite attends to her poetry. Geoffrey is back to teaching. I await his letter with trepidation, and thank you as ever for listening.

Your devoted friend,

Crawford

Wellfleet, Mass.
October 27, 1946

My dear son:

Quite frankly, I am puzzled. Throughout your long, vexatious silences, your mother and I have extended ourselves to you with money, presents, friendship and assistance. Have you forgotten the gavel that I posted to you from Nuremberg? Or that, four years ago, at your mother's urging, I intervened on your behalf with Secretary Stimson to assign you to a non-combatant Signal Corps unit? Had it been my choice alone, I would rather have seen you in officers' school. Your mother, having already lost Oliver, beseeched me to step in. Yet you now have the temerity to criticize my action. It occurs to you—does it not?—that my intervention may have saved your life.

I invited you to Nuremberg last January, but you didn't respond until June with a suggestion that we meet in Paris for a "bender," at a time when I was working day and night drafting our verdicts. But then, your thoughts on my career are a mystery to me. When I remarked over dinner with the Kalishes that I had worked for FDR, it was evident that your girl and her family knew nothing of this. You had not told them about my Nuremberg duties, a fact which would have interested them for obvious reasons. I have never expected you to kowtow. I am, however, astonished that you hold my achievements in such contempt.

On your recent visit you seemed utterly incapable of finding your tongue. Why? You know that I have always favored candor. I have not forgotten Justice Webster's exhortation when I was his clerk: "Treasure the truth, Boulton!"

Now that you have deigned to correspond, you spit out allegations you would never have the sand to tell your father face-to-face. You allege that I have behaved with something less than honor. Even my worst political detractors have never questioned my honor.

Nonetheless, in a sincere effort to extend my hand and quell this childish squabble, I shall answer your contentions seriatim:

1. Regarding your mother's comments after dinner with the Kalishes, I was probably as nonplussed as you at that moment. It may be

that you are partially correct, in the sense that further explanation to the Kalish family might have been warranted, and inasmuch as these people may have misconstrued Mother's words. But if you believe an apology was in order, why did you not leap into the breach? In your letter, you say (accurately or not; I will not quibble) that the Kalishes took offense. You certainly knew none was meant. Or did you expect me to apologize after Marguerite left the room? As you seem so bent on matrimony, you will perhaps understand if I do not take sides with strange people against my own dear wife, regardless of our occasional disagreements.

2. Regarding your claim of anti-Semitism in our home, I am simply astonished. My record as attorney general attests to my even-handed application of the law to all, whether colored, German, Jew or Oriental. It is my immodest hope that Walter Lippmann is correct in saying that history will view me as an A.G. who stood for civil liberties even in time of war. How do you wish to be remembered, Geoffrey? As the son who accomplished little but decided in anger that his New Deal father was a Klansman at the bone?

3. Regarding your delusion that my gardener and former tipstaff, Ugo, was a cog in some dark design to undermine your romance, this is nonsense, Geoffrey. Since I knew that Ugo was planning an excursion to the Catskills, I mentioned that your Jewish friends might be there coincidentally. He later remarked to me that the Kalishes seemed sturdy and full of life.

4. Regarding, finally, your emotional recitation of events long ago, I fail to see a basis for your claim that your parents lack "sensitivity." If you accuse me of too often answering the call of public service, then I plead guilty. A nation does not survive war and depression if its leaders stay in the nursery. The maids and tutors we recruited for you, at considerable expense, were young men and women of the highest calibre. It is you who said that Waldo Holcombe filled up the place left empty by little Oliver's death.

To your criticism of our conduct in that last, tragic event, I can say only that I acted to protect you. Should a boy of 11 watch a boil swell to the size of a peach on his little brother's neck? I think not. Should I have wakened you to listen to him scream for half an hour, ceasing only when the final morphia needle knocked him cold? Should I have told you how the blood-streaked pus splattered on my waistcoat and cravat as the ship's surgeon pressed his lancet through the boil? I think not.

You whine of isolation through your Millbrook years. I can only imagine how you would fare in my shoes at Groton before pumpings were outlawed. Imagine sitting with other boys of 10, 11 and 12 as the day's list of victims is read off, and praying to the Lord that today the half-drowned boy held upside-down beneath the spigot— his head submerged, his feet held high by two upperclassmen—will not be you. Then tell me your schooling was rough.

And if you believe your father was abroad too much, fancy me at age nine: or have your forgotten that my father passed away that year? We did not pule and languish long. Indeed, four years at Groton came and went before Mother even said my father's name again. And yet I can say immodestly that I turned out all right.

You contend that I stated, "You will never amount to a thing." Ask yourself, Geoffrey, for you may someday have a son: Was I in error if I said this, as you slouched about with baseball cards or played mumblety-peg, while the world roared past? You, who claim to favor candor as strongly as I do? I deny my words reflected "insensitivity." I only did my duty as a father.

I still believe you can attain great heights, when and if you buckle down to something of more consequence than teaching. I still regret that you so hastily rejected my offer to speak with Dean Harkness at Harvard Law. My offer still stands.

Father

Wellfleet, Mass.
November 11, 1946

Dear Judith:

Your note caught me unawares. It was never my intention to deceive you in any way. I told you many times of my devotion to

Marguerite, and I am puzzled that a woman of your superior wisdom could have misconstrued my words.

You had similarly denied any serious intentions. If your feelings changed at some point, I would have welcomed your candor. You knew my motto, "Treasure the truth," and you seemed to admire this in me. If you believed my heart had changed, why did you not speak more frankly before we parted?

There may be, I suppose, a whit of truth in what you say. At certain moments, your liveliness may have caused me to say wild words. I trust you will construe any such declarations as nothing more than well-intended compliments.

You are not the first person to tell me that my knowledge of justice does not extend to the realm of the heart. My wife and son have said the same of late. I suppose, in the end, I am a sour old man who was sweetened temporarily by your affection.

If you are ever in Manhattan to see your editors, please call. From time to time I ride the train from Boston to Philadelphia. I often stop in New York at Pennsylvania Station, where the railroad's private restaurant serves an elegant prime rib.

Your devoted friend,

Crawford

Contributors

Daniel R. Biddle is the politics editor at the *Philadelphia Inquirer*. He has worked in journalism as a reporter and editor for many years, at the Inquirer and at the *Cleveland Plain Dealer*. While at the *Inquirer*, he won a Pulitzer Prize and other national awards for his investigative stories on courts. He holds a degree in history from the University of Michigan, was a Nieman Fellow at Harvard University, and is the author, with Murray Dubin, of *Tasting Freedom: Octavius Catto and the Battle for Equality in Civil War America*. He and his wife, Cynthia Roberts, live in Philadelphia.

Gwen Florio's first novel, *Montana*, published in 2013, was awarded the Pinckley Prize for debut crime fiction, as well as a High Plains Book Award, and led to her Lola Wicks mystery series. Her short fiction has been nominated for the Pushcart Prize. A former reporter for the *Philadelphia Inquirer*, Florio now lives in Missoula, Montana.

Samantha Gillison is the author of the critically acclaimed novels *The Undiscovered Country* and *The King of America*. She regularly writes opinion, reviews, and travel features for national print and online publications, and has received a Whiting Award and a John Simon Guggenheim Fellowship in fiction. Gillison is currently working on a new novel, *The Control Question*. She lives with her family in New York City.

Romnesh Lamba is a senior executive at the Stock Exchange of Hong Kong and has always worked in finance. He has also lived in Bombay, Eton, and Philadelphia, where he began writing fiction as a student at the University of Pennsylvania. Between 1988 and 1991 he participated in several workshops at the Rittenhouse Writers' Group. His fiction has been published in *Confrontation*, *Columbia*, *Christopher Street*, the *Mississippi Review*, and the *Gettysburg Review*, and in magazines in India. He received a Fellowship in Literature from the Pennsylvania Council on the Arts in 1990.

Caren Litvin is a labor and employment lawyer in the Philadelphia area. She participated in workshops led by James Rahn for over fifteen years at the University of Pennsylvania and has been a member of the Rittenhouse Writers' Group since 2000.

Diane McKinney-Whetstone is the author of five acclaimed novels, *Tumbling*, *Tempest Rising*, *Blues Dancing*, *Leaving Cecil Street*, and *Trading Dreams at Midnight*. She has received numerous awards including the American Library Association's Black Caucus Literary Award for Fiction, which she has won twice. She has been a contributor to *Essence Magazine* and a lecturer in the writing program at the University of Pennsylvania. She lives in Philadelphia with her husband, Greg.

Lisa Paparone is a tax accountant and financial planner. She lives in Hainesport, New Jersey with her husband and three children, and volunteers at her children's school in various capacities, including eight years as a field hockey coach. She writes fiction when she can find the time. She has participated in the Rittenhouse Writers' Group for more than twenty years and finds that the workshop gives her the motivation and feedback she needs to keep writing.

Alice Schell grew up in south-central Pennsylvania and attended college and graduate school in New York. She taught English at independent schools before moving to Philadelphia, where she continued working as a teacher, then as an administrator in higher education. Her fiction was first published in *Story* magazine. She is the recipient of a Pushcart Prize and a National Magazine Award and has received fellowships from the Pew, Leeway, and Ragdale Foundations and from the Pennsylvania Council on the Arts.

Tom Teti is an actor working on stages in and around Philadelphia and throughout the eastern United States. He has been in and out of the Rittenhouse Writers' Group since 2000. His work has appeared in the *County Press, Philadelphia Stories,* the *Bucks County Writer, Apiary,* and the *Journal of the Coatesville Cultural Society,* and has been presented in readings at InterAct Theater and the Coatesville Cultural Society.

Saral Waldorf is a medical anthropologist who has lived and worked in Uganda, Lesotho, Cameroon, Malawi, Benin, Thailand, Turkmenistan, Malta, and England. Many of her stories reflect this background. Her fiction has appeared in the *Hudson Review, Commentary,* and twice in the *Southern Review.* She also has appeared in a fiction issue of the *Anthropology and Humanism Quarterly.* She is a widow with three grown children who also travel the world and two grandchildren who intend to do likewise.

Credits

Acknowledgments

THANK YOU to the folks who read drafts of this book in part or in toto: Stefanie Cohen, Leigh Jackson, Romnesh Lamba, and Alice Schell.

Thank you to Jane Gallen and Ross Murphy for keen, clear-eyed advice.

Thank you to the staff at Paul Dry Books for opening the door, then working meticulously.

Thank you to the Psychoanalytic Center of Philadelphia who taught me deeply about the hidden mechanisms of the mind, particularly Howard Covitz for his wisdom, guidance, and compassion.

Special thanks to Margetty Coe for her friendship, her invaluable reading and editing, and for her willingness to keep pushing me down the road.